STILL THE ONE

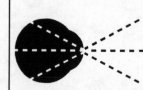

This Large Print Book carries the
Seal of Approval of N.A.V.H.

STILL THE ONE

JILL SHALVIS

THORNDIKE PRESS
A part of Gale, Cengage Learning

GALE
CENGAGE Learning·

Farmington Hills, Mich • San Francisco • New York • Waterville, Maine
Meriden, Conn • Mason, Ohio • Chicago

GALE
CENGAGE Learning®

LIBRARY OF CONGRESS CATALOGING-IN-PUBLICATION DATA

Shalvis, Jill.
  Still the one / Jill Shalvis. — Large print edition.
    pages cm. — (Animal magnetism) (Thorndike Press large print romance)
  ISBN 978-1-4104-7817-7 (hardback) — ISBN 1-4104-7817-3 (hardcover)
  1. Large type books. I. Title.
PS3619.H3534S75 2015
813'.6—dc23   2015009331

Published in 2015 by arrangement with The Berkley Publishing Group, an imprint of Penguin Publishing Group, a division of Penguin Random House LLC

Printed in Mexico
1 2 3 4 5 6 7 19 18 17 16 15

STILL THE ONE

ONE

Darcy Stone had never been big on rules unless she was breaking them. But that was the funny thing about nearly dying — it changed you, in a big way. So she'd taken a good, hard look at her life and decided that maybe a few "guidelines" wouldn't hurt.

Number one: Don't stress the little stuff.
Number two: Never let a certain man into your heart. Ever.
Number three: Don't take crap from anyone.

It was number three on her mind right now. Today's crap came in the form of one weasel named Johnny Myers, a dog trainer who lived two counties over from Darcy's town of Sunshine, Idaho, deep in the Bitterroot Mountains. Johnny was complete pond scum, not to mention under investigation for illegally importing and exporting exotic

7

animals.

It killed Darcy to do business with him, but if she didn't, he'd send the dog she wanted straight to the kill shelter.

"I'm not paying you seven hundred dollars for a service dog you intend to dump for not passing his certs," she said into her cell phone as she walked through the pouring rain and into work. Hell, she didn't have seven hundred dollars.

Her wet sneakers squeaked as she entered Sunshine Wellness Center and rounded the front desk. Cold had started to seep through her drenched clothes to her aching bones but she ignored this. "Make it two hundred," she told Johnny, "and you've got yourself a deal."

She didn't have two hundred, either, nor a way to even get out to Johnny's place since she no longer drove highways, but she'd worry about that later.

Johnny started sputtering with outrage as she shoved her wet hair back from her face, going still when her body suddenly went into hyper-alert mode.

Damn. Again? At this rate she could hire herself out as some sort of paranormal secret agent . . . except the only person whose appearance she could predict was AJ Colten.

Guideline number two, and the bane of her existence.

And sure enough, in walked her boss: six feet two inches of solid muscle, testosterone, and attitude. And damned if she didn't have a secret thing for all of the above. *Very* secret, since she'd gone there with him once — or nearly anyway — and had been burned big-time.

Never again, no matter how hot he was.

Luckily she had one heck of a poker face, because on a good day just a fleeting glance from AJ reminded her that she was a twenty-six-year-old sex-starved woman.

On a bad day, every single part of her sent urgent memos to her brain that she was practically a re-virginized twenty-six-year-old sex-starved woman.

It took everything she had not to look hungry.

Or even overly friendly.

AJ made it a lot easier by showing absolutely zero interest in her. The only thing she got this morning was a hooded glance that probably meant he was wondering why he'd even hired her.

She raised an eyebrow in his direction, trying for nonchalance while she soaked up the sight of him and the easy, confident way he moved his big body.

"Not a penny less than six hundred," Johnny said in her ear.

"Three hundred," she countered, tearing her gaze away from AJ. "And I'm cold and wet and almost late for work. If you don't want the money, tell me now, because I need to go."

Thanks to an unseasonably warm late fall putting Mother Nature in a mood, rain and wind slashed at the building. Darcy loved the rain. What she didn't love was a violent storm. Not only was she shivering, she undoubtedly looked like a complete mess.

Her life motto was dance like no one was watching, so she told herself she really didn't care what she looked like. Then she told herself that a few more times while watching AJ's mighty fine bod move across the room.

"Three hundred is a joke," Johnny complained. "I bet if I opened my e-mail I'd have ten offers that are better."

"You go take a look," she said. "I'll wait." While she did, she shoved her purse into the filing cabinet, but not before taking a surreptitious bite out of one of the two breakfast taquitos she'd grabbed on her way in.

When she realized AJ was heading her way, she nearly choked in her rush to swallow because AJ didn't approve of the love of her life — crap food. And as he was the boss, owning the Sunshine Wellness Center as well as being head physical therapist, she tried to play by his rules. Okay, not really, but she at least did her best to hide the evidence.

She booted up the computer and caught an accidental flash of her reflection on the screen.

Yep, she was a hot mess, alright, her long curls — usually her best feature, if she did say so herself — now resembled a frizzy squirrel's tail.

Good thing she didn't care.

Naturally, AJ was not a mess. Not that he ever was. Nope, as usual he'd defied the odds, the rain not daring to stick to him. And no squirrel-tail hair for him, either. His sun-streaked brown hair was short and silky smooth, and as he took in *her* hair, his lips quirked in an almost smile.

Bastard.

And then Johnny was back. "I've got plenty of e-mails with interest, so you ain't getting it for cheap."

It. Darcy forgot about her hair catastrophe, and AJ's lack thereof, and grinded her back teeth together. Guideline number three: Don't take crap from anyone. "Three fifty,"

11

she said. "Tops."

"Five hundred."

This wasn't going well. Plus, AJ was still looking at her, as always, aware of everything going on around him. She smoothed out her expression and added a professional smile. *Nothing to see here.*

He didn't return the smile.

Darcy attributed this to the fact that it was seven in the morning, and AJ hated mornings with the same level of passion that she herself reserved for doctors and exercise.

From the hallway that led to the offices, Ariana waved at AJ, all sweet and cute, pointing to the steaming mug of coffee on the counter waiting for him. The yoga instructor always prepared him organic coffee in the mornings.

Suck-up.

Organic coffee? It sounded as good as tofu or kale, not that AJ ever complained.

Sometimes Darcy wished that she could be described as sweet and cute, too, but she was usually too busy being her normal sarcastic and annoying self.

Ariana had other things on Darcy, too. Calm and steady and grounded, for instance. And she meditated, didn't eat choco-late — who didn't eat chocolate? — and was Zen at every turn.

Darcy couldn't have done Zen to save her life.

"You still with me?" Johnny snapped at her. "Five hundred. *Today.*"

Darcy turned her back on AJ and lowered her voice. "That's five hundred more than you deserve, you bloodsucking scumball —"

"You kiss your mama with that mouth?"

Darcy kissed her mama never. Her mother wasn't the kissing sort. "We're done. Good-bye —"

"Wait! Jesus, we're having a little fun-free enterprise here, no need to get all pissed off. Four hundred. Final offer."

"Done," Darcy said. She'd just have to find a way. She always did when it came to rescuing service dogs who, for a variety of reasons, needed to be "reassigned."

Some needed to be retired, either because the work was too strenuous or they'd lost their owners, or they simply couldn't keep up with the demands of their job. Most were sold to good homes, but not all. People had jokingly labeled these dogs as "career change" dogs, but Darcy knew the truth. They were throwaways.

And no one knew how it felt to be a throwaway more than Darcy herself.

In the past month she'd rescued three such dogs, each of whom had been let go by his owner but who still had so much to offer.

She'd easily placed them as emotional support dogs with people who needed them as badly as the dogs needed good homes. In this case that had been two military vets suffering PTSD and a woman who'd lost her hearing due to illness.

Word had gotten out, and now Darcy had a list of more people who needed emotional support or therapy dogs as well, people who couldn't afford to go through the usual channels.

There certainly wasn't a shortage of dogs or people who needed them.

But there was a shortage of funds, as these dogs, with their training and certifications, were expensive.

"The money needs to be here tonight or he's going to the pound," Johnny said.

Most likely he was lying, but he was a first-class jerk so she couldn't be sure. "No problem," she said, and hoped that was true. She disconnected and buried her nose in work.

"That was either a drug deal or a bookie," AJ said.

That was the thing about AJ — the Navy vet was the definition of stealth. And maybe she hadn't heard him coming, but she'd

14

sure as hell *felt* him. She ignored both her happy nipples *and* him. First, she'd dedicated one of her three guidelines to him. Second, he was one of the few people on the planet who could see right through her and call her on her shit.

No woman wanted to be with a man who could see right through her.

And then there was the fact that he had a 'tude bigger than hers and could back his up with an all-around bad-assery she couldn't begin to match.

Nope, if and when she decided to jump into the man pool again, it would be with someone sweet and kind and lovely and sensitive. Someone who'd fawn all over her and think she was the best thing to ever happen to him. Someone who hadn't rejected her.

"I don't do drugs," she said without looking up, using her most impressive PMS tone. "Or gamble."

"Sure you do. You gamble with your health when you eat spicy sausage taquitos from a convenience store for breakfast."

"Ha-ha," she said. "And for your information, I got the veggie ones."

He didn't say anything to this, and damn if she didn't finally cave and look up, right into his eyes.

Big mistake.

AJ had deep, warm eyes the color of a hazelnut, and when he wasn't being her militant hard-ass PT or her boss — in fact when he wasn't looking at her at all — they softened.

Not that there was anything soft about him right now.

And that was the thing about AJ. He was tough and strong, both inside and out, and he always, *always* knew what to do, in any situation.

Whether that came from being raised by a Navy captain or from his own military stint, she had no idea. She could ask him for help with Johnny and he'd step in and handle it without hesitation.

Which was exactly why she said nothing. This was her problem, not his.

"Let me guess," he said, his tone dialed to *Not Surprised.* "You're in trouble."

As that was usually the case, Darcy supposed she couldn't blame him for the assumption. "What I am," she said, moving past him, shoulder-checking him by pretend accident, "is none of your business."

He caught her arm and turned her to face him. "I don't just sign your paychecks. I'm your brother and sister's best friend. You're definitely my business. And," he went on when she opened her mouth, "I don't see how that's a bad thing, having people want to help you."

Of course he didn't. Because he'd never found himself in a situation where he needed help from anyone. But if she said so, he'd only disagree with her. It was his second favorite thing to do, right after driving her batshit crazy.

"And you ever hear of a jacket?" he asked, shrugging out of his and tossing it to her. "You look like a drowned rat."

"Aw, you say the nicest things." And she tossed his jacket right back at him.

He simply wrapped her up in it, jerking it closed, bending close to yank the zipper up.

"I don't need —"

"I'll lock you in it," he said, his voice still calm but utter steel. "You're shivering."

Actually, not anymore, she wasn't. But no sense in letting him know she enjoyed the warmth of his jacket or telling him he might have been right. This was the thing about AJ — he spent a lot of time being right.

Infuriating.

The jacket smelled like him — which was to say amazing — and held his body heat. Refusing to give in to the urge to press her face to the collar and inhale him in, she shoved her arms into the arm holes and scooped his schedule out of the printer tray to slap it against his chest.

His hard-as-a-slab-of-marble chest. She wondered if his other part-time receptionist, Brittney, ever noticed such a thing. Probably not, as Brittney had just recently gotten engaged. "Your first client is Ronan," she said. "He just pulled up." She didn't look into his face because doing so tended to make her stupid. She didn't know if it was his lean jaw, in perpetual need of a shave, or that wide, firm mouth currently set in a grim line, discouraging any casual conversation — which perversely always made her want to ask him about the weather just to watch his head implode.

Ronan walked in the front door, his left arm in a sling to protect his shoulder while he recovered. He'd been an army MP in Afghanistan when he'd been injured. He'd been medically discharged after treatment seven years ago but the shoulder had never been the same, so he'd recently had another surgery.

Another thing that had never been the same was Ronan himself. He suffered PTSD and had been having problems with going out in public because social situations made him anxious. He didn't like people, didn't like to interact. There were only a few that he could tolerate: Any of his army buddies.

And AJ.

Ronan's hard gaze looked over at them. His gaze immediately locked on AJ and, well, *softened* wasn't the right word but he definitely relaxed, as if just seeing AJ there had made it worth it to leave his house.

AJ sent him a smile and a welcoming nod. "Hey, man, good to see you today."

Ronan didn't return the smile but he did look less likely to rip someone's head off as he headed to the far corner of the big, open gym where he and AJ always started their sessions.

Darcy's leg ached from being cold and standing, and the pain made her grit her teeth. But when AJ turned his attention back to her, she hid her grimace. "What do you need money for?" he asked.

"I didn't say I needed money."

He gave her a *get real* look.

Right. Everyone knew that between her exorbitant medical bills and being unable to do her usual work — which until her accident had been travel writing for Nat Geo and the Travel Channel's websites — she was desperately strapped for cash. "It's not work related," she said, annoyed that she sounded defensive.

He leaned against the counter, pose casual, body calm and relaxed.

If a panther was ever calm and relaxed . . .

"What is it related to?" he asked.

She picked at a nonexistent speck of lint from his jacket.

"How much do you need, Darcy?"

Look at that, she had a ragged nail. She hoped someone here had a nail file or she'd be tempted to chew it off.

"A couple hundred?"

"No. And never mind." She moved to the filing cabinet. Or more accurately, *limped* to the filing cabinet, because now her entire body ached like a sonofabitch. She rubbed her leg without thinking and caught AJ's gaze narrowing in on the movement of her hand.

"Stress is bad for your recovery," he said quietly.

She dropped her hand. "I know how to take care of myself."

He arched a brow, and hell if that didn't really put her back up. She wanted to sit but her pride wouldn't let her until he moved off. And fine, yes, once upon a damn time she'd been shit at taking care of herself.

Case in point — wrapping her car around a tree on a stormy night on a deserted highway out in the middle of nowhere and nearly dying. But that had been eleven months ago, and a woman could change.

Or at least, she could be working on that change . . .

The door opened and Zoe strode in. Darcy's older sister was looking professional in a business suit, clearly dressed for a flight. As one of only two pilots for hire at Sunshine's local airport, Zoe stayed busy.

But thankfully not too busy, because she was carrying a bag of — yes! — Gummy Bears. Darcy's drug of choice.

Tall and willowy, Zoe had all eyes on her as she strode across the floor, sparing a smile for AJ.

AJ returned it, and without any warning, Darcy's heart careened off her ribs. It really wasn't fair that he looked like a fallen angel when he smiled. Good thing he rarely did.

"What's up?" he asked Zoe.

"Just here to visit your sweet, adorable, kind receptionist."

"She's not in today," AJ said, deadpan.

Zoe laughed.

And Darcy sighed. But then her sister handed her the Gummy Bears, which went a long way toward soothing her rumpled feathers.

"You've been here for two weeks without getting fired," Zoe said. "Impressive."

She was referring, of course, to the three days Darcy had worked at the local bar before being shown the door. "Hey," she said. "Putting false engagement rings in women's drinks as an early present from Santa was funny."

"Not to their boyfriends," Zoe said, and then stage-whispered, "and please don't try to punk AJ, okay? He means a lot to me, so if he kills you, it'll be all sorts of awkward."

"I won't go up for murder," AJ said. "They'd never find the body."

AJ humor. Darcy rolled her eyes. "Thanks for the goodies," she said to Zoe. "But I'm sure you have to go now."

"I've got a few minutes."

Great. Darcy looked at AJ. "Tell her I'm too busy to socialize. And you're too busy, too. Ronan's waiting."

As if on cue, Ronan sat up from where he'd been doing sit-ups and looked over.

"Hey, Ronan," Zoe called out with a warm smile. "How's your mom?"

"Done with chemo and looking better."

Zoe's smile brightened. "Oh, I'm so glad!"

Sunshine was too damn small, Darcy thought. Not only did everyone know everyone, but no one had ever learned to mind their own business. Darcy started to move back to her computer but AJ stepped in her way, ducking down a little to look into her eyes.

"Ice the leg," he said, and without waiting for a response, headed toward Ronan.

Damn, the man had a way of moving, his body shifting with barely sheathed loose-limbed power and grace, and both Darcy and Zoe watched him go.

"He's got such an edible butt," Zoe whispered. "Do you think he knows it?"

"I don't think he cares." Besides, his being hot didn't change the fact that he was a bigger problem for her than Johnny could even think about being. Johnny was just an asshole. AJ was . . . well, she wasn't sure what. Dangerous as hell to her well-being, for starters.

"So why do you do it?" Zoe asked her.

Darcy tore her gaze away from AJ's ass. "Do what?"

Zoe took her big-sister status very seriously. But then again, in spite of the fact that there were only a few years between them, Zoe had always been more maternal toward Darcy than their actual mom ever had.

"Bait him," Zoe said. "He's great guy. He's smart, hard-working, self-made . . ."

"Maybe you should date him."

Zoe laughed. "We're not suited."

"Because?" Darcy asked.

"Well . . . he's a bit alpha."

Yeah. Just a bit.

"We'd butt heads," Zoe said. "But I've always thought that maybe you two might . . ."

"A minute ago you were worried he might kill me."

"Well, sleeping with him might go a long way toward making sure he wouldn't."

Darcy snorted. "Go away, Z."

"In a minute. He did so much for you after your accident."

This was absolutely true. Darcy had had five surgeries, and once she'd been okayed for physical therapy, AJ had taken over her care. He'd been a drill sergeant but he'd also saved her life. She knew it. He knew it.

And wasn't that just the problem. She hated knowing that she hadn't been able to save herself, that she'd needed help. "You're right," she agreed softly. "He's done a lot for me."

"I mean look at you, Darce. You're walk-ing."

A miracle. Darcy got that. She was grate-ful for that, so very grateful he'd gotten her out of a wheelchair and onto her own feet again. Sure, she'd never win a track meet and she was always going to be somewhat unstable on her own two legs — especially the right one which still enjoyed buckling on her at the worst of times — but yeah. AJ would forever be a hero for what he'd done for her.

Which wasn't to say she liked him.

In fact, during her PT she'd actually hated him. She'd dreamed nightly about strangling him, drowning him . . .

Very satisfying dreams, too.

And if there'd been a few others, some that had involved a different kind of altercation altogether between them, of the naked and sweaty variety, well, those were her little secrets.

Across the large room, past all the exercise equipment to the mirrored wall, Ronan lay flat on his back now, working with a large rubber band around his ankles, doing strengthening exercises.

On his knees at his side, AJ guided him, and wrong as it might be, the sight of the two built guys working so hard together made her pulse race just a little bit.

During a quick beat of rest for Ronan, AJ glanced over the carved muscles of his shoulder to meet Darcy's gaze.

She stopped breathing.

At her side, so did Zoe. "I just don't get why you're so hard on him," her sister said.

"Actually, I think you've got that backward." *He* was hard on *her*.

Very hard.

And she resented that. It was almost as if he expected her to soften her edges, to be something she wasn't — like maybe one of those soft, sweet, bendy yoga instructors he was fond of dating. But though Darcy was working on herself, she was never going to be soft and sweet.

Or, thanks to her accident, bendy.

"Maybe you could just try a little bit harder to be more . . . friendly," Zoe suggested.

Darcy didn't have words for what she felt for AJ, but she was pretty sure "friendly" wasn't going to make the list. And yet if AJ had been there for Darcy in a huge way, so had Zoe. Always. So Darcy blew out a breath and managed a smile for her sister. "Sure," she said. "I'll try."

Two

Several days later, AJ was in the middle of his weekly game of rec league football. And since Sunshine was a place where only the rugged, the hardy, and the tough-as-hell resided, the "flag" part of the game had long ago been forgotten, making it a contact sport. Complainers were booted and banned. For life.

AJ's team consisted of old friends: Darcy's veterinarian brother, Wyatt. Griffin, a friend from high school. And the three brothers who ran the Belle Haven Animal Center: Brady, Dell, and Adam.

Their opposing team was a company of local firefighters who played fast and dirty.

Really dirty.

In the first half AJ took a hard hit and found himself flat on his back.

From the sidelines came the collective groan of the spectators. Sunshine took its sports seriously.

AJ rubbed his aching ribs and decided that probably nothing was broken. Just as well. Not even broken ribs would've gotten him benched — they had no substitute players tonight. He lay there a minute to catch his breath, staring up at the sky. Looked like it was going to rain again. He heard Wyatt call a time-out.

Wyatt's face appeared above him. "Haven't seen that in a while," his best friend said with a smirk. "Whatcha doing?"

"Just needed a quick rest," AJ said.

"Well, rest on your own time. We're down by three and I've got fifty bucks riding on this. Plus, Emily's watching."

Emily was Wyatt's girlfriend, and he was in the "show-off" phase of their relationship.

AJ lifted his head and eyed the crowd. Yep, the cutie-pie, new-to-town intern vet was indeed watching. In fact, most of the town was.

Emily, who was just as crazy about Wyatt as Wyatt was about her, stood up, waved, and blew him a kiss.

Wyatt grinned stupidly at her.

"If you blow her a kiss back," AJ muttered, "I'm taking away your man card."

But he was wasting his breath because Wyatt blew her a kiss back.

AJ flopped his head back to the grass and groaned.

"Hey," Wyatt said. "Which of us is going to get laid tonight? Me, that's who. In fact, I get laid just about every night, so who's got the man card now?" He offered AJ a hand up. "You going to tell me what your problem is?"

"In the middle of a time out here."

"They'll wait. Given your performance tonight, they think you're so old you need the rest, that buys us some time."

"Mind's not on the game, that's all," AJ said.

"No shit. Where's it at?"

Excellent question. Wyatt was easygoing and laid-back, which made him a great vet, and in fact, a great guy, but there were limits to what a man could say to his best friend. For instance, *My mind's on your frustrating, crazy-hot sister* wasn't going to fly, not if he wanted to keep his teeth where they were. "Work," he finally said, figuring it was close enough to the truth.

Wyatt's eyes narrowed. "It's not Darcy, is it?"

AJ resisted taking yet another look at the crowd watching. He didn't have to; he'd memorized her. She wore dark sunglasses on her clear jade green eyes and her honey-

29

colored hair had been left on the loose tonight, the curls wild and free, much like the woman herself. She wore sexy, painted-on jeans, boots designed to make a grown man drop to his knees and beg, and a formfitting, scoop-neck vintage Led Zeppelin tee. She was long-legged, hotter than the sun that hadn't bothered to show its face in weeks, and looked like the poster woman for the very best kind of trouble — trouble she could and had delivered.

And she was one hundred percent the most dangerous thing he'd ever faced, and that included his six years in the Navy. "No," he said. "It's not Darcy. She's . . ." Driving him right out of his ever-loving mind. "Fine. It's nothing. Let's finish this."

Wyatt's expression said *Nothing my ass*, but he nodded and they went back to the game.

By the time the game finally ended, they were filthy and a little bloody, but they'd won by three — no thanks at all to AJ. He sucked down water like it was going out of style as Wyatt sat on the bench at his side.

"Is it your dad?" Wyatt asked. "He have another skin cancer scare?"

"No," AJ said. "He's fine." Ornery as hell, but fine. "And I told you, nothing's wrong."

"Can't bullshit a bullshitter," Wyatt said.

"It's a woman. Right?"

AJ bent to the task of switching out his cleats for running shoes.

"Yeah," Wyatt said. "It's a woman."

Still ignoring him, AJ stood.

"Listen, not three weeks ago you helped me get my head out of my ass," Wyatt said. "Told me to go after the love of my life. I did and it worked out."

AJ sighed and turned to face him. "We were both drunk. You're just lucky I didn't suggest something stupid, such as running like hell."

"You never suggest anything stupid," Wyatt said. "You're the most logical, reasonable guy I know."

AJ pulled out his phone and looked at the time.

"My point," Wyatt said, "is that love isn't logical or reasonable."

"Gee, there's a news flash."

Wyatt stood up and pushed AJ's phone away, smiling when AJ narrowed his eyes in annoyance. "It's my turn to be Obi Wan, and that's because now I get that the right one isn't the right one unless she's driving you absolutely bonkers in the best possible way. And I gotta say . . . you're looking a little bonkers, man."

He had that right. "Let it go," AJ said.

"Fine. You don't want my help until you fuck it all up, I get that, too. But I'll be standing right here when you need me."

AJ shook his head. "Thanks for the warning."

"And not that you deserve the invite, but Emily and I are thinking about going camping up to Marble Flats this weekend. Her sister and her fiancé will probably come, too. We could get some of the guys and —"

"Can't," AJ said.

"You off to consult somewhere or heading to D.C.?"

Besides running the Sunshine Wellness Center, AJ consulted on physical therapy at military bases across the country, mostly within the special ops units. He also went to D.C. regularly to fight for better, longer PT care for injured vets. "Neither," he said. "I'm heading to Boise."

"That guy who's interested in your grant program finally set up a meet, then?"

"Yeah." AJ had been working on putting together grants to cover extended treatment for patients with extensive trauma cases who got cut off too early by their insurance companies. Unfortunately he had way too many of those cases and not nearly enough funding, so he'd gone looking for people willing to fund grants and had someone interested.

"I hope he bites," Wyatt said. "You need this. I don't know what we'd have done if Darcy hadn't had you at her back when her insurance ran out."

"She had all of us," AJ said, but knew Wyatt was right. If Darcy had quit PT when her insurance had stopped covering her treatment, she'd still be in a wheelchair. "This guy's got a wife who needed long-term PT care after an accident. He's a CEO of a team-building corporation, and he's having a weekend retreat for his employees. I've been asked to bring along someone I helped pro bono after they ran out of funds. Someone who'd have benefited from the grant program. My plan was to bring Seth."

Another of AJ's clients, Seth Williams had been in a climbing accident and worked his way back from an incomplete SCI — spinal cord injury — thanks to extended treatment.

"Seth agreed to that?" Wyatt asked, surprised.

Seth was so introverted and shy that he could barely go to the store, much less show off his motor skills on demand. "At first," AJ said. "But he just cancelled on me today. Said he appreciated everything I've done to help him but that he couldn't handle being on display."

"So how important is it to bring someone for show and tell?" Wyatt asked.

"Mission critical."

They both glanced up at the crowd still milling around. Zoe was there, messing with her phone. Ariana, too, and she smiled at AJ. *You okay?* she mouthed, gesturing to her ribs, silently asking about his.

AJ nodded that he was fine.

"You've got other options," Wyatt said quietly.

Yeah, on paper Ariana was the perfect match. She'd needed AJ's PT services five years ago for a shoulder rebuild. But he knew that she cared about him as more than co-workers and friends. And though he'd tried to return the feelings, he'd felt no chemistry. He could live without a lot of things, but chemistry wasn't one of them. "A weekend away with Ariana might give her the wrong message and screw up our friendship and working relationship," he said. "I don't want to hurt her again."

"I wasn't talking about Ariana," Wyatt said.

AJ followed his gaze to the side of the spectator stands, to where Darcy now sat on the grass, alternately stuffing her face with nachos from the snack bar and loving up on a young German shepherd.

Her laugh came to him on the wind and he pretended that didn't affect him, the sight of her having fun — which for the past eleven months had been rarer than him nearly screwing up tonight's game. "Never going to happen."

"Why not?" Wyatt asked. "She works for you."

More like she allowed him to pretend she worked for him. "She's not exactly on Team AJ at the moment."

Wyatt laughed. "We both know that Darcy isn't on any team, she's not a team player." His smile faded. "And we both know why."

Yeah, they did. Wyatt, Zoe, and Darcy's foreign diplomat parents had played a hell of a head game on all their kids, but most especially Darcy. From infancy they'd dragged her all over the world in the name of making better lives for others, giving her little to no supervision and then acting shocked whenever she'd found trouble.

Their response had always been to send her away to some tight-assed school in a country on a different continent than theirs and leave her there without communication — a total and epic parental rejection.

It was little to no wonder she had trust issues and a seeming inability to become emotionally attached to anything or anyone.

"These past eleven months have been good for her," Wyatt said. "I mean the accident was fucked up, but having her stick around Sunshine —"

"She didn't choose to stick," AJ reminded him. "She hasn't been healthy enough to chase stories around the world and write about them. If she could, she'd be gone, off traveling for work without looking back."

"Yeah." Wyatt scrubbed a hand over his jaw. "That was definitely true at first, but I think she's starting to enjoy a home life now. It seems like she's really coming around."

"To you and Zoe maybe."

Wyatt smiled. "She does seem to take some serious delight in screwing with you. What did you do to piss her off?"

"Breathe." But AJ knew exactly what he'd done and he was taking it to his grave.

"There's no reason why she wouldn't do this for you," Wyatt said. "Especially after all you've done for her."

"Any physical therapist would've done what I did. And I was paid for my services. She owes me nothing."

"You weren't paid for all of it," Wyatt reminded him. "You wrote off a lot of your bills after the insurance stopped paying. Given that, she'd probably jump at the chance to help you . . ." He trailed off at the look on AJ's face. "You never told her?"

AJ slid his hands into his pockets.

"You never told her," Wyatt repeated in disbelief. "Are you fucking kidding me? You insisted that Zoe and I not say anything to her because you wanted to do it."

"Whatever," AJ said. "You do the same thing at your work all the time. Do you tell your patients when you do pro bono work?"

"My patients are four-legged creatures who don't speak English. Jesus, AJ, she should know what you've done for her."

"She doesn't need to know." AJ met Wyatt's gaze. "Ever."

Wyatt opened his mouth but AJ pointed at him. *"Ever,"* he repeated. "Think about it. Like you just said, she's settling in for the first time in her life. She seems happy, even relaxed. She's finally on her feet again and feeling like she has some control back. I'm not taking that from her by making her feel like she owes me."

Wyatt blew out a breath. A silent, reluctant agreement. "Okay, I get that, but you could still ask her to do this for you."

AJ tried to imagine getting Darcy to dress up and go to a fancy dinner and play nice, helping him schmooze his potential financial backer. Unable to, he shook his head.

"Look," Wyatt said, "if getting this guy means anything to you —"

"It does," AJ said. "You know it does."

"Then tell her. She's got more heart than the rest of us put together. Appeal to that. You can convince her to do it."

As if AJ knew the first thing about successfully appealing to a woman's heart. "Have you ever talked your sister into doing something she didn't want to do?"

Wyatt laughed ruefully, conceding the point as they both looked over at Darcy again. She'd shoved her sunglasses to the top of her head and had the German shepherd sitting obediently in front of her, eyes on the doggy treat in her fist.

AJ hadn't seen the dog before but knew he must be the one Zoe had mentioned to him in passing, the "career change" dog Darcy had rescued from Asshat Johnny. AJ hadn't imagined she'd be able to handle a dog. But she seemed to be handling the animal fine.

Without even realizing his feet were on the move, AJ walked up to her.

"Play dead and roll over," she was saying.

"I'd need alcohol for that," AJ said.

She looked up at him, eyes cool. "I meant Blue."

"Blue" collapsed to the floor, ruining the

"dead" image by lolling his tongue, appearing to smile up at Darcy.

She burst out laughing.

And actually so did AJ.

Darcy cocked her head up at him. "Huh," she said. "Didn't know you could do that."

Ignoring this, and also the way her scent had come to him on the evening breeze, all soft, sexy woman, AJ crouched low and held out a fist for the dog to sniff. "Hey there."

Blue licked AJ's hand in greeting and then rolled over in silent appeal for a belly rub. AJ obliged, his mind doing the math. It was only a twenty-minute drive to Johnny's, but the guy lived off of Highway 64, a narrow, curvy, two-lane highway.

Which was where Darcy had crashed her car eleven months ago.

As far as he knew, she hadn't driven on a highway since, and she certainly hadn't been on Highway 64. "How did you get him?" he asked.

"Xander drove me."

AJ ground his back teeth together at the name but said nothing.

"I used the quarterly bonuses you gave out yesterday." She paused. "Thank you for that."

He nodded. No way would he admit that to help her without hurting her pride, he'd given out the bonuses for her sake.

"He failed his S&R training because swimming makes him anxious," Darcy said, and offered a treat to Blue.

He leapt to his feet and gently took the prize.

"Good boy," she said softly, and Blue melted into her hug, leaning into her, knocking them both to the grass.

Knowing exactly how much she still hurt, AJ reached for her. "You okay?"

With a laugh, she sat up. "I'm fine. Such a good boy, Blue." She hugged the dog tight and rubbed her cheek to Blue's. "What a good, pretty boy, yes you are."

"Aw, thanks, baby."

AJ craned his neck to take in the tall, skinny, leather-clad, tatted-up man who'd just appeared at their side.

Xander returned AJ's cool look with one of his own. He didn't like AJ much.

The feeling was absolutely mutual.

Blue, however, went nuts, giving a joyous bark at the sight of Xander, jumping up and down like a Mexican jumping bean.

"Yeah, yeah, you're pretty, too," Darcy told Xander. "But not as pretty as Blue — and you're late."

"Appointment went over," he said, and kept looking at AJ.

AJ kept looking right back.

Darcy divided a glance between them. "Seriously? Still?"

When neither man moved, she sighed. "You're both ridiculous." She looked at AJ. "Xander's giving Blue to his aunt as a therapy dog. She's been wanting one forever but couldn't afford to make it happen. We're hoping to get one for Tyson next."

Tyson was Xander's brother, and also a patient of AJ's. And AJ agreed, Tyson would probably get a lot out of a therapy dog, though AJ had his doubts that Tyson was ready for one. Tyson was barely ready for life as a paraplegic after a motorcycle racing accident had destroyed his spine a year and a half ago.

Xander took Blue's leash from Darcy, giving her a secret smile before turning back to AJ. "Heard you took a hard hit earlier."

"I'm fine."

Xander looked a little disappointed at that. Word around town was that he and Darcy were just friends, but there was nothing that said "just friends" in Xander's gaze whenever he looked at Darcy. Nope, he looked at her like she was lunch.

Not that it mattered to AJ.

Except it did.

The truth was that even though he had

absolutely no intention of making a move on Darcy, he didn't want Xander to, either. He realized this made him a complete and total dick, but he could live with that.

"Thanks for watching him for me, babe," Xander said.

"No problem," Darcy said. "I —" She broke off to send AJ a startled look. "Did you just . . . growl?"

"No." Shit, he totally had.

Above her head Xander smirked at him. *Asshole.*

Darcy bent low and hugged Blue good-bye one last time. When she stood, she steadied herself equally on both legs the way AJ had taught her so that she didn't continue to baby her bad leg and keep it weak. "I'll see you later," she said to Xander.

"Yeah, you will," he said, and didn't go away.

AJ didn't, either. He wasn't leaving first. Hell no. And he could stand here all night, too. Even if he wanted to curl into the fetal position and whimper over his aching ribs.

"Oh, for God's sake," Darcy said in exasperation. "I'm sure both of your penises are the exact same size."

Xander grinned.

"Go home," she snapped at him.

"As you wish." Xander brushed a kiss

right across her mouth and then he and Blue sauntered off.

Darcy turned to AJ and something flashed between them, something that most definitely *hadn't* flashed between her and Xander, though he was at a pretty big loss to say what it was.

Darcy sucked her lower lip between her teeth and suddenly he knew exactly what it was.

Lust.

Which was going to be a problem, a big one. "You going to order me home, too?" he asked, daring her.

She laughed. "Like you'd do anything I ordered of you."

"Try me."

THREE

Try him? *Try him?* Darcy thought about reminding him that she'd once done exactly that and he'd flat-out rejected her — a feeling she'd learned to be so at one with that it hardly fazed her anymore.

Mostly.

But her tummy quivered at the look in his eyes, even though she had no idea what it meant. Didn't dare give it much thought either because she'd long ago trained herself to stop wanting him.

Especially since sometimes, like right now, she was vividly reminded of her most embarrassing moment. It had been three months after her accident. She'd still been in a wheelchair and homebound — and going stir-crazy. It had been late, really late, and she'd been alone, selfishly needing someone.

Anyone.

She hadn't wanted to disturb her brother

or sister, not when they'd finally gone back to having their own lives after being with her nearly twenty-four/seven for so long.

So she'd called AJ.

He'd shown up ten minutes later looking sleepy and disheveled, like he'd literally rolled out of bed and rushed to her side. He'd forever earned a spot in her heart that night by not questioning her when she asked him to drive her to the bar for a drink.

Still in casts and various bandages, it had taken her a half hour to wrestle into real clothes. Real clothes being yoga pants that stretched over her leg cast, and her fave KISS tank top. After weeks and weeks of pj's, she'd felt infinitely more human and herself, especially after she'd added mascara and lip gloss.

AJ had rolled her from his truck to the bar, where she'd had two shots and absorbed the loud music and laughter like she'd been in prison. Afterward, they'd gone back out into the night.

It had been a clear, gorgeous one with a full moon and a million stars littered across the black velvet sky. She'd never forget staring up and inhaling deep the chilly air, and for the first time since the accident she'd felt . . . grateful.

Grateful to be alive.

She hadn't realized she'd been crying until she'd felt AJ's fingers on her. He'd hunkered down at her side, balanced on the balls of his feet as he cupped her face and whispered her name.

She'd pulled him in with her one good arm and kissed him.

And for one glorious moment he'd kissed her back with his firm, warm lips, a sexy low groan rumbling up from deep in his throat, the delicious glide of his tongue to hers, and then . . .

And then he'd jerked back. He'd shaken his head in disbelief before speaking. "This isn't going to happen, Darcy. This isn't *ever* going to happen, not with you."

Cue the humiliation.

Because she'd given it her best shot. She'd thrown herself at him, and he'd found her lacking. Worse, he'd refused to discuss it, apparently preferring to pretend it had never happened.

So after making him promise to never tell a soul, she'd done the same.

She'd been as good at that as she'd been at pretending the rejection hadn't hurt. Really good. After all, she had good practice since for most of her life she'd been dumped like yesterday's trash and she'd long ago learned to block off her feelings. She'd been good at that, too, and was able to do it with everything and everyone — except one man.

This man.

That night she'd made a pact with herself. She'd decided she didn't need to know why AJ affected her the way he did. She only had to steer clear of him enough so that it didn't become an issue. For the most part she'd done just that, except she hadn't been able to resist stepping on his every nerve whenever possible to make things more even between them.

The hardest thing was also the most embarrassing — making sure she never gave herself away by keeping her tongue rolled in her mouth when he was at work looking hot and sexy and confident.

Or on the football field looking dirty and hot and sexy and confident.

"I've gotta go," she said. "I —"

But Ariana had stopped at his side to give him a hug. The kind of hug that suggested familiarity.

Whatever. So AJ and Ariana had had a thing. Everyone knew that. They were well suited, what with AJ's calm, stoic attitude and Ariana's calm inner spirit. Hell, maybe they were still having a thing. Truth was, AJ had lots of things, with lots of women. That's what happened when you had that whole badass thing going on. Women tended to be stupid when it pertained to big and badass.

Herself included.

No matter that she told herself she preferred sweet and gentle, the truth was that she wouldn't mind being a little stupid with someone big and badass and sexy as hell. Problem was, she wasn't exactly at her sexiest, and hadn't been for a while. She walked like Lurch from *The Addams Family,* she was mean as a snake from not sleeping more than a few hours at a time due to the pain, and though she liked the thought of having wild monkey sex, the actual mechanics of it were undoubtedly beyond her now.

Bending, she grabbed her bag and slung it over her shoulder before starting to rise carefully back up. This was always the tricky part because when she didn't pay attention, her right leg tended to buckle and she often ended up face-planting.

She'd done so just last week at the grocery store checkout in front of the really cute checker, going down like a sack of potatoes. Even more mortifying, the cute checker had crouched at her side and said, "Ma'am, I've called the ambulance, stay real still."

Ma'am.

He'd thought her old enough to be called

ma'am, and hell, she'd certainly felt old. It had been a blow to her ego because there'd been a time when she could've batted her lashes, flashed a smile, and caught any guy she wanted, young or old.

Now? She didn't even have the energy for a self-serve in her own shower.

So yeah, she'd fall in front of an audience again over her own dead body, especially an audience that included the guy who'd probably give her a new list of strengthening exercises to do every day and then watch over her like a drill sergeant.

But before she could make the careful struggle, a large hand appeared in front of her face. Reaching out, she gripped AJ's hand, using it as a lifeline.

He didn't let go right away, either, just squeezed his fingers in hers, setting his other hand on the curve of her waist to help her gain her balance, silently reminding her to put equal weight on both feet. She concentrated hard, her gaze up as he'd taught her. *Feel the equilibrium.*

The directives had been drilled into her by AJ himself, who stood there quietly, respectfully letting her get to it by herself on her own timetable.

The opposite tactic of Xander. While he had a lot of really great qualities, patience wasn't one of them. He'd been known to pick her up, toss her in a fireman's hold, and carry her where he wanted to go rather than wait for her to get there herself.

It never failed to piss her off.

At least Ariana had moved off and no one was staring at her struggling. She hated that most of all — the sympathetic gazes. Hated. That was one thing AJ had never done: pity her.

Piss her off? Oh yeah. But not pity her. She supposed he got Brownie points for that. "I'm good," she said.

"I know."

He could be such an annoying alpha pain in her ass, but it was in moments like these that she realized just how important his steady, imperturbable disposition was, and had been, to her recovery.

He'd given her back her life.

And her dignity.

Damn him all to hell. "Well," she said, blowing out a breath and relaxing a bit. "This has been fun."

"Liar."

She choked out a laugh. "You know, I'm always a little bit disappointed when someone calls someone a liar and their pants don't catch on fire."

His eyes smiled. "You want my pants to

catch on fire?"

Not going there . . . "Any special reason why you were intimidating Xander back there?" she asked. "Or was it just for sport?"

AJ's gaze slid away to take in the retreating man in question, who'd been stopped by Ariana to talk. "You think I intimidated him?"

"Like you, he's hard to intimidate," she said. "But unlike you, he's afraid of me and my wrath so he backed off."

"And you don't think I'm afraid of you?" he asked.

Valid question. As far as she knew, just about everyone was afraid of her. Crazy Darcy. Bitchy Darcy. Wild Darcy. But she slowly shook her head. "I don't think you're afraid of anything," she said.

The corners of his mouth curved as if her statement amused him, but also maybe wasn't quite accurate. But she sincerely couldn't imagine the big, built, ex-military man standing in front of her being afraid of a damn thing.

And anyway, why was he here talking to her? He rarely did unless he had to. "Did you need to talk to me about work?" she asked.

"No. Well, yes, kind of," he said. "I'm going to Boise this weekend."

"To meet up with your potential grant sponsor. I e-mailed you all the hotel and registration info, for both you and Seth. It's a retreat weekend, did you know that? It's some big team-building thing for all the guy's employees. Be prepared for Seth to freak out when he sees how many people will be there."

"Yeah, about that . . ." AJ rubbed a hand over the sexy scruff on his jaw and it made a sound that reminded her how it felt to have a man kiss her. All over.

Damn, she missed sex.

"Seth already freaked out," AJ said.

"Uh-oh." She tried to read him but he could be military stoic and impenetrable when he wanted, giving nothing away. "What happened?"

"He said that he can't be on display."

Ah. Now she knew why he was still standing there talking to her. "Sounds like a problem for you," she said slowly.

"Yes. It is."

She stared at him some more, thinking, *Oh hell no.* Then she said it out loud just in case her expression wasn't clear enough. "Oh *hell* no, AJ."

"I didn't say anything."

"You were thinking it," she said, pointing at him. "You want me to go instead."

"I do," he said calmly.

She didn't realize she was shaking her head in the negative until he spoke.

"You've got an amazing comeback story," he said. "And since I was your PT, I can personally attest to your recovery and exactly how amazing it was."

"You want to profit from that?"

"No," he said, his voice still perfectly even, but something flashed in his eyes.

Disappointment? Hurt?

"I want others like you to profit from it," he said. "With donations for grants, I can help more people when their insurance cuts them off before they're ready to stop PT."

Emotion swamped her, unexpected and hot. Shame. A man like AJ would never try to profit off another. Never. "I'm sorry," she managed. "You're right. I shouldn't have said —"

"It's just one night," he said, clearly not wanting or needing her apology. "Just a dinner. I'll help you through it."

"But —"

"You don't want to be on display, either," he said. "I get it."

No, she didn't want to be on display. So badly she didn't. She still felt self-conscious when her sister and brother watched her walk, much less other people. And talking about her accident and the recovery? Her biggest nightmare.

And yet he wanted her to do exactly that, where so many strange sets of eyes would be on her.

Horror. "No —"

"I'll pay you," he said, still quiet, still calm in the face of her panic.

She just stared at him.

"Cash. A thousand bucks. That's enough for what, three dogs?"

Her mouth fell open. "Yeah, but . . . why? Why would you pay me?"

"Because you have a cause, and I'm a sucker for a cause that involves anything with four legs."

Oh, damn. Damn, that was a good answer.

He looked at the time on his phone. "I've gotta go. Think about it and let me know."

And then he was gone.

One night, she told herself. One dinner. And in return, money for more dogs.

How hard could it be?

She was afraid she knew the answer to that question.

That night she lay facedown on the tattoo table, her Queen tank top rolled up to just beneath her breasts, holding her breath as Xander worked his magic.

"Breathe, sweetness," he said.

"Can't." Her fingers were wrapped around the edges of the table so tight she was probably leaving permanent indentations. "Holy . . . crap," she gasped. "Holy effing crap."

He stopped the torture, aka the tattoo he was creating alongside the scar from her spinal surgery.

"You're sure you don't want me to try to cover the scar instead of going parallel to it?" he asked. "It'd be difficult to get rid of it entirely but I could cover it pretty significantly."

"No." She held up a hand when he turned his tat gun on again. "Not yet!"

He blew out a sigh and leaned back to give her a longer break, handing over a bag of Gummy Bears — was he a good friend or what?

"It's not that painful," he said. "And piercings are worse, and you've willingly pierced just about everything on your body."

"A *very* long time ago," she pointed out and tore into the bag. "When I was young and stupid." She'd long since taken out most of the piercings, way too much upkeep. "And I was intoxicated for all of them."

"You went through how many surgeries?"

"Those don't count, either," she said,

painstakingly pulling out the green Gummy Bears for consumption first since they were her faves. She'd eat the reds next and then the whites. She didn't acknowledge the yellows because they tasted like furniture cleaner, though in a pinch she'd eat them anyway. "I was under anesthesia so they didn't hurt at all."

"Recovery hurt," he said. "PT hurt. Having your parents not even come home from Somalia to see you in the hospital hurt."

Okay, so maybe *that* had hurt. Though it really shouldn't have. She'd long ago gotten used to being an afterthought, a throwaway. "I had my brother and sister," she said. "And you."

Their gazes met. They'd been friends for years, though they'd only recently connected again, ever since she'd found herself grounded in Sunshine for the past eleven months.

Xander had grown up here. After high school he'd backpacked through Europe before returning to his roots to take over his father's tattoo business.

Darcy's roots weren't connected to a place but to Wyatt and Zoe. And Xander, too, even though he'd been looking at her lately with much more than sibling-like feelings. Oddly enough, neither of them had ever acted on that, though most people in town thought otherwise. But she'd not been feeling well enough, and anyway, Xander almost always had a woman hanging around. Or several. Except, come to think of it, he hadn't had anyone around lately.

He was a damn good-looking guy, all long and lanky and lean, and badass, too, with all the tats and leather and shitkickers. So yeah, maybe she could see why people had assumed she'd dipped her toes in those waters.

But she wasn't ready.

"Why not?" he asked, voice low and a little rough, making her realize she'd spoken out loud.

She sucked in a breath. "Well, for starters," she said, her voice low, too, "my body still looks like Frankenstein's monster."

To his credit, his gaze didn't sweep downward to look, but instead remained on her eyes. "Your body is perfect," he said with nothing but sweet sincerity.

It wasn't often he did sweet, and that moved her. But she shook her head. "Okay, so I *feel* like Frankenstein's monster," she said. "I can't control much —"

He shook his head. "Excuses."

True enough. They both knew she wasn't embarrassed in the least by her scars. In fact, it was the opposite really. Her scars represented something to her. They represented her change. BS — before scars — she hadn't cared for herself all that much. She never gave her safety, or her future for that matter, any thought at all. She'd not had a death wish or been depressed, but she hadn't really seen herself getting old. She'd lived in the moment, always. Sometimes the moment had involved hanging off a mountain by a rope covering some new adventure for Nat Geo. And sometimes that moment had meant swimming with sharks off a South Pacific reef for the Travel Channel.

But something weird happened to a person when they nearly bought the farm. Turned out your life really did flash before your eyes. And in her case, all her adventures had as well. That's when she'd realized — almost all of those adventures had been experienced alone.

When she'd opened her eyes in the hospital, and then had faced all those long months of staring up at the ceiling while her body healed, she'd decided she had things to work on. Things that included learning to not only like herself, but to love herself as well.

She'd been working on the *like* thing, and

was starting to have some success. But the love thing . . . that was taking a little bit longer. Hence the real reason she wasn't sleeping with Xander. In her heart of hearts she knew he was falling for her and she refused to hurt him unless she knew she could fall for him back.

As for the new tattoo . . . No, she wasn't being self-destructive. Nor would she ever cover her surgical scars. Instead she wanted to complement it with her tattoo, which read in small, beautiful script: *I am the hero of my story, I don't need to be saved.*

She wanted to remember that every single day.

Xander was still just looking at her, clearly waiting for her to say something he'd actually understand, so she took his hand and brought it to her heart. "You're a good guy, Xander."

He stared at her. "Ah, fuck." He dropped his head to his chest on a low laugh. "The good guy speech." He lifted his head again. "If your next line is that I have a good personality, just kill me now."

"You *do* have a good personality," she insisted.

"Like a dagger," he said, and mimed being stabbed, but then he squeezed her fingers affectionately.

"And anyway," she said, squeezing him back, "you don't really want me."

Now he let his gaze meander down her body and his eyes heated. "Wanna bet?"

She smiled. "I'm talking about the me on the *inside*. I'm still a bitch, Xander. I mean I'm working on it, but I'm not going there with anyone right now, not until I'm ready."

At that, he brought their entwined fingers up to his mouth and brushed a kiss over her knuckles. "You are a bitch," he said with great fondness. "But I love that about you. And I'm a patient man. I can wait. Now lie down and suck it up. I'm on the clock."

She settled back on the table, relieved at the lack of awkwardness between them. She knew most women would say she was nuts. Being with Xander would be good. And easy.

And once upon a time that had been all she needed. Good and easy.

But it no longer felt like enough. His friendship meant too much to her. And she might be reckless, or at least have a reputation for it, but she was no longer stupid or thoughtless.

"Damn," she gasped as the sting of the tat gun hit her again. "Damn, shit, hell —"

"Deep breaths," he told her. "That's it, just keep breathing for me."

"Hey, man, you busy?"

At the sound of his brother Tyson on the other side of the privacy curtain, Xander lifted the tat gun off Darcy's skin. "In the middle of a tat for Darcy," he said.

Silence.

For whatever reason, Tyson had instantly decided way back when that he didn't like her, and it had stuck.

Xander sighed. "What do you need, Ty?"

A pause, and then a gruff, "Nothing."

Darcy's and Xander's eyes met. Nothing her ass. He needed something — money, a ride, whatever — and he didn't want to ask for it in front of her because he knew she hated how he used Xander.

"There's cash in my wallet in the right-hand drawer of my desk in the office," Xander said.

He got no response, no thank-you, nothing, just the sound of Tyson's wheelchair squeaking as he rolled off.

"Dammit, Xander," she whispered. "He's —"

"My brother," Xander said firmly.

"You're his *enabler*."

Xander pulled back, his face closed off, which she knew was to mask his hurt and worry about Tyson. The two of them were all each other had.

Darcy got that and softened. "I'm sorry," she said, reaching for his hand. "Ignore me, I shouldn't talk. After all, I drained both my brother and sister dry all year."

"Love is love," he said, and she knew he absolutely believed that.

What she didn't know was if believing it made it true.

FOUR

Early the next morning, AJ was at the gym with Wyatt at his side, both of them lifting weights.

"You ask Darcy about this weekend?" Wyatt asked, setting his weights down. "Let her know you needed her?"

"I told her, yeah."

Wyatt choked out a laugh and rolled his eyes, for a beat looking very much like his 'tude-ridden sister.

"What?" he asked.

"What, are you an amateur? You can't tell a woman what to do. You have to finesse it. You *ask*. You cajole or coax, or whatever you've got to do. And if all that fails, you have to make them think that whatever it is you need them to do is *their* idea."

AJ laughed. "That's . . . ridiculous. Not to mention manipulative."

"It works," Wyatt said. "You need to trust me on this, as I'm the only one of the two of us currently sharing a pillow with a female. *And* a bathroom. And since we're going there, why is it that guys get the bad bathroom rap when women use *all* the counter space? I mean, what do they need twenty-five different lotions for? How much skin do they have anyway?"

"You share a pillow?" AJ asked.

"You're missing my point," Wyatt said.

"That's because you have too damn many of them." AJ paused. "But for the record, I did ask Darcy." He paused. "I'm pretty sure."

"And . . . ?"

"And she's thinking about it."

"She'll do it," Wyatt said, sounding certain.

"Yeah? What makes you think so? We all know she's not exactly crazy about me."

Wyatt dismissed this. "You can't take that personally."

It felt pretty fucking personal.

"She's not crazy about *anyone* right now," Wyatt said. "But going with you is right and she knows it. Like I said, she just needs it to be her idea."

"And what makes you the leading expert on women?" AJ asked.

"Are you kidding? I've been through three generations of women — my grandma, my mother, two sisters, and now a live-in girlfriend." He looked smug. "I should teach a crash course in female. I'd make a fortune."

AJ didn't have sisters. Or a mother. Or a grandmother, at least not anymore. And though he'd had plenty of women in his life, none had been live-in.

"Think of it this way," Wyatt said. "I'm paving the way for you. My knowledge is your knowledge."

"Thanks," AJ said dryly. "And does this knowledge extend to how to coax your sister into behaving this weekend if she comes with me?"

"Negative. No one's knowledge extends that far."

Terrific.

Darcy woke up to laughter. Someone was having good times without her. Several someones, by the sound of things. Zoe and . . . a man.

This was pretty unusual because Zoe wasn't on the man train right now. She had her reasons and no one had been able to talk her out of her male moratorium.

Darcy spent a few moments in her usual morning fog, staring at her ceiling trying to wake up.

She was not successful.

"Woof!"

The joyous bark shocked her into near cardiac arrest and was accompanied by two big paws hitting her bed. Turning her head, Darcy found herself greeted by a very slobbery tongue that licked her from chin to forehead.

It smelled like Pup-Peroni treats.

"We talked about this," Darcy told Oreo, Zoe's dog. "No kissing until we brush our teeth. And by our, I mean your."

Oreo sat back on his haunches, smiling wide. He was huge, as in Bernese mountain dog huge.

Darcy supposed if she couldn't wake up next to a really hot guy, Oreo would do.

He'd been recently rescued from a dog-fighting ring — by Emily, Wyatt's girlfriend. Zoe had taken one look at Oreo and it had been love at first sight. And he was a good dog, though he still needed some rehabbing. After being neglected and abused for so long, he wasn't the biggest fan of men. Just the other day the mailman had come to the door and Oreo had broken Zoe's bed trying to get under it to hide. He tolerated Wyatt okay but that was probably because *every* animal on the planet tolerated — and genuinely loved — her veterinarian brother.

66

He was like Dr. Doolittle or something.

"Woof."

"Yeah, yeah, I'm getting up." She sat and winced.

She was sore as hell, but this had become her new norm, being stiff and achy as an eighty-year-old in the mornings. Getting out of bed was an Olympic sport, but she managed. Straightening slowly, breathing deeply, she glanced at herself in the mirror. Yikes, her hair looked like she'd stuck her finger in a light socket. Turning her back to the mirror, she lifted up her cami and contorted herself to see the perfect, beautifully rendered tattoo running alongside her scar.

More laughter drifted up from downstairs. Thanks to the questionable insulation in the walls, one could hear every creak and groan the place made. One could also hear every move made — a bummer on the many nights she'd attempted to sneak out of there without being caught by a nosy sister or brother.

She and her siblings had inherited the hundred-year-old Victorian from their grandparents after they'd both gone to the big Bingo game in the sky. Since Darcy's accident, she'd shared it with both Zoe and Wyatt, but over the past month Wyatt had been sleeping mostly with Emily at her house a few miles away. This left Darcy and Zoe, neither of whom knew the first thing about geriatric-house upkeep, though they did their best.

Okay, so Zoe did her best. Darcy, not so much.

But she did love it here, in the first real home base she'd ever had, even if you couldn't use the toaster or a blow-dryer without blowing a fuse. And forget charging your phone and tablet at the same time. In fact, forget having enough bandwidth out here in the boondocks to even warrant having multiple electronic devices, because it wasn't like you could use more than one at a time, especially with the myriad of pot growers in the area using up all the watts and bandwidth.

She didn't care, she was happy here. Surprisingly so. She'd never have guessed that she liked having her siblings so close, that they could all get along. Or that it would mean so much to Darcy that they did. The way they'd been there for her after her accident had meant everything to her. Everything. They were a real family, which never failed to nail Darcy in the gut. In a good way. In the very best way.

Oreo whined at her, wanting her to go with him downstairs to join in the fun he felt he was missing out on.

Darcy knew if anyone in the kitchen was using water there'd be no hot water for a shower, so she didn't even attempt it. She simply followed her nose — bacon! — downstairs with great hope.

Not one to lead, Oreo trailed after her, his nails *click, click, click*ing on the ancient, battered old wood floors, occasionally goosing Darcy in the back of the thighs with a cold, wet nose to hurry her along when she stopped to stretch her leg.

Zoe stood at the stove flipping bacon and Darcy got excited, though that excitement dimmed considerably at the sight of AJ doing the same for pancakes on the griddle.

Damn. She couldn't escape the man.

They had music going from Zoe's iPod — Macklemore's "Same Love." Zoe was performing the rap portion into a wooden spoon, complete with what Darcy assumed Zoe thought was gansta dance moves.

For his part, AJ had taken on the female singing lead, using a really bad falsetto.

They looked ridiculous. For one thing, Zoe couldn't dance to save her life. And for another, AJ might be hot but he was tone-deaf.

And yet for a single heartbeat Darcy felt a pang of . . . what? It had better not be jealousy because that was ridiculous, and yet . . . it felt an awful lot like she'd been bitten by the green-eyed monster.

It was just that most of the time AJ was taking care of the wellness center and his patients, and also traveling to consult on military bases across the country. His life was pretty serious.

Zoe's, too. She had a lot on her plate trying to keep this house together on a shoe-string budget, working too many hours, and she'd made a second career worrying about Wyatt and Darcy.

So it wasn't often that Darcy saw either of them blowing off steam, and yet here they were, going a little nuts, letting their hair down with each other in a way she'd not been privy to. Something tightened in her gut at that. Yep. She was jealous of their easy friendship. Totally and completely jealous.

With the loud music and their even louder singing, AJ couldn't have possibly heard her approach, but he suddenly looked up and locked eyes right on her.

Zoe turned and smiled in surprise. "Hey," she said, breathless. "Hungry? I mean it's turkey bacon and whole wheat pancakes because Mr. Won't Pollute His Body With Crap here wouldn't let me pull out the pork and white flour, but actually it all tastes pretty good."

Darcy had never been picky when it came to food, especially food she didn't have to cook. But suddenly she wanted to be somewhere else. *Anywhere* else. "No, I'm good, but thanks."

Oreo barked. He was feeling sorry for himself and the lack of bacon that had fallen into his mouth.

"You sure you're not hungry?" Zoe asked Darcy, who understood her sister's shock because she was almost always hungry.

She didn't let herself look at the pancakes. "Nope."

"I suppose that's due to the empty bag of potato chips I found on the counter this morning," Zoe said. "Middle-of-the-night munchies again?"

"Yep," Darcy said, avoiding AJ's steady gaze. God forbid he'd ever be tempted by something like trans fats. "A girl needs to keep her strength up."

"I had carrots and celery cut up in the fridge," Zoe said. "I thought you were going to try and go for healthy snacks on your middle-of-the-night prowls."

"Hey, I dipped the chips into your cottage cheese," Darcy said. "That's healthy, right?"

Zoe didn't look amused. In fact, she looked worried. "You're not sleeping again."

Again? Still . . .

"Honey, you need to try the things the doctors suggested," Zoe said. "Yoga, and long, warm baths, and reading before bed to wear out your brain, something frothy and fun like a good, juicy romance."

None of those things appealed. In fact, all of those things made her feel grumpy.

Or grumpier.

AJ didn't say anything. He was like that. Quiet when it mattered. He knew when to push and he knew when to back off. He knew just about everything, damn him.

Which reminded her that she needed to give him an answer about Boise. Her belly quivered at the thought of going. She hated being the center of attention, but not nearly as much as she hated talking about her accident. Purposely recalling those long, terrifying months of not knowing when or if she'd ever walk again, or the equally long months that had followed, during which she'd worked her ass off every single day in PT with the man in front of her.

She hated the thought of facing any of it, and yet AJ needed her to do exactly that.

One dinner.

That's all he'd asked. Actually, it's all he'd ever asked of her. Well, that and her blood, sweat, and tears as he'd pushed, coaxed, and bullied her into walking again.

The house phone rang and Zoe flicked off the music and looked at the caller ID. "It's work," she said. "I'll take it in the other room." She grabbed the cordless receiver and moved into the living room.

Darcy took the few steps to the island and pilfered a piece of turkey bacon. Huh. Zoe had been right. It wasn't bad. She might've even admitted so out loud except she was getting an odd vibe from AJ. "What?" she asked him.

"You're . . . not dressed."

She looked down at herself in her little cami and boxer set. Her nipples thrust against the thin material like they were trying to make a break for it.

Yikes. She crossed her arms over her chest. "Sorry. I smelled bacon."

AJ gave a slow shake of his head. "Don't be sorry. I'm not."

Wait. Had he just . . . flirted with her? Unsure, she searched his features, but he was back to the food, flipping pancakes, eyes hooded from her.

Sensing the tension, Oreo hid behind Darcy's legs and whined.

AJ set down the tongs in his hand and crouched low, whistling softly.

Unbelievably, Oreo wriggled so much his

73

back end became a blur as he scooted to AJ and leaned into his touch.

Or maybe not so unbelievably. After all, Darcy knew the wonder of AJ's calming touch firsthand. There'd been several times during a PT session when she'd gone off the rails. As in completely lost her collective shit.

Each time, AJ had crouched at her side and spoken to her in that soft but steely voice that could melt the North Pole, sliding his big, warm hand to the nape of her hot and sweaty neck, gently squeezing, rubbing away her stress, bringing on other emotions she didn't want to face right now.

Or ever.

She turned to go. "Come on, Oreo. We're out."

Oreo didn't come on. He stayed in the warm, strong circle of AJ's arms.

Fine. She'd go without him.

"Running off?" AJ asked.

"Yeah. I've gotta . . ." She gestured vaguely behind her in a way that could have meant anything: taking a shower, watching paint dry, getting a lobotomy . . . because watching him stroke Oreo made her want to be stroked, too.

By him.

Oreo tilted his head up and sent AJ an

adoring look.

"Benedict Arnold," Darcy muttered to the dog — *and* her own libido. "Come."

Oreo whined, like *Please don't make me leave the new love of my life.*

"He doesn't like discord," Darcy said.

"Does he know you live in that state?"

Wasn't he a laugh a minute? Thankfully Zoe came back into the room.

"Sorry, I've got a flight change, and then Mom called." She looked at Darcy. "She and Dad are heading to Istanbul next week. They wanted to let us know they'll be out of touch."

"Aren't they always?" Darcy asked.

"Pretty much." Zoe took in the way that Darcy and AJ stood practically nose to nose with Oreo in between them looking worried. "What's up?"

"Nothing," Darcy said.

AJ didn't say anything.

Zoe divided a look between them. "It feels like something."

No kidding . . . "AJ needs a favor," Darcy said. She met his easy and relaxed gaze.

She, on the other hand, felt the opposite of easy and relaxed. Heat flickered through her whenever he was around, and even when he wasn't and she only thought of him. And she spent way too much time thinking of him, wondering if he knew how to use that big body of his in bed.

She suspected he did. "I'll go," she told him.

"You'll go where?" Zoe asked.

Darcy waited for AJ to explain but he didn't. Of course not. He wanted her to say it. "To Boise to meet a potential bigwig interested in funding AJ's grant program."

Zoe turned to AJ and grinned. "Yeah? You got someone interested?"

"Yeah," he said, but he hadn't taken his gaze off Darcy. "And he's asked that I bring along someone I've treated after their insurance cut them off."

"Aw," Zoe said. "And Darcy's going to pay back a favor for a favor. Nice."

"Wait — What?" Darcy asked, and turned to AJ just as he was making a slicing-finger-across-the-throat motion to Zoe.

Zoe was staring at him in confusion as she answered Darcy. "For all the pro bono physical therapy work he did when your insurance stopped paying at four months —" She broke off when AJ shook his head in disgust.

Yep, definitely missing something, Darcy thought, not liking where this was going. "I thought you and Wyatt covered me," she said to Zoe.

76

Zoe sighed. "AJ wrote the bills off." She turned to AJ. "I'm sorry, but you said you'd tell her. I just assumed she knew."

"I hadn't gotten to it yet," AJ said, looking resigned to having this conversation, the one about how he'd not only saved her life but also not gotten paid.

Darcy could scarcely breathe. "You . . . you wrote the bills off? But that had to be hundreds of dollars of treatment, or more."

"Forget it. Oh, and the dinner's dressy. And we're going with no drama so don't bother packing any."

Zoe winced. "Maybe I should go, too. I can pack food for the trip, it'll be fun."

Darcy was struggling to contain herself. Her inner bitch really wanted to come out but . . . *he'd written off her PT bills.* "I'll skip the drama if you skip being an ass."

"I'm not sure either of those things are possible," he said. "But while we're in negotiations, let's put this on the table — no crazy."

"Okay," Zoe said. "I'm definitely coming with."

"Maybe you should print me out a list of rules," Darcy said to AJ, ignoring Zoe. "Like when I talk to you, should I say 'Sir, yes, sir,' or not speak at all?"

"I mean I have work," Zoe said. "But it's

no big deal for me to cancel a few flights."

"Not necessary," AJ said to Zoe as he poured himself a mug of coffee and leaned back against the counter to take a leisurely sip. "And as much as I like the 'Sir, yes, sir,' " he said to Darcy, "let's go with door number two — not speaking at all."

Okay, this wasn't going to work. Darcy was working at paying off her debts. She always paid off her debts, but this one might kill her. "Do you want to approve my wardrobe as well?"

"Yeah," Zoe said, pulling out her phone. "So I'll just start cancelling some flights right now —"

"No," Darcy told her. Having Zoe the Worrier there would make everything worse. "Thank you but we'll be fine."

"Fine dead, or fine in prison?"

AJ smiled, albeit a little grimly. "Fine fine."

Zoe didn't look convinced but she nodded. "Well . . . it's really nice of you to help him out," she said to Darcy.

Nice had nothing to do with it. Darcy waited for AJ to mention that he was paying her a thousand bucks to go, something she would absolutely refuse now — but he didn't say a word. She looked at him pointedly.

He looked right back at her from those

impenetrable hazelnut eyes.

A point in his favor, she thought reluctantly. "He offered to pay me," she told Zoe, and had the pleasure of catching a flash of surprise from him.

He'd underestimated her. She was well used to that. "A lot of money," she added. "That he's no longer going to pay me now that I know what he did for me."

"I'm sorry," Zoe said. "I'm going to ask again. Are you two *sure* this is a good idea? It's a long car ride, and we all know that the two of you don't exactly . . ." She trailed off, grimacing again when both Darcy and AJ just looked at her. ". . . get along," she finished.

Silence. Because why argue the truth?

Zoe looked uncomfortable.

Not AJ. In fact, Darcy had never seen the guy look uncomfortable, ever. It didn't matter what he was doing, calmly digging into her knotted muscles while she swore and cursed at him, plowing his way across the football field with the guys, or running the wellness center and all the people in it with his endless, legendary calm — he never looked anything less than completely confident.

She could hate him for that alone.

AJ took another sip from his coffee while

with his other hand he turned off the burner under the bacon pan, expertly flicked the pieces onto a plate layered with paper towels, and walked the plate to the table.

"Coffee?" Zoe asked Darcy. "I made you decaffeinated in the hopes you'd sleep better."

"Did you serve AJ decaffeinated?"

"Hell no," AJ said. "Coffee without caffeine is like sex without a woman." His phone went off. He looked at the screen and then moved to the door. "Gotta go."

"But you didn't get to eat," Zoe said.

"Next time." He glanced back at Darcy. "Let me know if you change your mind."

"I don't go back on my word," she said. And plus now she owed him, which really chapped her hide.

Zoe shifted uneasily. "Listen, there's got to be someone else who could do this for you, AJ. Maybe someone who . . ." She broke off and glanced guiltily at Darcy.

"Maybe someone who what?" Darcy asked, eyes narrowed.

Zoe winced. "Maybe someone better suited to handle the social pressure of representing AJ's work."

Darcy sucked in a breath and tried to act like that didn't hurt more than her aching leg.

"Honey, I'm not trying to hurt your feelings," Zoe rushed on when Darcy stared at her. "But this is really important to him and you're good at lots of things, but social stuff isn't one of them. And then there's the problem that the two of you don't exactly see eye to eye."

They saw eye to eye just fine, Darcy thought grimly. And for three glorious minutes they'd once seen lips to lips, but hey, he hadn't wanted her and she could deal with that. Someday. When she was old and gray and no longer had estrogen in her body. Maybe. "I *am* a representation of his work," she said.

AJ, clearly knowing better than to get in the middle of a sister "discussion," remained silent. If he had any reservations about bringing her, he kept them close to his vest.

Like he did just about everything — except for how he felt about her. He'd made that pretty damn clear. Whatever. She'd deal with that, too.

FIVE

AJ left Zoe and Darcy's house and told himself things were all good. Darcy was going to go to Boise with him.

Sure they'd be trapped together for the long car ride, but he couldn't obsess about it.

Nor would he obsess about what Darcy had been wearing when she'd stumbled into her kitchen fresh out of bed — a thin cotton cami and holy shit *short* shorts.

He shook the memory off with shocking difficulty and pulled up to the small ranch house where he'd grown up. The neighborhood hadn't changed much. Still a hardworking, blue-collar street, the vehicles were mostly American-made trucks better cared for than the yards.

AJ's dad had renovated the house a decade back during one long summer with AJ's help.

They'd nearly killed each other, several

times over.

Retired Navy Captain James Mitchell Colten hadn't softened much over the years. If anything, the opposite had happened. Back when AJ had been a little kid missing his mom after she'd died, his dad hadn't known what to do with him. So he'd gone with what he knew and had treated AJ like one of his good little soldiers. Except AJ hadn't exactly been good.

There'd been a lot of pretty rough years with badass 'tude going head-to-head with badder-ass 'tude. Because in Captain Colten's house, talking back hadn't been tolerated.

Suck it up, soldier.

That had been his dad's favorite line, but in hindsight AJ knew the guy had done the best he could. AJ had done his best, too. And because he'd never been good at following orders and the chain of command, he'd not gone the career Navy route as his dad had wanted.

And still hated.

But they'd gotten better at compromise with time. Or maybe AJ had just come to understand his dad and the man's need for rules. After all, without them, chaos reigned.

He had his own rules, and for the most part he abided by them. The lone exception had been almost taking advantage of what Darcy had offered that dark night eight months ago.

He let himself into his dad's house and wasn't too surprised to find him already up, showered, and dressed. Years ago he'd been as tall as AJ, though age had robbed him of a few inches. Age had also softened much of his bulky muscles, but he still could kick ass when he wanted. He stood staring down at a pan full of frying sausage.

Not turkey sausage, either.

"Dad," AJ said. "The doctor was clear about your cholesterol —"

"It's all new age bullshit. A man can't live without sausage."

"Actually," AJ said, "a man could live a lot longer without sausage."

His dad glowered at him and jabbed a fork in his direction. "I've put in my time. If I want to go to the big buffet in the sky by way of sausage, I'm entitled. Besides, there's nothing else good to eat for breakfast."

AJ went to the refrigerator that he'd personally stocked for the man and pulled out the already cut-up fruit and a container of yogurt. "You said you'd eat this."

"Fruit's for fairies."

"Dad." AJ pinched the bridge of his nose. "You can't say shit like that."

His dad tossed up his hands. "I can't eat what I want to eat, I can't say what I want to say. And I can't even remember the last time I got to boss anyone around."

"It was me, last weekend, remember? You made me build those shelves for you. You yelled at me for two straight days that I was doing it wrong, and you had a great time doing it."

"Oh yeah." His dad smiled and nodded. "That was fun." He limped to the cabinet and pulled out a box of Ding Dongs.

Jesus. "Dad, where's your cane?"

"Cane's for sissies." He twisted around and looked at AJ. "Or can't I say sissies anymore, either?"

AJ took a deep breath. "Your cane is to help keep you upright until your knee fully recovers from your surgery. If you fall on it right now, you'll make everything worse."

"I won't fall. I'm not that old. I'm only sixty-five."

"You're seventy, Dad."

His dad stopped and blinked. "You sure?"

"Yeah."

"Well don't tell anyone. I just signed up for a . . . whaddya call it . . . an online gig thingie."

AJ stared at him. "An online dating site?"

"Yeah. And I told everyone I was sixty-five." His dad very purposefully unwrapped a Ding Dong and shoved it into his mouth, looking absolutely rapturous. "Goddamn. This is better than sex. And I don't need a fucking blue pill for it, either."

AJ kicked out a chair for his dad. "Let's hear it."

"Hear what?"

"I want to know what's really going on here."

"What do you mean?"

"You're acting like a little kid," AJ said.

His dad shrugged. "Maybe I figured it was about time I pay you back for all those years you were such a rotten kid. And speaking of kids, you going to make me a grandpa or what?"

AJ went brows up. "Looking to terrorize a whole new generation?"

His dad smiled. "I'd be good at it. You'd best hurry though. Apparently I'm older than I thought, and if you wait until after I bite the bullet, I'll be pissed off and haunt you from my grave."

"Then it's a good thing you're not dying anytime soon," AJ said. "You're too stubborn. And you know I'm not dating anyone right now."

"Son, you've gotta use it or lose it."

AJ scrubbed a hand over his face. He

turned and went back into the living room, hunted up the cane from the foyer, and brought it to his dad. "Use this," he said.

"Now who's bossy?" his dad said, but took the cane.

AJ went to the stove. He drained the sausage and served it to his dad. He peered into the box of Ding Dongs — only one left. What the hell, he thought, and served that to his dad as well. "Enjoy it," he warned. "It's your last breakfast of its kind."

"Sure," his dad said too easily, and AJ just shook his head. He didn't need kids. He had his dad . . .

Darcy held two part-time jobs, one at AJ's Sunshine Wellness Center and also one at Belle Haven, Sunshine's local animal center, where she filled in twice a week. That was today's job. After she showered and dressed, she walked to her piece-of-shit Toyota, which moaned and groaned when she cranked over the engine. The morning had dawned cold and icy, and her car didn't enjoy either.

Neither did she. Rain, yes. Ice, no. The roads felt slick, and since she had not yet been able to get back onto a highway, she had to take the back roads, which had her saying "oh crap oh crap oh crap" like a mantra.

To get over herself, she tried to think of something, anything else. The first thing that came to mind — how AJ had looked in his faded Levi's and soft navy T-shirt that clung to his perfect back as he sang in her kitchen with Zoe.

He'd danced like no one was watching. Like he didn't give a shit about what anyone thought.

And damn. Damn that was both a surprise and attractive.

What the hell was going on with her today?

She cranked the music and tried to relax but her favorite radio station wasn't coming in, so she ended up on a candy pop station listening to that damn *Frozen* song and singing about how the cold never bothered her anyway. She was really owning the lyrics and getting into it when a deer dashed out from the woods and stopped right in the middle of the damn road, staring wide-eyed at Darcy.

Darcy let out a string of every bad word she knew as she slammed on the brakes.

The deer blinked and bounded off.

Darcy dropped her head to the steering wheel and gulped in air.

A car came up behind her and honked and

took three years off her life.

"Yeah, yeah, bite me," she yelled and carefully eased onto the accelerator. "It's all good," she told herself and tried to channel her inner Ariana. "Just clear your mind."

But as it turned out, she really didn't have an inner Ariana, because her heart stayed at heart attack level all the way into work.

She finally pulled into the Belle Haven parking lot, where both Wyatt and Emily worked as vets. Darcy had started off working here as a favor to Dell Connelly, one of the owners, a month or so ago when she'd finally been well enough to work again. Since she couldn't do what she used to do, she'd been forced to take what she could get.

It had turned out to be a decent gig. She ran the front desk accompanied by Peanut, the mouthy parrot that perched at her elbow, and Bean, the grumpy cat asleep on her printer. At her feet lay Gertie, a one hundred pound Saint Bernard and the heart and soul of the place.

The heart and soul of the place was currently snoozing, snoring loud enough to wake the dead.

The day flew by, and near the end, Adam Connelly — Dell's brother — stopped at her desk.

"You ready?" he asked.

Adam was ex–National Guard, worked in Search and Rescue training both people and dogs, and was just about as tough as they came. Today he wore cammy cargoes and a military green T-shirt and a dog tag that read: *Allergic to bullshit, bullets, and bitching.*

She stared up at him. "Ready for . . . ?"

"I'm teaching a puppy class. You're assisting."

"I am?"

He gave her a rare smile. "Yeah."

Ten minutes later they stood outside in the yard facing their class. Darcy sidled up to Adam. "You seriously need assistance?" she asked disbelievingly, because the class seemed to be made up of four women and four adorable puppies. "You've been to the front lines. How bad can this be?"

"Bad," he said. "Your job is to watch my six."

"Your back?"

"My virtue," he said.

She rolled her eyes but hey, he was the boss. If he wanted to pay her to stand there and protect him, who was she to argue?

"Watch and learn," Adam said. "It's not about training the puppies; it's about training their humans."

He turned out to be right. Within twenty

minutes, two of the puppies had turned into escape artists and were on the loose, racing around in the mud, spooking a few horses in the pen and generally wreaking havoc.

Their owners stood there wringing their hands, so Adam and Darcy divided and conquered to capture the little wriggling heathens.

Adam had no problem capturing his, but then again he had strength and agility on his side.

Darcy, on the other hand, felt like a baby giraffe who'd just found her legs. Twice she dove for the damn puppy and twice she missed.

And landed in the mud.

Adam laughed so hard he had to bend over, hands on his knees.

She narrowed her eyes at him.

This only cracked him up all the more, a sight to behold because he was normally a pretty serious guy. When he'd finally controlled himself, he came over and offered her a hand, which she took.

And then pulled him down into the mud with her.

"People have died for less," he said mildly but she told herself she wasn't worried.

Much.

Then the still-on-the-loose puppy raced

for the fence and the horse standing behind it with its ears pricked up, stomping a foot in irritation. When the horse lowered its head and snorted in the puppy's face, the puppy squealed, jumped, and did a one-eighty in the air, diving right into Darcy's arms.

"Got you," she said triumphantly on her knees, covered head to toe in mud.

The puppy was still running in place in her hands, wriggling and squealing like a baby pig.

"Maybe this will teach you to listen," Darcy told it. "Hush now."

The puppy actually stopped struggling and relaxed, and Darcy flashed a triumphant smile at Adam. "See? This isn't so bad at all."

That's when the puppy peed on her.

Adam grinned. "You're right. This job isn't so bad at all."

By the time Darcy got home, most of the mud — and puppy pee — had dried, making movement even more difficult than usual. She had a raging headache and her body throbbed at each pulse point from overuse. She needed a hot shower, bed, and utter silence.

But she walked into the house to the scent

of BBQ and the sound of music and laughter.

Wyatt and Emily were there, and some of Zoe's friends as well. She remembered that she'd had a text from Zoe. She glanced at it and yep, sure enough, Zoe had given her a heads-up.

People were scattered throughout the living room, but Darcy's gaze went straight to the tall, built man leaning against the mantel.

AJ, a beer in hand, smiling at something Remy was saying to him.

Remy was a good friend of Zoe's. A beautiful petite redhead, who was perfectly toned from all the time she spent at the gym trying to get AJ's attention. She was pretty and funny, and her legs always worked — and she probably was never covered in mud and puppy pee.

"Hear you're going to Boise," Wyatt said when he came up to Darcy's side. "So AJ got his head out of his ass and asked you. That was my idea, by the way. Ask you, not tell you. You know, coax."

"Coax?" Darcy asked.

"Yeah, sort of let you think it was your idea. Women like that."

Darcy stared at her brother, who was so smart and also a complete idiot. "Who told you that garbage, Dr. Phil?"

"It's Women 101, aka having two sisters and a really hot girlfriend," Wyatt said.

Emily, who'd come up behind him, smacked him on the back of his head. "Women 101?"

He rubbed the back of his head. "Did you not hear the really-hot-girlfriend part?"

Emily looked slightly mollified as she gave Darcy a hug and then froze, nose wrinkled. "Uh . . ."

"I know," Darcy said, backing away from everyone. "I'm a wreck. I need a shower."

Everyone went back to whatever they'd been doing, taking her at her word. Except for one person.

AJ, of course. He saw everything, always, and he certainly saw right through her. She wasn't sure if she was annoyed or secretly thrilled when he broke away from Remy and caught her before she vanished.

"Hey," he said, hand on her arm, turning her to face him. He looked her over very carefully, taking in the mess that was her Styx tank, her jeans with all the questionable stains on them, and her battered, mud-covered boots.

"Don't touch," she warned. "I'm disgusting."

Reaching out, he pulled something from

94

her hair. She didn't want to know what.

There was something in his gaze. A seriousness, and . . . irritation? Well, that wasn't exactly new, so she shouldn't be surprised that she'd managed to piss him off without trying. She looked around for a distraction but no one was paying them any attention, especially Wyatt, who had Emily in a clutch, kissing her, slow and lingering, with as much eye contact as lip contact.

Something deep in Darcy sighed. "Well," she said, "this has been fun but I'm going to go hazmat myself now."

"In a minute." Holding her still, AJ met her gaze.

Annoyingly breathless, she tried to disappear. "I don't have time for this, AJ."

"You have a damn minute." He reeled her back in, smoothed the hair away from her face, and peered into it. "You okay?"

And just like that, she came undone. She always did when he looked at her like this, his eyes dark and assessing. Controlled and, yeah, still cranky but also . . . warm. Caring. There was never any doubt of that, though she was hard-pressed to understand why.

She knew exactly how hard she was to care about. "I'm good," she managed.

He shook his head, not buying what she

was selling.

"I ran a puppy training class with Adam," she said. "I'm covered in mud, questionable muck, and most definitely puppy pee, and I ache from head to toe, especially the head part. And now that you know everything there is to know, I'm going to the shower and I'm not coming out until next week. When I do come out, I'm going to hunt down my purse, which I think I just dropped by the front door, grab some Advil, and go straight to bed. If that meets with your approval, of course."

And then, without waiting for his response, she took the stairs and escaped into her bathroom, where she locked the door, stripped, and cranked the hot water.

Just before she stepped in there was a knock. Only one person would dare, and she didn't have the energy to deal with him. "Go away."

"Open up."

AJ, of course, and he didn't sound any happier than he'd been a minute ago. Well, he could join her damn club now, couldn't he? She shook her head, realized he couldn't see her, and cleared her throat. "Why?"

"I've got Gummy Bears."

She wrapped herself in a towel and cracked open the door. He stuck his foot in, muscled the door open, and strode in.

"Hey!" She tightened her grip on the towel and glared at him. "And where are the Gummy Bears?"

"I lied." His face was quiet, calm. Almost blank. Which, as she was beginning to learn when it came to AJ, meant he was feeling the exact opposite, proven when he turned his hand up, palm out, revealing a bottle of Oxycontin.

Hers.

"I found your purse for you," he said. "No, you didn't have any Advil in it. Just this."

She stared at the bottle.

"You told me you were done with the painkillers months ago."

She blinked in surprise, both at the question and at the tone in his voice. Cold. Angry. "Yeah," she said carefully. "And I am."

After as many surgeries as she'd had, she'd gotten a little too attached to her painkillers. In fact, she couldn't sleep without them.

And since she'd given them up two months, one week, and four days ago — not that she was counting — she hadn't slept since.

The last refill on her prescription had come due yesterday, and in a moment of panic she'd refilled it just to have it. Sort of like a security blanket. She got that it made no sense to anyone but her. But nor was it anyone's business except her own. "How is this any of your business?"

He didn't answer.

She didn't need him to; the answer was painfully obvious.

He thought she had a problem.

"Not that this is any of your concern," she said, trying hard to control her anger, "but I have them for comfort, basically. I'm not taking them."

He just looked at her, face blank.

"Look," she said. "Count them if you need to. Or don't. I don't care what you think." Unlike him, she didn't have a blank face, which infuriated her. She snatched the bottle from his palm and tossed it to the counter. Only she missed and the bottle hit the mirror and ricocheted off, nearly beaning AJ in the head. Would have nailed him if he hadn't caught it in midair.

"Do you know why I keep these?" she asked.

"To hit people in the head?"

"Get out."

"Darcy —"

Nope. She didn't look at him, because if she saw pity she'd have to kill him. She took the bottle for the second time and gave him a nudge that was much more like a big, fat shove, knowing that when he indeed moved, it was only because he allowed it. Then, to make herself feel better, she slammed the door on his nose.

Six

The next day AJ worked his ass off at work, seeing clients back to back to back, managing staff, running a fitness workshop with Ariana, and handling the virtual mountain of all the usual behind-the-scenes crap at his desk. He'd been so busy he didn't have time to wonder if his head was on straight.

A good thing, as it was most definitely *not* on straight. In fact, thinking about the Boise trip, it was about as unstraight as it could get.

A knock at his door had him looking up from his computer.

"Going to meditate," Ariana said. "Thought you might join me."

She was forever trying to get him to meditate with her. AJ appreciated that she got a lot out of it. And he also appreciated that a lot of their clients got a lot out of it. But he didn't. Every time he tried, his mind wandered to all the shit he should be doing with his time. "Sorry. I've still got a lot to do."

She smiled. "You know what they say about all work and no play . . ."

"Yeah, yeah, but I also have one client left for the day."

"Tyson? He just cancelled."

AJ frowned. "Any reason why?"

"Yeah, he said he was over it."

AJ had been working with the guy for months, and though Tyson still had a shit attitude, AJ had thought that maybe they were finally getting somewhere.

Apparently not.

He pulled out his phone and called him.

"What?" Tyson answered in a tone that suggested the caller could and should go fuck themselves.

"We had plans," AJ said.

"You had plans. Me, not so much."

"The key is constantly working at those muscles," AJ said. "You know this. When we work hard, you get more mobility each time."

"We?" Tyson repeated. "You mean when *I* work hard, and I'm tired of working hard." He blew out a breath. "Listen, this isn't your problem, so forget it. Forget me."

Most of AJ's clients actively wanted to get better. Not Tyson. He honestly didn't appear to care if he recovered or not. Not that this mattered, because AJ refused to give up on him. "Come in or I'll drive to you."

There was a beat of silence. "Why?" Tyson finally asked. "What the hell does it matter to you?"

"A lot. You're going to get some more improvement, Tyson, even if you don't believe it."

"But I'm always going to be in this fucking chair."

"You still have two working arms and a brain, right?" AJ pressed.

More silence. Pissy silence.

"Look," AJ said more gently, "your doctor said there was room for physical improvement, and it's my job to help you get it. Why not go for it? Unless you're enjoying the solo pity party?"

"Fuck you. Hard."

"Tell you what," AJ said. "Let's strengthen your arms and shoulders and then you can try."

Tyson choked out a laugh. "You're an asshole."

"I know. You have a ride here?"

Another pause. Then a long, drawn-out exhale. "Yeah."

"Great," AJ said. "I'll be waiting."

Tyson swore and disconnected, and AJ left

his office, walked down the hall, and into the gym. It would take Tyson at least a half hour to get here, not long enough for a real workout but he'd take what he could get.

He needed to blow off some steam.

Wyatt was there at the bench press, and by the looks of him, he'd been there awhile. AJ took the machine next to him and started pumping.

Wyatt slid him a look. "Problem?"

"Nope. No problem. No problem at all."

"Say it one more time and maybe I'll believe you."

AJ just kept working the weights, eyes open. Every time he closed them he could still see a certain woman in her pj's standing in her kitchen looking sexier than he could possibly have imagined.

When had Darcy gotten so sexy?

"Did you seriously just ask me that?" Wyatt asked.

AJ nearly dropped the weights on his face and just barely managed to not kill himself. "Um, what?"

Wyatt stared at him. "Zoe's worried about this weekend," he finally said. "And now maybe I am, too."

"I'd never put Darcy into a situation she can't handle."

"Actually, Zoe's worried that it's a situation *you* can't handle," Wyatt said.

"I'll be fine." One could hope.

"Remind me again — when have you ever successfully handled Darcy?"

Shit. "I don't plan to handle her at all," AJ said. "She just needs to be herself. That's all I'm asking."

Wyatt was quiet a moment, and AJ went back to the weights, thinking they needed a subject change quick.

"You two have always rubbed each other the wrong way," Wyatt said after a minute. "Since I can't even remember when." He met AJ's gaze. "Come to think of it, I don't even know why."

AJ stayed very busy with the weights but could see from his peripheral that Wyatt didn't do the same. In fact, Wyatt got up and stood behind AJ like he was going to spot him.

AJ tilted his head back and met Wyatt's upside-down face staring down at him. "What?"

"Is there something I should know?" Wyatt asked.

"About?"

Wyatt's eyes narrowed. "My sister."

Yeah, there was a lot he should know. Like the fact that AJ couldn't stop thinking about her. That they'd had a near miss. And she smelled like heaven. All important details, but they paled before the biggie — he wanted her. "No."

Wyatt pointed at him. "You hesitated." He stopped AJ from pumping, holding the weight down on AJ's chest. "What was the hesitation?"

"Can't. Breathe —"

"Answer the damn question."

"I've already told you," AJ managed to say past the weight on his chest. "Nothing's going on." He met Wyatt's gaze straight on and let out the rest. "But you should know, I want there to be."

Wyatt stared at him for a long beat. "You want there to be," he repeated. He went back to his bench and sat hard, rubbing his chest.

AJ sat up, rubbing his, holding eye contact with Wyatt because this was important. Getting this right, being honest, was important to him. And the easy part. "Yes," he said. "I want there to be."

There was the slightest wince on Wyatt's face, like maybe he'd rather be having a root canal right now than discussing this, without drugs.

"So then why the fuck do you two fight like cats and dogs?" Wyatt finally asked.

And now for the hard part. "I don't fight

with her. She fights with me."

There was a long beat while Wyatt processed this. "Explain."

"A while back she came to me and wanted to . . ." AJ hesitated, unsure how to tell his best friend that his baby sister had wanted a quickie in the parking lot.

His silence must have spelled it out for him, because Wyatt scrubbed a hand over his face and muttered "Christ" beneath his breath.

"I turned her down," AJ said quietly.

Wyatt dropped his hand and stared at AJ, the implications chasing each other across his face. "You rejected her?"

"Would you rather I hadn't?"

"Yes. No. *Shit.* I don't know." Wyatt dropped his head into his hands. "Did you do it for me?"

It was AJ's turn to scrub his hands over his face. "I told myself I did it for her. That I couldn't give her what she was looking for."

Wyatt's eyes sharpened. "Meaning?"

"She didn't want *me*," AJ said. "She wanted oblivion. And I couldn't give her that."

"Why?"

"Jesus, Wyatt —"

"Yeah, I am going to need to scrub my

brain with bleach after this conversation, too," Wyatt said. "Just finish it."

"I refused to be a one-night stand for her. Okay?" AJ shoved his fingers into his sweaty hair. "That never would've worked."

"Because . . . ?"

AJ stared at Wyatt, hoping like hell this wasn't going to change a damn thing between them, because Wyatt was the brother he'd never had. "Because I have feelings for her. I always have."

Wyatt didn't move a single muscle for a long moment. Then he let out a shaky breath. "Why didn't I see this coming?"

"I didn't want you to see it. I didn't want to feel it."

Wyatt took that in. "You could've told me. You can tell me anything."

"Yeah? Like your shirt's on inside out?"

Wyatt looked down at himself and let out a wry laugh. "Emily and I shared a ride into town this morning."

"And your fiancée didn't happen to notice you were dressed incorrectly?"

Wyatt actually flushed. "I started out with it correct, but then we got held up by the train and . . ." He shook his head and tugged off his shirt, righting it. "Never mind. And nice job on the distraction technique."

"So . . . we okay?" AJ asked warily.

"We've been together a long time."

"And yet you asked Emily to marry you and not me," AJ said.

Wyatt's lips quirked. "She's prettier than you."

"No doubt."

Wyatt's smile faded as he met AJ's gaze. "Hell. Yeah. We're okay. We'll always be okay." He paused. "She really doesn't know how you feel about her?"

"No." Hell no. She'd make his life a living hell.

"So all she knows is that you rejected her," Wyatt said.

"Yeah."

"And Darcy, being Darcy, didn't take the rejection very well," Wyatt guessed.

"Not well at all," AJ confirmed.

Wyatt actually grinned.

"What?"

"You've got to spend a lot of hours in the car with her this weekend," Wyatt said.

"That's funny?"

"Very."

"I thought you said you were okay with it."

"I am," Wyatt said. "Doesn't mean I want it to be easy for you."

Darcy had been working on training Oreo for an hour — with less than wondrous results — when AJ pulled up. He parked his truck on the street and crossed the yard to where she sat in the grass.

"We're in a showdown," she said, nodding her chin at Oreo, who sat facing her. "I'm trying to teach him to stay."

"He looks like he's got the hang of it," AJ said.

"Because I'm holding a doggie cookie. He's like every other man on the planet. He can be bribed."

"Sounds like you've got us all figured out," AJ said.

"Yep." Every single one of them but him. "Zoe's not here."

"I came for you."

Her heart had started a heavy thumping the moment he showed up. He wore faded Levi's and an untucked button-down, and she thought no one wore clothes quite the way he did.

And he thinks you're a druggie.

"Wanted to make sure we're on for the morning," he said.

"You mean am I still going to show myself

109

off to your money guy?"

His expression didn't change. He was one of the few people she couldn't easily rattle. She didn't know what to make of that. Never had. "Said I would. I don't go back on my word, AJ." She rewarded Oreo with a cookie. "Now let's work on come," she said. She stepped back to the edge of the grass. "Okay, Oreo. Come."

Oreo sat.

AJ crouched on the balls of his feet and whistled. "Come," he said.

Oreo ran to him, tail wagging, tongue lolling, staring adoringly up into AJ's face.

AJ rubbed Oreo up and down until the dog was nothing but a puddle of boneless goo.

Darcy tried not to be jealous and failed yet again. "So is that all you wanted to know?"

"For now."

"You mean there'll be more later?"

AJ met Darcy's eyes. He looked grim. Resigned. "To be determined," he said.

His frustration didn't give her near the satisfaction she'd thought it would. Because if he had to spend the long car ride with her, she had to spend it with him as well.

It would be a miracle if they both survived.

"Be ready to go by seven A.M.," he said,

and left.

Oreo cried.

Darcy sighed. "You'll get over him," she told the dog. All she needed to do was the same.

SEVEN

At seven the next morning, AJ stood outside Darcy's house in a freezing mist, leaning against his truck. He knew better than to rush a woman, but they really needed to get going to allow for any unplanned incidents on the road.

Although considering Darcy was one really big Unplanned Incident, it probably wouldn't matter when they left.

He was in for a rough time today and he knew it. If there'd been any other way — any other way at all — he'd have taken it. But he needed her.

He'd been raised to show no weaknesses, and that usually worked for him. But when it came to anything having to do with one Darcy Stone, he instantly went off axis.

The front door of the Victorian opened and Darcy stepped out wearing a formfitting, thigh-length sweater, leggings, and boots. Zoe stood in the doorway looking worried.

"Let's get this drama-free adventure over with, shall we?" Darcy asked.

"She hasn't had caffeine yet," Zoe warned.

AJ looked Darcy over. "You think caffeine's going to help?"

Zoe laughed, blew him a kiss, laid one on Darcy's cheek, and vanished back inside.

Darcy went on the move, walking with an uneven gait, signaling that she was tired, possibly to the point of exhaustion.

She still wasn't sleeping. Why, if she was still taking pain pills, wasn't she sleeping?

As she stepped off the porch it began to sleet in earnest, and she looked up at the sky, a slow smile crowding the exhaustion away from her face.

She loved the rain, always had.

Pushing off the truck, he strode forward to take the duffel bag from her. "You're not supposed to carry anything over five pounds," he reminded her.

Her sleepy gaze locked onto his and he felt both a stirring and a discomfort.

Yeah. He had a hell of a long day ahead of him.

"It's been eleven months," she said.

Eleven months and two weeks. He took a step closer, ordering himself not to breathe her in, but damn he loved the way she smelled. He shouldered her bag and held out his hand for the purse hanging off her other side.

She relinquished her purse without a word.

Another sign that something was wrong. He'd expected her to be pissy, but it wasn't temper he saw.

"Hey," he said, moving closer, bending to see into her face. "You okay?"

"Terrific, never better." She hit the first step and her leg buckled.

It was instinct for him to reach for her, but at his movement her head whipped around like Carrie in the horror film and she gave him a *back off or die* look.

He lifted his hands.

She put earbuds into her ears and hit play on her iPod. Then she very carefully gripped the railing on the porch and took the second step.

Killing him. He looked at the time on his phone and eyed the distance to his truck, torn between keeping his big trap shut and mentioning that not only were they in a hurry, but a fall on the slippery steps would be bad. "I'll carry you," he said.

She pretended she couldn't hear him over her music and made it to the third step, completely drenched now. Her hair loved

114

this weather as much as she did, the curls rioting around her face.

Two more steps.

AJ watched, holding his breath, hands itching to help. Jesus. How did Wyatt and Zoe do this every single day?

When she nearly bought it on the last step, he had to shove his hands in his pockets to keep them off her.

She held still a moment, fighting for balance — which she won. And the cocky smile she sent him over her shoulder was worth every second of the torture.

"Did it," she said, clearly proud of herself. "And this time I didn't eat dirt."

He'd been with her just about every step of the way since her doctor had approved PT. He'd seen her flat on the mats at his wellness center, writhing in agony as he dug into her scar tissue to loosen it up. He'd seen her fighting her way through the pain as she worked the weights and stretches he'd given her. He'd seen her stand up out of her wheelchair and take her first steps again.

All of it had moved him.

Deeply.

It was why he did what he did. He never got tired of being such an integral part of someone's recovery.

But now, right this very minute, watching her do a triumphant dance, which included a very carefully orchestrated hip boogie and body shake that had his eyes going straight to her sweet ass, made his day.

"Nicely done," he said.

She slid him a look, and he had no idea if it was the morning huskiness of his voice or something else, but she blinked in surprise at him.

And then turned left instead of heading to his truck. She walked to the middle of the grass in her yard and . . .

Lay down on her back. Despite the fact that the air was chilled and the ground even colder, she stared up at the sky and smiled as the rain hit her.

He stared down at his feet, blew out a breath, and tossed her bags into his truck. Then he joined her, sprawling out on his back on the — oh, perfect — wet grass next to her. Their arms touched and she reached for his hand, squeezing his fingers. "Perfect start to the day, right?"

The wet grass was seeping through his clothes as drops of rain splashed right in his eye. They had a long drive ahead of them, but all he could feel was her fingers in his, and then there was her smile.

Brighter than the sun that hadn't come

out in weeks.

The front door of the house across the street opened. An older woman in a thick bathrobe and curlers peered out. "What the hell are you crazy kids doing?" she yelled.

Darcy laughed her musical laugh. "Being crazy kids," she yelled back.

The woman muttered something and slammed her door.

"She'll call the cops," Darcy said. "And poor Kel will have to come out and investigate."

Kel was the local sheriff and a friend of AJ's. "We're not doing anything illegal," he said. "Stupid, yes. Illegal, no."

Darcy shrugged. "Mrs. Willingham likes to cover all her bases when it comes to me." She blew out a sigh and sat up. "We've got eight point five minutes to get out of here."

A few minutes later they were on the highway. "I'm not even going to mention how disturbing it is that you know the exact response time for the police to get to your house."

Darcy leaned forward, peering out at the long stretch of narrow two-lane road ahead of them. "Where are we going? This isn't the way."

"We have to take back roads today. Turns out they're repaving the main and the detour they've set isn't the best way to get there."

"Back roads?" she asked. "Isn't that going to take longer?"

"Yeah."

Her silence spoke volumes on her opinion of the matter.

"We there yet?" she asked five minutes later.

"Funny."

She squeezed the excess water out of her hair and stripped out of her sweater, which left her in a ribbed neon pink The Who tank.

To drown out the silence — and to keep himself from staring at her skimpy top — AJ turned on the radio. Rap blared through the cab.

Darcy leaned forward and changed the station. Vintage rock filled the cab. With a smile, she began to sing along to Van Halen.

He flicked the station back to Eminem.

"My fillings are going to fall right out of my head," she said and changed the station again. Bubblegum pop this time.

She sent him an evil smile that he knew better than to trust. Plus, he was pretty sure it was Justin Bieber, and he hated himself for even knowing that. "And I'm going to need fillings just from listening to this," he said. "Use your iPod."

"I'm doing you a favor," she reminded him. "The favoree picks the tunes."

"I'm driving. Driver picks the tunes."

"Fine," she said. "Pull over. I'll drive."

He pulled over to the side of the highway so fast that she squeaked in surprise. Biting her lower lip, she made a show of looking over her shoulder. "You're going to get a ticket."

"You wanted to drive," he said. "Well worth a ticket."

Silence, which he let fill the interior of the truck because they both knew one undisputable fact — she hadn't driven on any highway since her accident. She was cleared to drive and she drove around town when she had to, but she'd made every excuse not to go further. She was a woman who leapt without looking first, who always took a dare, who thrived on challenges, and he loved that about her. He *missed* that about her. He removed his seat belt and reached for hers.

"You're an asshole," she said softly and clutched her seat belt to her.

"Much as I'd love to listen to you whisper endearments in my ear, we're on a tight schedule," he said. "You've changed your mind, then?"

Ignoring the question, she cranked up the

radio again. This time Poison blared out, singing "Talk Dirty to Me."

Shaking his head, he pulled back onto the highway.

"You know," she said, a loaded fifteen minutes of silence later, "most people baby me through all this stuff and my new milestones. Not you."

"Not me," he agreed.

"You just plow right through the shit, expecting miracles out of me. I annoy you that much?"

He glanced at her in surprise. "Annoyance doesn't play into it at all."

"Uh-huh," she said dryly to the passenger window.

He passed an old couple doing fifty miles an hour before continuing their conversation. "I do it because I care," he said.

She snorted.

He looked at her again, starting to get pissed off that she kept thinking the worst of him. "And also because I believe you can do anything you want to do."

He could feel her surprise, and again he met her gaze because he wanted her to see that he wasn't kidding. "There's more to life than simply surviving a car wreck," he said. "You need to *live*. Even if it means

120

you're going back to doing stuff that scares me."

Her mouth twitched. "Nothing scares you."

"Wrong," he said. "*You* scare me."

She looked at him again. He could feel the weight of her stare as she studied him.

"I'm not going to ever baby you," he told her. "I realize you've got your brother and sister and friends all wrapped around your pinkie, but that's not my style."

She stared at him some more. Then she changed the station again and cranked it up.

Country this time.

As someone sang about his tractor and his dead dog and his wife sleeping with Santa Claus, AJ considered offing himself. It would be less painful. He looked at the time.

Only five and a half hours to go.

Perfect.

Twenty minutes later he glanced over at the sound of Darcy's low laugh. She was texting, her thumbs flying, a big smile on her face.

Damn, he thought, staggered. That smile was a hell of a good look on her. "Who you texting?"

"I'm not texting. I'm sexting."

"Sexting," he repeated.

"Yes. It's the act of sending sexually explicit content via text."

"I know what sexting is." He pulled out his phone and made a show of glancing at the screen. It was dark.

"Not you," she said.

"Who?"

No answer. More thumb flying, and then another laugh.

Don't get sucked in, you don't need to know. She's fucking with you, just stay out of her vortex. This was what his common sense told him. But his common sense wasn't in charge. "Who?" his dick asked.

She gave him a long look.

And . . . kept on sexting.

And cracking herself up. This went on for another half hour before AJ took the next exit. They were out in the middle of nowhere, but there was a gas station and a convenience store, and he needed more caffeine.

"What's wrong?" she asked. "You've got to go to the bathroom already? Weak bladder?"

He shoved the truck into park and slid her a look that would've intimidated anyone else.

Not Darcy. Of course not Darcy.

"They have meds for that, old man."

122

He grated his teeth as he tossed off his seat belt. He had a good life, he told himself. Hell, he had a great life. He had a thriving business, his own home, and he did alright in the women department as well.

So why the hell he let this one get to him, he had no clue. "I don't have to go to the damn bathroom," he snapped. "And I sure as hell don't have a bladder problem."

"Hey, it's nothing to be ashamed of. It's not like I questioned the size of your —"

He shoved out of the truck. "Wait here," he said curtly, and started to walk off. At the last minute he went back for the keys and yanked them out of the ignition.

She laughed. "Nice show of trust."

"There's trust, and there's stupidity," he said, and strode into the convenience store. He bought a coffee, a Gatorade, and, because he knew his passenger, he also bought a bag of Gummy Bears. He'd bribe her to shut up if needed.

When he got back to the truck all he could see was an iPad in the passenger window. "What the — ?" He moved closer and stared. "Are you fucking kidding me?"

Darcy was using the iPad as a sign and it read:

Help, I'm being held captive by a diabolical madman with a weak bladder!

EIGHT

AJ confiscated the iPad, which turned out to be his. Darcy had liberated it from the backseat. "Nice job on spelling *diabolical,*" he said.

"I used spell check."

He slid into the truck and touched the iPad screen to activate it, looking to see what she might have messed with. He half expected to be locked out of the thing, but no. She'd been online checking her e-mail, which she'd not signed out of. He saw e-mails from both Nat Geo and the Travel Channel.

"Talking to work again?" He didn't want to think about why that made his gut hurt. When she left Sunshine, he'd celebrate.

"Just enough to get two big 'no thank you, we don't want you back's," she said. She shrugged. "I've been replaced. It happens. Let's go. Time's a'ticking."

He didn't start the truck. "I'm sorry."

"Don't be. It's not like I'm in a place to go gallivanting across the world anyway." She gestured to his phone, which he'd left in the console. "And while we're on the subject of you snooping, you got two text messages. First one's from your dad."

"I wasn't snooping."

"I was. Your dad said he found the spot for next month and there'd be no arguments." She looked at him. "You must hate it when he bosses you around."

"Nah," AJ said. "He's a grumpy old fart, but we're good."

"What spot is he talking about?"

"For ice fishing. We always take a winter trip."

She seemed surprised. "Wow. That's kinda . . . cute."

"Not cute," he said. "Manly."

She grinned. "Sorry, it's cute. Manly would be alligator hunting or something. And I thought your dad was this hard-ass Navy captain who busts your balls all the time."

"He is."

"But you still go fishing together," she said.

"And camping."

"So you . . . like each other."

He met her gaze and saw the genuine

curiosity. "Liking each other doesn't usually play into things," he said. "But he's my dad."

"I get it," she said.

His heart squeezed because he knew she didn't get it at all. Her dad hadn't even shown up when she'd nearly died. He'd certainly never spent any time renovating a house with her or taken her camping.

"Your second text was from Ariana," she said. "She wants you to know she created a new meditation tape for you."

He still hadn't used the last two she'd made him.

"Oh, and she'll be thinking of you," Darcy said. "Apparently while meditating. Although I thought the whole point of meditating is to *not* think."

He shook his head. "Is that what this mood is about? Ariana?"

Darcy stared at him and then turned away to look out the window. "I'm not in a mood. This is just me being my usual ray-of-sunshine self."

There was something in her voice now that had him taking a second look at her. "You don't like Ariana."

"No, I do," she said. "She's a lovely person. Kind and gentle, caring . . . bendy."

He raised a brow. "Bendy?"

"Yeah. You know anyone else who can wrap both of her legs around her own neck when she's doing her yoga stuff? If I was a guy, I'd think that was . . . something."

AJ opened his mouth, and then shut it. "Not touching that one with a ten-foot pole."

She shifted, looking irritated. "Look, forget it," she said, doing a dismissive gesture with her hand. "I just meant some people are bendy and some people aren't, and I'm sure if a guy had a choice, he'd pick bendy, that's all."

He wasn't sure what was going on here. But then again, this was Darcy. When it came to her, he always operated in the dark.

"She's helping me, you know," Darcy said. "You asked her to give me some yoga stretches and she did. They're working, although I'm not ever going to be bendy."

And that bothered her, he could tell. That he'd actually followed her convoluted, twisted logic scared him to death, but that was a concern for later. "Darcy, you know that Ariana and I aren't —"

"Hey," she said, holding up a hand. "Who-ever you're doing, that's your own business. I don't care. Not in the slightest. Not even a little tiny bit. Let's blow this Popsicle stand."

He turned her to face him again and made a point of looking over her features.

"What the hell are you doing?" she asked.

"Checking to see if your nose grew on that lie."`

She rolled her eyes. "I don't care if you're with Ariana."

"Okay, good. But I'm not," he repeated.

"You were."

"Yes," he agreed. "Past tense."

She crossed her arms, her body tight. She couldn't have put herself into a more defensive position. "You don't have to explain yourself to me," she said.

"Happy to hear that." He smiled when she huffed a little to herself in her seat, grumbling wordlessly beneath her breath.

She was jealous. He couldn't believe it but didn't dare say it out loud because he liked his nose right where it was, thank you very much. But damn. She was jealous.

"It's probably because of your crappy taste in music, right? She dumped you?"

"Okay, how about a truce for the rest of the ride?"

Her eyes went wary. "What did you have in mind?"

He pulled out the bag of Gummy Bears and she lit up. "Maybe," she said, and reached for the bag.

129

He held it out of reach. "Nope. Truce or no Gummy Bears."

She laughed, and that was the thing about Darcy. She had the most amazing laugh. It was full bellied and like music to his ears, and absolutely, one hundred percent contagious.

"You should use the facilities first," he said. "We won't be stopping again."

"Even if I irritate you?"

"You won't."

"How do you know?"

"Because I hold the Gummy Bears. Which means I've got you right where I want you."

She studied him for a long beat. Then sent him a smile that made him nervous as hell before leaving the truck. Her limp was definitely pronounced but not nearly as bad as it had been earlier.

Her phone sat in the cup holder, buzzing with incoming texts like it was having a seizure. He picked the thing up to set one of his Gatorades in there and, shit. Yeah. He glanced at the screen.

Xander.

She was sexting with Xander.

The passenger door opened and Darcy went brows up at the sight of him holding her phone. "Learn anything?" she asked, struggling to get up into the cab of the truck.

AJ had his hand on the door handle to get out and go around to help her when she bared her teeth at him.

"Don't you dare," she said. A painfully long minute later, she finally relaxed into the seat, damp with perspiration and breathing heavily. "Not one word from the peanut gallery," she panted.

He just handed her the Gummy Bears.

"Didn't eat any, did you?" she asked.

"Never fear, your bag of citric acid, dyes, and sugars is intact."

"Okay then." Surprising him, she turned the radio back to hip-hop.

He didn't question the good fortune. He just hoped it lasted.

It did, but only because she fell asleep. It had taken her a while to get comfortable though. She'd tossed and turned and tossed some more. Eventually she laid her head on the console between the two front seats and shifted around miserably.

Reaching behind them, he pulled out a pillow he'd packed for her. "Lift up," he said.

She settled onto the pillow with a sigh and was gone in what appeared to be three seconds. Like completely out cold, limp, unmoving, breathing heavily and deeply.

Knowing how rare it was for her to get into a good sleep, he sighed a breath of relief for her. And because the sun had come out and was in her face, he lowered her visor.

Her face was relaxed and she looked . . . Damn. With her smart-ass mouth closed, she actually had a sort of girl-next-door innocence thing going, looking younger. And sweet.

Pain free.

Her arm slipped off the console. AJ carefully replaced it, and though she twitched, she didn't awaken.

With her arms bared by her tank top, he could see a few of the scars on her exposed right shoulder and biceps where she'd been cut by the windshield on the night of the accident. They were fading and he was grateful for that. Not because they took away in the slightest from her natural beauty, but because he knew exactly what scars could do to a person, how the daily sight of them could make getting over what had happened to her even more difficult.

She shifted in her sleep, stretching one of her legs up on the dash. She'd long ago kicked off her boots and socks. Her toenails were painted sky blue alternating with bright pink. Her right foot was still badly scarred. It had a plate in it and had required a skin graft over the top.

She was lucky she hadn't lost it.

In her sleep, she sighed. A sweet, endearing sound that softened him when he didn't want to be softened. Didn't want to think of her as anything other than the woman who drove him nuts. Didn't want to entertain that they could have something more.

There were a lot of reasons for that, the biggest one being that he'd already been in love with a woman who'd been through a terrible tragedy, and she'd dumped him because she couldn't believe herself lovable after.

He knew reckless Darcy wasn't too far off the same mark as Kayla, and he didn't plan to go there with another woman ever again.

"You're thinking too loud," Darcy murmured sleepily. She sat up and blinked at him, her eyes heavy-lidded. "You're regretting bringing me." She rubbed her eyes. "Buyer's remorse, right? Don't worry, it happens all the time."

His gut took a hit, as did his heart. If he could, he'd have cheerily strangled her parents for putting her default setting at *defensive* and *always braced for rejection*.

How hard could it have possibly been to give her even a little bit of genuine love and attention, much less affection? Instead they'd treated her as an afterthought, proving to her time and time again that she was worth zip to them.

"I don't do regrets," he said.

She thought about that for a minute. "You're not even a little bit worried about tonight?" she asked. "Or don't you do worry either?"

"Oh, I worry," he said.

"About?"

You, he nearly said. *Your pain, your recovery, your happiness, and why you still feel the need to carry around pain meds like a security blanket.* "Plenty."

"Such as . . . me behaving tonight?"

He didn't answer on grounds that it might incriminate him.

She shook her head. "You really think I'd screw you over tonight. Good to know where you're at, AJ. Thanks for the trust."

"Darcy —"

"Oh no," she said, her face to the window on her side, watching Idaho go by. "Don't try to be nice now, you'll ruin my mood. Just tell me flat-out what you need from me, okay? Tell me right now and then do me a favor and don't talk to me again until we get there."

"I need you to be available, receptive to

questions, and . . ."

She turned her head and eyed him. "And?"

"Charming wouldn't hurt."

She narrowed her eyes. "You don't think I can do charming?"

Honestly? He had his doubts.

She blew out a breath. "Whatever. So is that it, then? Be available, receptive to questions, and charming?"

"Yes."

"Fine." She turned forward, expression resolute. "I'll keep my part of the bargain. You just make sure you keep yours."

"Darcy —"

She pointed at him. "No talking."

NINE

When they finally arrived at the hotel that afternoon, Darcy slid out of the truck before AJ even shut off the engine.

"Wait," he called out to her. "It's raining again —"

Darcy couldn't wait. Nope, she needed to escape the tight confines of the truck where she'd been hyperalert to his every movement for the past six hours. Actually, seven, because they'd been blocked by a five-car pileup and had sat on the highway for an hour.

A very long, silent hour.

She'd spent the time soaking up the way AJ's hands took the wheel, how his broad shoulders remained relaxed under any circumstances, even when he'd been cut off by some lady who was older than dirt. Twice.

And then there was his scent. Logically she knew it was his soap or deodorant or whatever and not really his skin, but damn.

It should be effing illegal for a guy to smell that delicious. It was distracting, for one thing. And for another, it just wasn't fair. A woman was programmed to go all soft and melty when a guy smelled that good. And this was the last guy on the planet that she'd ever want to be soft and melty for.

He thought she was a pain in his ass. And a possible druggie. Both were insulting, but only one actually hurt. She'd worked so hard, done everything he'd asked of her, followed his exercise regime, his eating plan, everything. Okay, maybe not the eating plan, not entirely. But he'd been a big part of helping her wean herself off the pain meds in the first place. In fact, he hadn't wanted her to do it as soon as she had.

His way had been smarter, of course, and more logical. But she'd needed a clear head. And that he could actually think she'd gotten hooked and was hiding it . . .

Yeah, he'd opened a big can of 'tude with that one. Mostly because she was still in pain and not sleeping at all, and she'd give her *good* leg to take some Oxycontin.

So yeah. Her feelings were completely hurt, which surprised the hell out of her since she'd long ago realized she felt things at a different level than other people.

Which was to say less. She felt less than most.

She didn't know why or how, it just was.

So the fact that he'd managed to get in past her walls and cause pain? That sucked.

She was thinking all this and not paying a whole lot of attention to her body. All she wanted was to get away from AJ, who clearly wasn't feeling any of the things she was feeling.

And didn't she hate that, too.

But unfortunately, her right leg had other ideas.

From the long hours in the truck it had tightened up, and as she put her weight on it a sharp, air-stealing, vicious cramp gripped her and her knees gave way.

And she hit the wet pavement hard.

She heard AJ swear. Then his truck door slammed and he was there in the pouring rain, his hands on her, holding her still.

"I'm fine — Ah, shit." She gasped at the fire racing up and down her leg while his fingers dug into the twitching, cramping muscles.

Crouched at her side on the balls of his feet, in an easy grace that she couldn't have managed on her best day, AJ's skilled hands worked their magic as the agony washed through her.

"Breathe, Darcy," he instructed, his voice a quiet command that she automatically obeyed. "Deeper."

She'd long ago learned to ride the wave and let it take her, but it was still a very long two minutes before she could relax even marginally and nod her head. "I'm okay. I can get up."

Ignoring the rain, their wet clothing, and the valet guy hovering and shifting uncomfortably on his feet because he probably hadn't been trained on what to do about a woman lying on the concrete, writhing in agony from cramps, AJ kept his hands on Darcy. As he rose to his feet, he pulled her up with him, holding her still a moment, his gaze locked on hers. Probably taking her temperature and pulse by osmosis.

She looked down at herself. Since she hadn't put her sweater back on, her tank was wet, drenched through, giving everyone a show.

AJ's gaze dropped, took that in for himself before he shrugged out of his lightweight jacket and wrapped it around her.

"Thanks."

"Yeah." He cleared his throat and paused, like he'd lost his thoughts. "No problem."

Yeah, definitely. Mr. Calm, Stoic, Always in Charge's cool façade had definitely just slipped a little. This fascinated her and gave her more than a little grim satisfaction.

Maybe she *wasn't* in this crazy state of stupid lust by herself.

"You okay now?" he asked.

"Yes." Because between discombobulating him and being cocooned in his deliciously warm jacket, it was practically Christmas morning for her.

To his credit, AJ recovered quickly, and with a gentle squeeze of his hands, stepped free of her.

Back to normal. She bit down on the disappointment and had started to walk by him when he spoke.

"Proud of you," he said.

Her feet faltered, and this time it had nothing at all to do with her faulty legs.

Darcy took in the sight of the hotel in front of them. It was a huge, overstated affair with a big circular drive that was meant to simulate entering the wilds of the Bitterroot Mountains. There were hundred-gallon planters with trees lining the entrance and huge pens exhibiting disturbingly lifelike wildlife in their habitats.

"Jesus," AJ muttered as they passed a mountain lion frozen in the act of taking down Bambi, huge teeth and all.

"Welcome to Idaho," Darcy muttered back and made him laugh. She stared at him, realizing that he didn't do that nearly enough. *Don't get sucked in,* she reminded herself. *You're mad at him. Stick with that.*

"Wait here," he commanded, giving her another reason to be mad at him — he was bossy as hell.

He led her to a seating area in the lobby. He dropped their two bags at her feet, and strode off to the check-in desk.

In charge of his orbit, and hers.

You're just here because you know you owe the man this much at least, for all he's done for you. All she had to do was survive a few hours more˙ and then hopefully she'd be in her own hotel room watching some good TV for the night, and then in the morning it would be back to *The Real World,* Sunshine Edition.

Two long, denim-clad legs appeared in her field of vision and she looked up . . . and up, because damn, AJ had a long, built body.

He held out a room card.

She narrowed her eyes. "We're not sharing a room."

"Oh hell no," he said. "I want to be able to sleep with both eyes closed."

She snorted and pushed to her feet, gritting her teeth at the usual burn of pain slicing down her body.

AJ didn't rush her, just gave her the moment she needed. He did however take her bag, shouldering it along with his, gesturing with his chin to the bank of elevators.

At her floor he stepped off along with her and she found herself holding her breath as he walked her to her room. In front of her door he waited while she used her room card. He dropped her duffel bag just inside for her without stepping a foot into the room. She felt a ping of . . . something. Maybe irritation that it was so easy for him to walk away from her. In any case, her inner bitch took over and she slipped out of his jacket — slowly — and handed it back to him.

For the briefest of beats his gaze skimmed over her body and a muscle in his jaw bunched.

Good enough. Feeling better now, she smiled.

"Lobby in a half hour," he said. "Rest for a bit, whatever you need to do."

She saluted him, and he shook his head and strode off.

Blowing out a breath, she watched him go.

"Staring at my ass isn't resting," he said without looking back.

Dammit. She slammed her door, pretty sure she could still hear him chuckling. She hated when he got the last word.

A half hour later she'd showered, had contorted into a pretzel to treat her new tat with the required ointment, and dressed in a killer black dress she'd commandeered from Zoe's closet. The FMPs were her own, though she hadn't worn them in eleven months, hadn't worn any heels at all. She pulled them from her bag and hugged them close. "Missed you, my precious."

But her feet were sending serious doubt vibes.

"Look," she told them. "I need them tonight, okay?"

Her feet had no response.

Whatever. Surely she could manage for a half hour without wanting to go crying to her mama. She needed the extra height advantage. At five foot seven, the four-inch heels would put her on much more even ground with AJ and provide some desperately needed feminine power and sass.

She *really* needed sass. Especially since she was up against one undisputed truth — she couldn't change someone's mind about her.

She'd learned that early, along with the fact that she couldn't make someone love her, so hell if she'd try. It had never worked growing up, and she'd learned it didn't matter anyway. There'd been a one-strike rule at their house. If you screwed something up, you were done.

Granted, they'd lived in some seriously badass places. Liberia, Bolivia, Jordan, Hungary, Indonesia. The rule had been simple — fit in and blend. Or get in trouble and get sent to a boarding school in Switzerland until the next transfer.

Her siblings had gotten the hang of fitting in; they'd been naturals. And as a reward, both Zoe and Wyatt had gotten to go visit their grandparents in Sunshine much more often than Darcy.

But whatever. It was long ago over and done, and she was who she was: a little cynical, a little snarky, and a whole lot hard to love.

She got that about herself, she really did. She just didn't like to be reminded of it.

Slipping into the heels, she stared at herself in the mirror over the dresser.

As good as it got, she decided.

She grabbed her little clutch, shoved her phone and pepper spray in it — always prepared — and left her room.

She pushed the button for the elevator, and when the doors opened she gasped.

AJ stood inside in a suit and tie, and holy sweet baby Jesus, *who knew?* She'd seen him in jeans, she'd seen him in sweats, she'd seen him in basketball shorts, and once, years ago, she'd seen him in the buff when they'd all gone skinny-dipping up at the lake.

But she'd never seen him in a suit. He looked . . .

Damn.

Edible.

And just like that, her little pep talk and resolve not to care whether he liked her or not flew right out the window.

TEN

AJ held the door open for Darcy, doing his best to keep his tongue in his mouth, but he wasn't sure he quite managed.

"Thanks," she said, brushing up against his arm and shoulder as she stepped into the elevator.

His free hand came out to stabilize her, a purely instinctual move. He didn't give a thought to the fact that she hated to be helped because he *couldn't* give a thought to anything.

Holy. Shit. Hotness.

Her little black dress — emphasis on little — just about killed him. The bodice was short, snug, and, at first glance, modest.

Second glance, not so much.

She bent over and fiddled with her heels, which had a strap around her ankle and screamed SEX. So did the way the hem of her dress rose up on her thighs, high enough that his eyes nearly popped right out of his head. "What are you doing?" he managed.

"Nothing." Still bent at the waist, she shifted to her other heel, during which time he pressed his fingers into his eye sockets to keep his eyes in his head.

She was all leg and silken skin and crazy gorgeous hair, and he attempted to steel himself against her but he failed. He'd been wrong, oh so very wrong, when he said he'd be able to handle her. He couldn't, not in her yoga pants, not in a sexy little black dress, not at work, not in his truck, not in an elevator, not in anything anywhere — he couldn't do it, Sam I Am.

She straightened and sent him a searching look. She'd piled all that long curly hair on top of her head but several silky strands had escaped, brushing her temples and shoulders, giving her a just-got-laid look. Her lips were siren red and he knew it made him a pig, but all he could think about was her mouth and how her lips would looked stretched around his —

"We're on time still, right?" she asked.

He had to clear his throat to answer. "Yeah." *Jesus.*

The door slid shut and silence filled the elevator while they stared at each other. To keep his hands to himself, he backed to the wall.

"So," she said, looking like she was mentally cracking her knuckles. "What are the rules here? Kiss ass? Sit, shake, and roll over on command? Tell everyone how you saved my life? Obey your every order?"

Her sarcasm helped him roll his tongue back into his mouth. "I will ask you to kiss someone's ass never," he said. "Same for sit and shake and roll over. And you know damn well I didn't save your life. But as for the obeying me? That. Lots of that would be great."

She narrowed her eyes and opened her mouth, undoubtedly to slay him with her tongue, but his phone buzzed.

"It's Wyatt," he said, staring down at the screen.

"Saved by the bell," she said. "Answer it, what's wrong with you?"

Good question. No good answer . . . "Hey, kind of busy," he said to his best friend.

"Did you really just tell me that you were all for me obeying you?" Wyatt asked.

AJ blinked. "Um, what?"

"You butt dialed me again. You know how I love it when you talk dirty to me, but obey you? That's a kink I did not see coming from you."

Darcy, clearly able to hear her brother, snorted.

148

A beat of heavy silence came from Wyatt. "Was that Darcy?" he finally asked, his voice not nearly as amused now.

Shit. "We're in the elevator at the hotel in Boise, heading down to dinner."

Another pause as Wyatt clearly took in the fact that AJ had been talking to Darcy when he'd said the obey thing. "What's going on?" Wyatt finally asked.

Darcy leaned over AJ's arm and spoke to the phone while her scent drifted tantalizingly into his head.

"He wants me to obey him and call him sir," Darcy told Wyatt ever so helpfully. "I think that's grounds for beating the shit out of him, right?"

AJ gave her a long, hard look that didn't cow her at all. In fact, she smiled at him. A sweet, innocent smile that was complete BS. He blew out a breath and rubbed the back of his neck. "She's kidding," he said to Wyatt.

"No, I'm not," Darcy said.

"Christ," Wyatt said. "I don't want to know."

AJ grimaced.

"And you might've been right on this one," Wyatt said.

He meant, of course, that asking Darcy to

do this *was* a bad idea. *No shit.* "A little late now."

"We'll discuss it when you get back," Wyatt said.

"No need," Darcy said.

"Not you," Wyatt told her. "Me and AJ."

Darcy narrowed her eyes at the phone. "No, you won't," she told her brother. "I was kidding about beating the shit out of him, Wyatt. Don't you even think about getting into the middle of this, you hear me?"

AJ opened his mouth to intervene but she put a finger in his face. "Wyatt," she said. "You got me?"

"I got you," Wyatt said. "I got that you're both insane." And then he disconnected.

AJ stared at Darcy, a little surprised at how vehemently she'd stepped in and . . . what? Defended his honor?

"You going to tell me what your problem is?" she asked him.

Since he wasn't sure where to start on the list, he decided to plead the fifth.

"Look," she said. "I'm here because of you. But you've had a stick up your ass since you picked me up this morning."

"*I've* had a stick up *my* ass?" he asked in disbelief.

"Yeah," she said, jabbing a finger into his chest, hard. "You. You want to tell me how to remove it?"

No one could crank him up as fast as she could. No one. He snatched the finger currently boring a hole in his chest and pushed it away from him. Or he meant to. Instead he held on to her hand, holding her arm out from her body to look her over.

"What?" she snapped.

"That dress."

Her eyes narrowed. "What about it?"

"I said we were having dinner with a potential donator. I said we needed to impress him — not put him into cardiac arrest."

"So this is about what I'm wearing?" She looked down at herself. "Would you rather I wear a potato sack?"

Yes, but that wouldn't help. His heart was thumping against his ribs. Either he was stroking out or he needed to kiss her. Suddenly he couldn't see getting through the night, or even the next five minutes, if he didn't. "Yes," he said, his lust running amok, burying the last of his good sense. Not that there had been much to start with.

"Hey, I look damn good in this dress."

He met her gaze and heat coiled low in his belly and headed south from there. He took a moment to take in her features, those wide greener-than-green eyes, the flush on her cheeks, her delicious-looking mouth. He heard her quick, sharp inhale in response, and knew no matter what was going on between them — temper, resentments, whatever — in that moment she wanted him as much as he wanted her.

Well, she could have him however she wanted him, and if she wasn't sure in what way that might be, he had plenty of ideas for the both of them. God, she drove him up the wall, batshit crazy, in the worst of ways and the best of ways.

She stared right back at him, torturing her full lower lip between her teeth. Fact was, her mouth had been his undoing from the first time they'd kissed, in that bar parking lot. "Baby, good doesn't begin to even touch how you look in that dress."

Utter confusion filled her gaze.

Don't do it, soldier, he ordered himself. *Don't. Go. There.*

But either his hands had a mind of their own or they overruled his brain, because he gripped her arms.

Apparently he was totally going there. "You look hot as hell."

Still confused, she shook her head. "And that's a problem because . . . ?"

He pushed her up against the wall of the elevator and slid a hard thigh between hers.

152

"Oh," she breathed. Staring up at him, her fingers slid along the nape of his neck and into his hair, holding him to her.

Not necessary. He wasn't going anywhere. To prove it, he lowered his head and kissed her, soft at first, until she moaned, muttered something against his mouth, and slapped her hands to his chest. For a beat it could have gone either way, her shoving him clear or pulling him in.

In, he thought. God, please *in* . . .

As if she could read his mind, she slid her hands inside his suit jacket and fisted his shirt at his back, holding on tight.

And then they were fighting to get closer to each other, the kiss now hard and demanding, her mouth wet and hot and desperate on his.

And that's when he knew. One kiss wasn't going to be enough. Nothing short of stripping her naked to run his mouth over every inch of her would be enough, and he doubted even that could satisfy him.

God, she was the sweetest, hottest thing he'd ever tasted and she was right there with him, lost in the kiss. And even though he was a guy who never forgot his surroundings, he did exactly that.

The elevator disappeared.

Hell, they could've been on the moon for

all he noticed. His heart kept skipping beats and he couldn't get close enough. The taste of her made him realize he'd been starving for this, for her, and the way she melted against him in such soft, delicious, *perfect* surrender went straight through him in waves of intense pleasure.

He had absolutely zero reason to be doing this, not one single good reason, in fact had entire volumes of bad reasons. Not that this stopped him. The low ache in his body kept demanding more, so he pulled her in a little closer, a little tighter, opening his mouth wider on hers, needing to get inside of her, even if just for a moment.

And again, she was right there with him, moving against him, her breasts pressing into his chest as she made the sexiest sound of acquiescence he'd ever heard. Sliding a hand down her back, he cupped her ass and then the back of her thigh, lifting her leg, drawing it up around his waist to rock into her. "Darcy."

A helpless moan of arousal was her only response as her dress rose to dangerous heights. Her fingers were very busy in his waistband, gliding beneath, driving him right out of his ever-loving mind, because in another few seconds she'd have him in the palm of her hand, literally, and he'd be hers.

Rocking her hips to his, rubbing against the erection now threatening to burst his zipper, she was giving him a little taste of what she'd be like in bed. He wanted to hike her dress up to her chin, tear off whatever she wore beneath, and bury himself inside her. Instead he buried his face into the curve of her neck and groaned. *More.* That's all he could think. Not ready to surface, he slid his fingers into her hair and held her head as he once again kissed her, slowly, thoroughly, with long, lazy strokes of his tongue that had her practically climbing up his body.

He liked that, a whole lot, and going with the insanity plea, he was heading beneath her dress with nefarious intent when he heard someone's throat clearing.

Darcy shoved clear of him so fast his head spun. AJ was much slower to disengage, but yeah, the elevator doors had opened.

They were still on Darcy's floor.

"No worries," the man standing there said, looking embarrassed. "I'll . . . take the next one."

The doors closed.

"You never pushed the lobby button," Darcy said, her voice husky.

Right. Jesus. He tore his eyes off of her and punched the button for the lobby, barely resisting thunking his head against the steel doors a few times. He probably could have convinced himself that it had been just a kiss — if she hadn't looked at him right then.

It was the damnedest thing, but time seemed to stop.

Darcy swallowed hard but held the eye contact, nibbling on her lower lip, and God help him but he figured out exactly what this and the warning bells going off in his head were. Yeah, he knew, and he so didn't need this, didn't want this, but that didn't seem to mean a damn.

You. Are. So. Screwed . . .

Neither of them spoke on the ride down, the only sound being their still-labored breathing. AJ decided to take some comfort in the fact that she appeared to be having just as much trouble as he was. As the elevator slowed and then stopped, he reached out and hit the Close Door button and held it.

"What are you doing?" she asked.

"We should talk about it." He pointed to the wall where he'd pinned her and pillaged like a madman. Not that he'd been alone; he was pretty sure he still had the indentations from where her fingers had dug into his back.

But she was shaking her head. "Not necessary. I don't know what that was but I'm
going with denial. It *never* happened."

"But it did," he said.

"No." She exhaled a long, shuddering
breath. "The thing to remember here is that
I annoy the hell out of you and you make
me angry."

"Yeah, I noticed that when you had your
tongue down my throat," he said.

If looks could kill . . . "Are you telling me
that was all me?" she asked in a tone that
suggested he was an inch from death.

"Are you telling me it was all *me*?"

"Oh my God." She slapped his hand off
the Close Door button. "Let's just get out
of here before I strangle you."

The doors opened but he held her arm. "I
want to hear why you want to pretend this
didn't happen."

"Trust me," she said. "You don't want to
know what I'm really thinking."

"I do."

"Fine," she said and tossed up her hands.
"You're . . . remarkable. And by remarkable
I mean remarkably egotistical and —" She
broke off as another couple got onto the
elevator.

Darcy stepped off and started to walk,
stopping only to send a glance back at AJ.

"Hurry, I want to get this over with."

They were in the middle of the bank of elevators, alone. "Need a minute," he said.

"Why?"

He just looked at her.

Her gaze ran over him and he knew the exact moment she saw the problem because she stared at the obvious bulge behind his zipper. "Are you kidding me?"

"Oh, and you're not turned on?" he asked.

"Nope." She crossed her arms. "Not in the slightest."

He leaned in so that their mouths were nearly touching, marginally satisfied by her intake of breath and the way her gaze dropped to his mouth. "If we had even a minute of privacy," he said, "I'd prove you a liar."

Pushing free of him, she let out an annoyed sound and strode off toward the bar and grill in that dress and those heels, both his greatest fantasy and his biggest nightmare.

Halfway to the lobby she slowed.

He had no idea if she wanted to apologize or kill him. It could go either way.

Still not looking at him, she let out a long, unsteady breath. "AJ?"

He braced himself and schooled his features. "Yeah?"

"You really did save my life."

That was just about the last thing he'd expected her to say. She flashed him a quick, unreadable look. "But that changes nothing about how little I want to be here with you."

He nodded. "Understood."

The truce was over. He got that. He was going to just hope for the best. His potential grant partner was Trent Gibson, a genius IT guy who'd sold his software company several years ago for a staggering amount of money, more money than "my grandchildren's grandchildren could ever spend" as he'd told AJ.

The guy was fifty-five, self-made, and on top of his world. Or had been until his second wife had been terribly burned in a car accident. Physical therapy had saved her life.

Trent claimed that without his substantial wealth she never would have gotten the extended care she'd needed. As a result, she'd talked Trent into giving money to help others less fortunate than she. Trent's only stipulation had been that he got to personally meet and approve the physical therapists he awarded grant money to.

AJ had contacts throughout the country, good friends in the business, and he'd been mentioned to Trent several times over. He and Trent had spoken on the phone and via e-mail, and though Trent came off a little full of himself, no one could fault the guy's philanthropic spirit.

As for whether AJ's program would get to benefit from it, that all rode on tonight.

And on Darcy, the woman who'd just given him a hard-on in an elevator.

So his head wasn't exactly on straight as the three of them ordered drinks and dinner. In fact, his head was seriously fucked up. Darcy had him spinning. For one thing he had no idea what would've happened if the elevator doors hadn't opened when they had.

And for another, was this a random thing for Darcy, or had she felt it, too?

And while he sat there half lost in his own remembered lust, something shocking happened. Darcy carried the conversation. She held Trent's interest and . . . well, was the opposite of her usual snarky self. She laughed at the guy's jokes, smiled sweetly when he rambled on and on about how much money he'd made and the expensive colleges he planned on sending his kids from his first marriage. She asked questions as he pulled out his iPhone and flipped through hundreds of pictures of their lives on yachts and exotic islands and the like. In short, she was sweet and charming and wonderfully genuine — all while managing not to look at AJ or address him once.

Still, she kept her end of the bargain, and on top of that, it was a whole other side to her that she hadn't let him see before.

This didn't help him get his head on straight in the slightest.

And then dinner was cleared and in a lull of the conversation, Trent said to Darcy, "Tell me about your accident."

Oh Jesus. This was it. AJ held his breath because Darcy didn't talk about her accident, ever. It was a taboo subject and he got that. He really did.

It wasn't an easy subject for her.

Hell, it wasn't an easy subject for him. He'd been with Wyatt when the call had come in. He'd held a sobbing Zoe at the hospital while they'd waited for news from the trauma team that had worked on Darcy for twelve straight hours.

He'd watched Wyatt completely lose it in the ER parking lot, and AJ had done his best to pick up the pieces and hold on to them all until both Wyatt and Zoe could get it together.

Which hadn't happened until the surgeon had come out and told them she'd survived and that if she woke up in the next twelve hours, her chances were twenty-five percent.

Darcy had woken up eleven hours and fifty-five minutes later.

Stubborn as always.

But shockingly, Darcy didn't freeze up at Trent's question. She did however dodge it and skipped right to her physical therapy. She told Trent in great detail how she believed AJ had single-handedly gotten her walking again. How the insurance money had cut off after four months but that she'd still been in a wheelchair at that point. How AJ had continued to work with her on his own dime, and that if he hadn't, she'd still be in the chair.

Trent soaked up every single word, clearly fascinated, clearly impressed with her. "Remarkable," he said, unknowingly using the same word Darcy had flung at AJ earlier.

For the first time all night, Darcy looked right at AJ.

And, oh shit, there was a storm of trouble brewing in her eyes.

"You clearly have a deep bond," Trent said, clueless to the weather change.

Darcy nodded and reached for AJ. It was only years of soldiering that kept him from flinching, as he was pretty sure she meant to kill him.

Instead she squeezed his hand and . . . leaned in to kiss him gently on the mouth. "You're right," she said to Trent. "AJ is remarkable." Her gaze still locked on AJ, her eyes filled with trouble. "*Utterly* remarkable."

AJ held his breath. Surely Trent could see right through this ridiculous display of made-up affection.

But Trent seemed surprisingly touched. "Love it," he said. "You remind me of myself and my wife, the two of you are so obviously connected in spite of all the challenges you've faced. Amazing, really."

Darcy leaned back with a demure agreement. "Amazing," she said.

As if she had a single demure bone in her body.

The elevator ride back up to Darcy's room was entirely different than the one on the way down. For one thing, she was in it alone.

For another, she was exhausted.

She'd done her best, and yeah, she'd gone over the top, but there'd been a method to her madness. Trent loved only one thing more than himself and his money, and that was his wife. Darcy had gotten the idea to appeal to that softer side of him by using her relationship with AJ.

Her *fantasy* relationship with AJ, that is.

The two men had gone on to talk in great detail about some of AJ's other patients. By the time the waitress had cleared their plates and offered dessert, Darcy couldn't keep her eyes open.

AJ had noticed immediately and had started to excuse them to Trent, but she'd insisted she could go up to the room alone and get herself to bed.

She figured they were all safest that way. And by all, she meant herself.

Before the elevator opened she had her heels off and dangling from her fingers as she limped to her room. The second she shut her hotel room door, she dropped the heels to the floor. Halfway to the bathroom, she let the black dress fall as well.

With a whimper of relief, she picked up the hotel room phone. She hadn't eaten much at dinner and was still hungry. She ordered her standard comfort food — mac and cheese.

Then she practically crawled into the shower. She stood there beneath the hot spray until her locked muscles loosened slightly. Then, too tired to stand any longer, she turned off the water, barely managed to dry herself off, and staggered naked out of the bathroom, her only plan to drop into bed and pass out.

She took one step into the room and stopped short at the sight of AJ sprawled out on her bed, still fully dressed, his arms up behind his head, his feet casually crossed. His tie was gone, his collar open. He'd taken his sexy Mr. CEO look from day to night and her heart took the same leap.

Swearing, she whirled back to the bathroom, slamming the door, which she barely heard over the thundering of her heart in her own ears.

ELEVEN

AJ had broken into Darcy's room for a most excellent reason, but hell if he could remember it now as she came out of the bathroom bare-ass naked.

And Darcy naked was the distraction of a lifetime. Steam from her shower swirled around her willowy, toned body, a body that could make a grown man sink to his knees and beg.

Had he thought her dress heart-attack inducing? Because her dress had nothing on the sight of her without it.

"Get out," she yelled through the bathroom door.

Ah yes, now he remembered why he was here. She'd lied to Trent, made him think things that weren't true, things that couldn't possibly ever be true. "So you don't want to sleep with the man you find remarkable?"

"Okay, so maybe I took that a little further than I meant to," she said through the door.

"You mean you lied."

Silence, and then a rustling, and then the bathroom door opened and she reemerged wearing a towel wrapped around her body, tucked in between her breasts. "Look," she said, "it worked, right? He wanted us to have the kind of relationship he and his wife have, and I gave him that."

Her hair was loose and still wet enough to be sending little rivulets of water down her shoulders and chest, soaking into her towel. Not that he was noticing, or counting each and every single drop as it vanished.

"We have a problem," he said.

Her eyes zeroed in on his crotch, and the unmistakable bulge there. "Again?"

"Not that," he said, and rose off the bed.

"Oh, no you don't. Stay away. I mean it," she said and pointed at him. "You stay right over there and don't even think about coming any closer. Your lips might fall on mine again."

True story, although her lips had been right with him the first time — not that he was stupid enough to point that out.

"You need to go," she said.

"You were limping when you left dinner."

"I always limp."

"I wanted to make sure you were alright," he said.

"You ever hear of texting?"

"You ignore my texts," he said. "Maybe I should sext."

"Look at you with all the funny lately." She turned away. "I'm fine. I did what you asked. Now let yourself out."

"Damn," he said. "You're really good at that."

"At what?"

"Pushing people away."

A knock sounded at the door. "Room service!"

AJ opened up, signed for the delivery, and kicked the door closed. "Didn't we just eat?"

"Sometimes a girl just needs mac and cheese." She took the tray, lifted off the cover, and still in nothing but a towel, scooped a big bite. And then another. "Oh my God," she moaned in that voice she used in his dreams, like *Yum, AJ, I want to eat you up* . . .

After a few bites, she looked over at him. "You're still here why?"

"At dinner you mentioned the view from this floor," he said, "and Trent mentioned he was on the same floor as you."

"Yeah. So?"

"So after we finished tonight, we hit the elevator together."

"Uh-huh. Still not getting why you're here

being a perv."

He inhaled slow and deep. It didn't help. "You pretended to be in love with me."

"Yeah. And I pretended to love kissing you, too. So what?"

He met her gaze, trying to work out the best way to deal with this. He could leave her alone the way she so clearly wanted. His bruised ego could certainly use the break from her. But something was telling him to stay, that she needed him.

Which was ridiculous. She didn't need anyone. "First of all, he expected me to be sharing a room with you, and second . . ." *Don't do it . . .* But he did. "There was *nothing* pretend about that damn kiss," he said. "Not tonight, and not the first time we kissed, either."

She sucked in a breath. "We agreed to never discuss that."

"Actually, I never agreed to any such thing."

"No?" she asked, her voice glacial. "Well, clearly it sucked so bad that you didn't want to discuss it."

Since her tone didn't match her words it took him a minute to catch up. She couldn't actually believe that, could she? It didn't make sense. It was so past time to bail on this conversation before they went down a path he didn't intend to travel. Ever. "We're not doing this now," he said.

"Of course not."

"What does that mean?"

"It means whatever you say goes," she snapped.

"If only that were true."

Her eyes were lit and her body language screamed that she was spoiling for a fight, and damn if it didn't turn him on — which was not the appropriate response, he told himself. But his self wasn't listening. "Lie facedown on the bed," he said.

She choked out a laugh and crossed her arms, which plumped up her perfect breasts to mouth-watering proportions. "In your dreams."

"You're limping," he said. "You're holding yourself in a way that says you're in pain. We both know I can help with that."

She stared at him for a long beat and finally moved to the bed — which spoke volumes on how bad she must hurt. She lay flat, head on her arms, eyes closed.

He drew a deep breath and sat at her hip. Her hair fanned away from her face, wet and silky. Her face was drawn, her mouth a little pinched.

Yeah. She was in bad shape.

He began to slowly massage her spinal

cord over her towel, very purposely keeping her covered. "What the hell was tonight really about?" he finally asked.

"You'll have to be more specific."

The towel kept rising up the backs of her gorgeous thighs. He kept tugging it down. "You pretending we were a couple."

"I told you, I was trying to help you."

"I'm a little fuzzy on how lying to Trent helps me," he said.

"Look, if it's a problem for your high moral standards, then tell him I've got some condition where I speak out of turn, like Tourette's."

He decided to drop it. For now. Mostly because with his hands on her like they were, he was afraid he might be tempted to wrap them around her throat and strangle her.

Twenty minutes later she finally let out a shuddery sigh and relaxed. "Thanks," she murmured and rose, heading to the mini-bar. "Make sure you bill me in full for that, no more pro bono."

He ignored that. "You know they charge you a mint just to open that thing."

"Take it off my pay." She perused her choices and settled on a mini bottle of scotch.

"You already had two drinks at dinner."

She turned and gave him a deceptively bland look. The wild cat before the strike. "And?"

"And alcohol and pain meds don't mix, Darcy."

Her easy expression vanished. "I knew you'd get to it."

"To what?"

"To pissing me off." She pointed to the door. "Get out, AJ."

He didn't move as she took a long pull on the bottle. "Why are you still here?" she asked. "I asked you to go."

"You didn't ask," he said.

"Fine. Get out — *please.*"

His smile was as grim as her tone. "Better. But I'm still not going anywhere."

She just stared at him. "You know, most people run from me," she said. "As fast as they can."

"I'm not most people." He waited until she looked at him. "I didn't think you were taking the meds or you'd be a lot more mellow. I just wanted to be sure."

"Whatever."

"You going to stick with the story that the elevator kiss was pretend?"

"Yep," she said, popping the *P* sound, her eyes flashing with a dare.

His brain shut down and his body took

over. He strode close, put his hands on her arms, and hauled her up to her toes with some harebrained idea that kissing her again was going to fix this.

It was not.

Not even close.

Nose to nose she stared at him, her eyes both challenging and wary at the same time.

"Fuck," he said and let go of her, backing away, not quite trusting himself. "My point is —"

"Oh, goodie. There's a point."

Okay, that was it. He yanked her back in, hard. It was a selfish, asshole move, but then she sort of melted against him and he felt like he'd just won the lottery. Fisting his hands in her hair, he kissed her until she was letting out little, sexy-as-hell, panting whimpers and trying to crawl up his body. "Pretend though, right?" he murmured against her lips.

She shoved free. "Forget it. Let's go home."

He walked to her window and pulled open the shades.

Snow fell in heavy white lines, slashing through the night, and her mouth fell open.

"They're calling for at least six inches," he said. "The pass is closed until morning."

She stared at him.

Feeling guilty as shit and having no idea why, he shoved his hands into his pockets. Christ, now *he* needed a drink.

"Fine," she said. "So we're stuck until morning. Doesn't mean we have to be stuck together. Let yourself out." And then she turned her back on him.

Any words he might have uttered backed up in his throat because, casual as you please, she dropped her towel and bent to her bag. Jesus. He was still tongue-tied when she pulled on a big T-shirt and a pair of panties before facing him, one brow arched.

Right. She wanted him gone. Good idea. *Great* idea. He headed to the door, paused, had a mini argument with himself and lost. Or maybe won. In either case, he left her room and was striding toward the elevator when he heard his name. Turning around, he saw Trent in the hallway, carrying an ice bucket.

"You out to get that lovely lady of yours something?" Trent asked.

AJ's mind froze. "Uh . . ."

"Ice?"

AJ recovered. "Right. Yes. Ice." He looked down at his empty hands. Shit. "Forgot the bucket."

Trent grinned. "Going to be tricky without

174

it. But I'm glad I caught you. I was just telling my wife about you and Darcy. Summer
was too shy to come down tonight, but once
she found out that you and Darcy were a
couple, she got excited. She wants to have
breakfast with you two before you head
out."

AJ pictured trying to talk Darcy into
breakfast and rubbed a hand over his jaw.
"We're going to get an early start so —"

"Summer wants to meet you," Trent said
and moved closer, speaking in a conspira-
tor's tone. "And to be honest, AJ, I always
get her whatever she wants."

Hell. "I understand but we have a long
drive and both of us have work to get back
to."

"Let me repeat," Trent said, still smiling
but speaking firmly. "*Whatever* she wants,
AJ."

"Sure," he said, thinking what the hell,
this was Darcy's fault anyway. "Okay."

Trent clapped him on the shoulder and
smiled approvingly, and . . . didn't go away.
AJ finally realized the guy was waiting for
him to go back into Darcy's room — *their*
room — for the ice bucket.

This just got more and more fun. AJ
returned Trent's smile and walked back to
Darcy's room. Staring at the door, he blew

out a breath, lifted a hand and knocked once.

It took her a painfully long moment to answer, which was better than what he'd feared — that she wouldn't answer at all.

When she pulled open the door, she stared at him. "Sorry," she said. "I already gave at the office."

AJ barely got his foot in the door before she tried to slam it.

"Seriously?" she asked when he pushed his way in. "What if I'd screamed?"

"Then you'd have ruined all your hard work lying at dinner tonight," he said, and turned back to wave good night to Trent.

Trent returned the wave and went into his own room.

Finally. AJ shut the door and thunked his head against it.

"You're going to knock something loose," Darcy said. "And you're on the wrong side of the door."

He thunked his head a few more times.

"What the hell is wrong with you?" Darcy asked.

"Many, *many* things." He turned to face her. "Trent told his wife about us and Summer wants to meet you. We're having breakfast with them in the morning before they head off to their first team-building event."

She just gaped at him. "What?"

"You heard me."

"Okay," she finally said. "Here's what we're going to do, you're going to leave and I'm going to pretend you didn't come back."

"We've got to do this, Darcy."

"We? We're not a we!"

"You let them think we're a we," he said. "So, for better or worse, we're a we."

"Oh my God." She walked over to the door and thunked her head on it.

"What are you doing?"

"Seeing if this works." She straightened, her hand to her head. "It doesn't, by the way. You should've told Trent I've maxed out on the amount of time I can be in your presence and be nice."

"Yeah, that was on the tip of my tongue." He shook his head. "You're right, this is impossible. Forget it. I'll just tell him it was all a lie and —"

"Wait." She hesitated, her eyes suddenly worried. "Do you think that'll change his mind about you?"

"No one wants to invest in a liar, Darcy."

"Dammit!" She shoved her fingers into her hair, making the curls a little crazier than usual, and that was saying something. "Okay, whatever," she said. "Breakfast. But I want *real* bacon, AJ. None of this fake shit

177

you're always trying to push on me."

"Turkey bacon isn't fake," he said. "It's just healthier."

"Well, I want unhealthy bacon, okay? And *you're* buying. We eat, then we go."

"Fine."

"Fine." She pointed to the door. "See you in the morning." Without waiting for him to leave, she moved to the dresser and picked up a tube of some sort of ointment.

When it slipped from her fingers, he scooped it up for her and looked at it. It was what you used on a new tattoo. "Where is it?"

"What?"

He gave her a *get real* look.

"My back."

He pointed to the bed. "Sit," he said, and nudged her to the bed. "I didn't notice it when you dropped your towel."

"Because that's not what you were looking at."

True. Sitting behind her, he lifted her shirt and took in the new tattoo.

I am the hero of my story, I don't need to be saved.

The words ran in a perfectly straight, beautifully scripted line alongside her spine. Not on her surgery scar, but alongside it. "Xander's work," he said.

"Yes," she replied stiffly, clearly braced for something but hell if he knew what.

"Why not right on the scar?" he asked, feeling a little tense himself.

He couldn't help it. He had a history with scars and the mental anguish they could cause. He'd been in love with Kayla for three years during his stint in the military. They'd gotten lucky to be stationed together and he'd thought they'd spend the rest of their lives together.

Halfway through their tour of duty, she'd nearly been killed in an explosion that had rocked her Humvee halfway to Mars. She'd been one of the lucky ones and had survived, though she'd suffered burns to her throat and chest. They'd left scars.

Battle scars, he'd thought at the time. Proof that she was still alive. At least that's how *he'd* seen them.

Not Kayla. She'd always been beautiful, model beautiful, and as it turned out, she'd believed her beauty was only skin-deep. When her first reconstructive surgery didn't eradicate the scars, and the second and third surgeries didn't either, she'd gone off the deep end and dumped him. She refused to be loved.

Especially by a man who'd fallen in love with her when she'd still been stunning —

179

even though he'd thought her all the more beautiful for the imperfections. She'd been unable to believe him. Unable and unwilling.

And their relationship had detonated.

It had been five years now, and he'd be the first to admit that for at least half of that time he'd stayed out of relationships with other women in the hopes that Kayla would let him back in.

She had, but it had been a disaster of such epic proportions that *he'd* been the one to walk away that time.

Which was a big part of what held him back from Darcy, if he was being honest with himself. Darcy didn't see herself as lovable either, though with her it had little to do with the visible scars on the outside and everything to do with her scars on the inside.

Her fucking parents, of course, who'd taught her that she wasn't worth a thing.

"I wasn't trying to erase my scars," Darcy said now. "I didn't get the tattoo over them on purpose."

He lifted his gaze and found her twisted around to look at him. "Why?" he asked, hearing that his voice sounded tight. Grim.

She looked forward again and when she didn't immediately answer he figured she wasn't going to answer at all, but then she spoke.

"Just before the accident, I'd . . . lost myself a little bit," she said softly. "And then . . . after I plowed my car into a tree, I had a big wake-up call. I guess I just don't feel the need to hide that, or the scars."

He stared at her proud, squared shoulders and realized what she was braced for — his judgment. Which was never going to happen, especially since both her words and her inner strength completely undid him. "You're shaking."

"You know that happens when I'm tired," she said.

He squeezed some of the ointment onto a finger and carefully stroked it over the tattoo.

She shivered and goose bumps rose on her gorgeous skin.

He had to clear his throat twice to speak. "Cold?"

"No."

He went still for a beat and then capped the ointment, tossing it aside. "It's beautiful," he said. *You're beautiful . . .*

How many times had he said that to Kayla? It wasn't the package that made a woman beautiful, not even close, and yet she *had* been.

So was Darcy.

And now *he* was the one braced for Darcy to break down over his words. But she didn't.

In fact, she laughed.

And like everything else Darcy did, she went big and uninhibited. She tossed back her head and gave that throaty laugh that always went straight through him, lighting him up, warming him from the inside out even though he hadn't been aware of feeling cold.

"You're just saying that because you feel bad you saw me naked," she finally said.

"Actually, bad is just about the last thing I'm feeling." He could close his eyes and still see her walking out of that bathroom in nothing but steam.

She craned her neck to look at him. "What *do* you feel?"

"More than you want to know," he said, and because being on the bed with her was a temptation he didn't need, he rose and went straight to the minibar to grab a scotch for himself. And then on second thought he took a second so that he had one for each fist.

"What happened to that stuff being too expensive?" Darcy asked.

He snorted. "Like everything when it

comes to you — out the window." He opened both bottles and, with a sigh, handed her one.

"So," she said, clinking hers to his in a toast. "Here's to what happens in Boise stays in Boise?"

"Works for me."

TWELVE

Darcy hadn't meant to lighten the mood or make things easy between them. She was already in way over her head and she certainly didn't want to make matters worse by letting AJ think she was enjoying anything about this.

And plus the relaxed air gave far too much importance to the night. She didn't want to give importance to *anything* involving tonight. Tonight should've been just about doing AJ a favor.

But then there'd been that kiss.

AJ took life pretty damn seriously, and whatever he did he tended to excel at. He most definitely excelled at kissing.

God only knew what he could do between the sheets.

But that's not what she kept thinking about. Nope, she was thinking about when they'd gone to dinner and she'd watched him talk passionately to Trent about his work, about the people who needed him . . .

It had been humbling, and she'd realized exactly how much he had on the line tonight, and how much he deserved the opportunity, how many others could benefit.

"AJ?"

"Yeah?"

"Why do you do it?"

"Put up with you?" He shook his head. "No idea."

She rolled her eyes. "No, why are you a PT? What made you start Sunshine Wellness Center?"

He met her gaze. "Pretty deep question."

"I figure there's a deep answer. You don't do anything lightly, *or* just for the hell of it."

He looked at her for a long minute. "It's for my mom."

Darcy didn't know much about his mom other than she'd passed away a lot of years ago. "She had rheumatoid arthritis, right?"

"She had a bunch of health problems but the RA is what she suffered from the most. She did a lot of PT, especially in the end. I was just a little kid," he said quietly. "But I hated that I couldn't save her."

She let out a long breath and softened to him when she hadn't intended to. "So you save others. You help others."

He shrugged those broad shoulders, and at his modesty she softened even more.

He finished his drink, set the bottles down, and stood. Without his jacket and tie, he looked a little disheveled and a lot bad-ass.

He kicked off his shoes *and* her heart rate. "What are you doing?" she asked.

"I'm exhausted. I'm getting ready for bed."

Some of her happy scotch buzz drained. *"Here?"*

"Yep, and you can thank your little stunt for that."

They both eyed the bed.

The sole bed.

"Well," she managed. "I hope you like to sleep in bathtubs."

"I'm not sleeping in the bathtub, Darcy."

Damn. Why did the way he said her name always give her happy nipples? "Well, you're not sleeping with me."

"It's a big bed," he pointed out.

She crossed her arms over her chest, confused by how she could feel both pissy and aroused at the same time. "It's not *that* big."

He stared at her and she had no idea what he was thinking. She rarely did. AJ kept his own council. But clearly he'd decided on one thing — he didn't mind keeping them on par with their normal relationship, which was to say competitive and combative.

He smiled. "You're afraid you can't control yourself."

God help her, she knew she couldn't. "You wish!" And with that brilliant comeback, she strode into the bathroom, shut the door, and stared at herself in the mirror. "You will *not* jump his bones, you hear me?" she whispered to herself. Then she hauled the door open and strode back out there carrying a bath towel. This she rolled up and placed in the middle of the mattress before pointing to one side of the bed. *"Stay,"* she said.

He arched a brow and crossed his arms over his chest, making his biceps bulge.

Stupid sexy biceps.

"Stay?" he repeated in disbelief. "I'm not a dog."

"Hmm."

He looked amused. "What is that supposed to mean?"

"It means the jury is still out. What about pj's?" she asked. "You packing pj's?"

"I don't wear any," he said.

Oh boy. Now she had that image in her head, AJ all sprawled out in her bed wearing nothing but what God had given him, and God had been generous. And if that wasn't just perfect, now her heart was pumping but good, and judging by his smug expression, he knew it, too. Rat-fink bastard. "A toothbrush," she said desperately. "You don't have a toothbrush."

"You're stalling the inevitable," he said. "You must really be worried you can't control yourself."

Dammit! "Just . . . don't touch my side!" She stormed back into the bathroom because she needed a moment to find her composure. She took her time, slathering on lotion, combing her hair, doing everything she could think of to stall, hoping he'd be asleep when she ventured out there. When she finally did, the lights were off.

Good sign.

She tiptoed to her side of the bed and stared at the vague outline of one damn fine and damn annoying man.

He didn't speak.

And she wasn't about to. Near as she could tell, he'd left the rolled towel in place and was on his side facing away from her. Not moving. Steady breathing. Hopefully dead to the world. She gingerly climbed into the bed still wearing the only pj's she'd brought. A man's large, beefy tee.

AJ's.

She'd stolen it from his office locker at the wellness center because it was soft. And okay, because it smelled like him. Luckily he'd never noticed, and she *really* didn't want to explain why she had it. She could just remove it, because honestly? Being naked seemed a lot less revealing than him finding out she'd stolen his shirt.

But getting naked again seemed like tempting fate.

And she was done with the tempting-fate portion of her life.

She tried to calm her mind but her mind didn't get the memo. Did he really sleep naked, or had he been just teasing her? She couldn't tell but this was suddenly an issue bigger than world peace. She *needed* to know.

He seems like he's deeply asleep, a little voice said inside her head. You could take a teeny, tiny, little peek . . .

Bad idea. No way would she do that. Nope. Biting her lip, she stared at AJ's still form. Very still. Ah, damn. She was totally going to peek. Carefully she shifted and . . . lifted the covers.

Too dark to see anything.

She rolled to her back and tried to fall asleep, but the alcohol had juiced her up a little bit and her thoughts raced, making her toss and turn.

When the light suddenly came on, she squeaked.

AJ had sat up and hit the bedside switch. The covers slipped and pooled at his waist, revealing his bare chest and a set of ripped abs that made her want to drag her tongue from his chin to his belly button and beyond — *way* beyond.

Not a single sign of clothing, either. Which meant she now had her answer to the burning question.

Gulp.

"What's wrong?" he asked, sounding fully awake and alert.

She didn't know if this was because he could come awake in a blink, or if he'd never been asleep. Hell, maybe he didn't need sleep. Maybe he wasn't even human. That would explain a lot. "Nothing's wrong."

"Then why aren't we sleeping?"

"No reason. Shh," she said. "Let's go back to sleep."

"Did you want to try to get another peek at me first, now that the light's on?"

She narrowed her eyes. "I *knew* you were awake, you big faker!"

"Whatever, Peeping Tomina. And what

were you hoping to see anyway? Or should I guess?"

She felt herself flush. "Don't flatter your-self, I don't need to peek at you. All guys look the same in the buff."

"I can promise you that's not true," he said.

Oh boy. If she'd ever needed a subject change, it was now. "If you must know," she said. "The truth is I can't get comfortable."

He didn't blink. "And?"

She sighed and admitted the real truth. "And I stiffen up at night and get all achy. I can't fall asleep unless I take something. Which I didn't do tonight."

He *did* blink at that. His jaw got all bunchy, too.

She lifted her chin. "Not like you think," she said. "Not the pain meds."

"Darcy."

"I don't take them, AJ."

God, the concern in his gaze just about did her in. Which was the *only* reason she spoke the hard-to-admit truth. "I don't take them," she repeated. "I keep them, yes. It's a comfort. Like mac and cheese. Because at one time they were as important to me as that. And sometimes, I still want them and I pull them out and look at them and remember. I remember how shitty I feel when I take them, and how little they help. I keep them around because looking at them makes me feel sick, and I . . ." Dammit. She cleared her throat. "And sometimes I just need to look at them, that's all."

He didn't express disbelief. Or pat her on the head and tell her that her craving for them would pass. He didn't blow off her feelings. And she was grateful because it meant she didn't have to kill him.

"What do you take to sleep then?" he asked.

"Benadryl or melatonin. Something non-addictive."

"Every night?"

"A lot of them."

He scrubbed a hand down his face, and the sound of his palm brushing over the stubble on his jaw made her remember that he was maybe, quite probably naked.

He twirled his finger in her direction. "Lie down. On your front."

"Why?"

He went brows up at her suspicion. "Didn't we already play this game? I'll work on your tight muscles."

"Oh," she said. And what was that flowing through her? Disappointment? No, that couldn't be.

He was looking amused again. "What did

you think I was going to do?"

"I don't know."

"Uh-huh. Keep that up and you'll be a boy made of wood answering to the name Pinocchio." He tossed aside the covers and she didn't even pretend to look away.

He wasn't naked but nearly. His black boxer briefs covered his goodies in a disturbingly impressive way. She swallowed hard. "How are you going to give me a massage without crossing the great barrier reef?" she asked, pointing to the rolled-up towel between them.

He tossed the rolled-up towel to the floor.

Okaaaaaay.

"Facedown," he said.

To her dying day she would totally deny the fact that his authoritative voice turned her on. Some things needed to be taken to the grave. Still, she followed his directive and rolled over, pressing her face into the crook of her arm. "It's mostly in my —"

"I know where you hurt," he said, and proving it, put his big, warm hands right on the spot at her lower back that always caused the most pain.

She shouldn't be surprised. He'd been taking care of her body for eleven months now. He probably knew her every single inch better than she did, especially since she still hadn't gotten the hang of using her legs again and they often felt like appendages that didn't quite belong to her in the first place.

His hands stilled. "Is this my shirt?" he asked, a tone of disbelief in his voice.

Face still buried, she grimaced. "No."

"Seriously," he warned, "your nose is going to start growing."

She opened her mouth to retort to that but then he straddled her thighs, carefully keeping his weight off of her and on his knees.

He shoved the beefy tee up as high as it would go, baring her back to his gaze.

She sucked in a breath and was thankful she'd put on panties, though she was seriously wishing they didn't say *CHEEKY* across the ass.

Not that it mattered after her earlier inadvertent show . . .

There was a beat of utter silence and then a male snort. "True story," he said.

She opened her mouth to say something . . . well, cheeky, but then his hands began to move.

And good Lord, the man had a set of hands.

She couldn't hold back her low moans of relief as he rubbed and pressed and stroked at every single spot that hurt.

Leaving her a puddle of quivering goo.

"Relax," he murmured.

Yeah, right. He had two powerful thighs straddling hers, surrounding her by testosterone and pheromones, and he wanted her to relax. "I am," she said.

Another snort. "Close your eyes, Darcy."

"No, I'm —"

"Jesus, woman. For once just do something you're asked without argument."

"Fine." She closed her eyes. "And thank you. I mean that. It feels amazing and it's helping the cramping, but I still won't be able to sleep —"

"Shh."

She blew out a sigh and shut up.

And then, remarkably, fell asleep.

AJ worked Darcy over until she was limp as a noodle and so dead asleep to the world that she didn't so much as twitch when he finally slid off the bed.

Her skin was reddened from his hands but he knew she'd gotten relief from his effort. His gaze locked on her tattoo and his chest tightened.

She'd left the scar. Kind of like a huge, big fuck-you to the world, and it amazed him.

And made him proud as hell of her.

She was one of the most confounding, frustrating women he'd ever met. And the absolute bravest.

He carefully pulled the shirt down over her back and ass.

Cheeky.

He shook his head as he tugged the covers up to her shoulders, tucking her in.

She'd sleep now.

Not him though. His hands had been one hundred percent professional while he'd worked over her but his brain not so much.

He stepped into the bathroom, shut and locked the door, and cranked the shower. The hot water felt soothing, but there was no soothing his aching body. "You're a dumbass," he told his erection.

His erection had no response.

AJ bent his head, letting the water hit the back of his neck and shoulders as he wrapped a soapy hand around himself. His own form of sleep medicine.

Ten minutes later he was back in the room, his body temporarily sated but his mind no more relaxed than before.

Darcy hadn't budged an inch.

Glad that at least one of them could sleep, he carefully slipped into the bed and stared at the ceiling.

You could go back to your own room.

He had absolutely zero excuse for not doing exactly that as he turned on his side and studied the woman next to him in the dark.

She was breathing deeply and evenly, and with the ambient light sliding in from the gap in the shades, he could see her expression was calm.

Relaxed.

An expression he didn't get to see on her all that often. Seeing it now tightened his chest. He blew out a slow, careful breath and closed his eyes.

When he'd been a soldier he'd been able to order himself to sleep. It was a skill born of years of military training and necessity, as was the ability to tell himself to wake at any given time or for any given reason.

So that's what he did now.

Told himself to sleep until Darcy stirred.

Darcy woke up at some point in the middle of the night and found herself lying on top of a big, still body that was radiating heat like a furnace.

AJ.

He was flat on his back, just lying there innocently sleeping. And she? She had literally draped herself all over him like a blanket.

Damn.

Holding her breath, she tried to pull back but his arms tightened and she stilled. "AJ?"

"Mmmph," he said and didn't budge his arms of steel.

"AJ!"

His answer was to roll her beneath him and kiss her.

Deep.

Hot.

And wet.

And good God, her body helplessly rocked up into his because of that mouth.

Letting out a groan of pleasure, he slid his hands inside her shirt and up, until the tips of his fingers brushed the undersides of her breasts.

And then he went utterly still.

"Shit," he said.

THIRTEEN

"Gonna give a girl a complex," Darcy murmured.

AJ shook his head to clear it but that didn't help. Christ, had he just basically molested her in her sleep? Given that his hands were beneath her shirt, the answer was a big, fat yes.

"Shit," he said again, brilliantly repeating himself, and rolled to his back.

"That's quite the expansive vocabulary you've got there."

"I thought I was dreaming," he said.

With a laugh, Darcy hit the lamp this time. Her hair was Girls Gone Wild and the tee she'd stolen from him slipped off one creamy shoulder.

Her nipples were just about boring holes in the soft material and made his mouth water.

Jesus. He settled his arm over his eyes to block the view. He could feel most of his business hanging out in the chilly room air because at some point in the night she'd hogged all the covers. He needed to right them and get her back to sleep before she started asking questions he didn't want to answer.

"You dream about me?" she asked.

Like that one. "Shit," he said for a third time and sat up.

"That's so annoying."

He slid her a look. "What?"

"How when you sit up your abs do that stupid sexy guy crunch thing because you have no body fat, you bastard."

She might as well have been talking at him in Chinese. He rolled out of the bed and stalked toward the bathroom.

"Aw, don't go away mad," she said, sounding amused. "Just go away."

He slammed the bathroom door in tune to her low laugh.

The next morning Darcy pushed the lobby button and felt the elevator begin to glide. She stared at the numbers on the display as they raced toward the ground level, incredibly aware of AJ standing at her side.

He'd been gone when she'd woken up a half hour ago. She hadn't yet addressed the teeny tiny stab of disappointment that had hit her. By the time she'd come to terms with his absence and the winter wonderland outside the hotel window, he'd been back in her room with a coffee in each hand.

She'd gratefully downed the caffeine but still didn't feel ready for this breakfast gig. She hadn't been nervous last night at dinner. She'd still been pissy about being there in the first place.

But apparently she'd moved past the pissy stage into the anxiety stage.

"Do we need to talk about it?" AJ asked. His voice was still morning gruff, which somehow slid across every single one of her nerve endings. And apparently she had many.

"No," she said firmly. The less talking the better.

He turned her to face him. He wore jeans and a gray Henley, looking disturbingly laid-back and easygoing and . . . hot.

Dammit.

"We don't need to talk at all," she assured him. "In fact, let's practice not talking, all the way home."

"Okay," he said, annoyingly game. "But there's something you should know."

Great. "I'll behave myself." Probably.

He shook his head, a tiny quirk at the corner of his mouth suggesting that he

201

sincerely doubted her ability to behave herself. "Not that," he said, and waited a beat, his hazel eyes holding hers prisoner. "We got more than the forecasted six inches."

Uh-oh. "How much more?"

"There's two feet of fresh powder on the summit."

"And?"

"And it's still coming down," he said. "The pass is still closed."

She stared at him and then dropped her head back and stared at the ceiling. "Seriously?" she asked karma, fate, destiny . . . whoever was in charge of the joke that was her life. "What did I ever do to you?"

"Besides drive me crazy on a daily basis?" AJ asked.

"Not you!"

Now he did laugh. "You talking to God?"

"Trying." She met his gaze. "I'll call Zoe and make her fly her boss's plane down here to rescue me right this very minute."

"You don't want her flying in this weather."

Yeah.

Dammit. "Fine. We eat quick and get on the road before it gets any worse. Got me?"

"Got you."

Finally they were in sync.

The elevator door opened and she stepped off, only to be yanked back into AJ, who had a grip on the back of her sweater. "I still think we should talk," he said, staring down into her face.

"Sure. When hell freezes over." And with that she shrugged free and marched into the café.

Trent was seated at a table with a pretty, petite blonde two decades younger than him. She smiled a shy greeting. When she did, only the left side of her moved. The right side was marred by scars and skin grafts that stretched from her forehead to her neck.

Darcy's chest squeezed. She didn't realize she'd frozen until AJ came up behind her and put a warm hand at the small of her back, nudging her forward.

"Summer," Trent said, "this is AJ, the physical therapist I've told you so much about, and also the love of his life, Darcy."

Darcy nearly swallowed her tongue on the "love of his life" thing, and when she coughed, AJ slid her a look that said he wouldn't mind if she did swallow her tongue.

"AJ and Darcy," Trent went on, "meet the love of *my* life: my wife, Summer."

At the sweet words, Summer beamed at

him and then gestured to the empty seats. "Join us," she said. "I'm starving."

Trent leaned in and kissed her scarred cheek. "That's because we worked up an appetite this morning."

She smacked him lightly as she laughed, a sweet, musical sound. "At the hotel gym, you silly man. You always leave that part off."

Trent just grinned at her.

Darcy and AJ sat and the two men engaged in conversation about the storm. A waitress came and brought coffee and tea, and Summer leaned forward toward Darcy. "We have the two most handsome men in the room."

Darcy glanced around and saw a lot of other handsome men but her gaze caught on only one — the man sitting on her other side.

"And your man is particularly gorgeous," Summer whispered.

Yeah, and that it was true didn't help. "That's a beautiful necklace," she said in a desperate attempt to change the subject, nodding to the huge solitaire hanging from Summer's neck.

"Oh, isn't it?" Summer ran her finger over the diamond. "It was supposed to be my engagement ring, but then I got into the accident and . . ." She set her right hand on the table. Like her face, it was scarred, her fingers gnarled like a woman in her nineties instead of mid-thirties.

Little flashes of what Summer must have suffered hit Darcy in strong images. Strong, because she had an unfortunate amount of images in her brain to draw from. *You're recovering,* a voice inside her head said. *Soon nothing will show of your accident — unlike Summer, who'll always bear those scars.*

From beneath the table AJ squeezed her fingers. She squeezed back, grateful for the silent support, and drew a careful breath. "It makes a stunning necklace," she said. "It's like it was meant to be that way."

"I think so, too," Summer said and her smile faded. "After the accident, I wasn't sure how I was going to get back to a happy place. It's hard to be happy when every inch of you is in agony twenty-four/seven."

Trent stopped in mid-sentence from his conversation with AJ and grabbed her hand. "Honey, you don't have to go back there or talk about it. AJ and Darcy will understand."

"I want to talk about it." Summer looked into his eyes. "I want to tell people how you saved my life."

"But I didn't," he said. "I wasn't even in

town when that drunk driver hit you head-on." His voice hardened. "Or I'd have killed him with my own bare hands."

"No, stop that," she murmured. "We've been over this. I'd never have wanted that. He got what he deserved; he's sitting in a jail cell. And I meant you saved me *after.* You were there with me every second of recovery, through rehab, through surgeries, through everything including paying for the PT I so desperately needed, even after my insurance company cut me off."

Darcy's gaze got caught in AJ's and she couldn't look away.

Trent shook his head. "Anyone would have —"

"No," Summer said firmly, bringing their entwined fingers up to her mouth and kissing her husband's palm. "No one else would have, or could have." She looked at AJ and Darcy. "I was only an admin, making barely forty thousand dollars a year. My parents are elderly, and my sister and I help support them."

"Summer," Trent said carefully. "Honey, you're upsetting yourself —"

"No, I'm telling a damn story," she said, making Darcy smile because the woman wasn't blond fluff at all, but had real grit.

She loved grit.

Summer smiled at him to soften her words and went on with her story. "We'd only dated a few times, Trent and I. We barely knew each other. And yet I woke up after two days in a coma and there he was at my side." She stared at Trent, her eyes going shiny. "And he never left. From that moment on we were together, just like that. Before he even knew if I was any good in the sack."

Trent winced.

Darcy laughed. Yeah, she liked this woman.

A lot.

"By the time I got out of the hospital," Summer said, "I'd lost my job. I wasn't well enough to get another." She paused to swallow hard. "And the worst part was still to come. Physical therapy."

Darcy nodded at this. It was true. The accident, the surgeries, the hospital visits . . . all pieces of cake compared to the sheer agony of physical therapy.

"If Trent hadn't stepped in and covered my costs," Summer went on, "I'd still be in bad shape. I'd never have gotten better." She spoke fiercely, holding on to Trent's hand.

Still looking at AJ, Darcy's throat tightened so that she couldn't speak. *Same goes,* she wanted to say.

AJ gave a small head shake and she could practically hear his words in her head. *I didn't save your life. You saved yourself.*

"No way," Trent said, voice husky. "You're too stubborn to have not gotten better."

Summer laughed and blew her nose. "And people wonder why I love you."

"People wonder?" Trent asked, smiling.

Summer smiled, too, through her unshed tears. "I'm sorry, I didn't mean to get emotional. But I worry — how many people don't have a man like you in their lives when they need one?"

Trent slipped an arm around her and gave her a hug. "You flatter me, sweetheart."

"I don't flatter anyone," Summer said. "I tell the truth." She met AJ's gaze across the table. "You treated a friend of mine, someone I met in the hospital after my accident. Michelle Barnes."

AJ nodded. "I did. I still do."

"When Trent told me about you," Summer said, "I did my research. You take in new clients, whether they can pay or not. And when they can't, you match them up to sponsors and get them grants. Like a scholarship."

"As much as I can," AJ said.

Summer, looking visibly moved, nodded.

"And then you fell in love with your own Summer," Trent said.

Darcy had been staring at AJ, but she broke the eye contact as Summer reached for her hand. "You found love in spite of what happened to you," Summer said. "Real love. Can I ask . . . is there going to be a wedding anytime soon?"

Darcy opened her mouth and then shut it. She'd never felt like a bigger fraud. "We're not in a hurry," she managed.

"I guessed that," Summer said. "Seeing as you're not yet even wearing a ring."

Darcy hid her hands beneath the table, feeling like she was a kid again and about to get in trouble. In the old days that had meant getting sent away. Now the only thing that could happen was that she would blow an incredible opportunity for AJ, a man who maybe drove her insane just by breathing but was also a man who'd given back her life.

If she screwed this up for him, she'd never forgive herself.

She'd lose their friendship for certain, and in that moment she was startled to realize that the friendship meant more to her than just about anything else in her life. She turned her head to find his gaze still on her.

209

He cocked his head in an unspoken question.

She shook hers. "Some things don't require a ring," she said to Summer. "Some things just are."

AJ didn't move or let his expression change but she sensed his surprise.

Did he think she didn't understand love? Maybe she didn't trust love, but she understood it just fine.

Summer smiled. "I know exactly what you mean. And I couldn't help but notice that you're still limping. Will you tell me about your accident?"

Darcy stilled. Damn. "I . . ." *Damn.*

AJ slid an arm around her. "We should really go check the roads and see if we can get out."

Saving her. As he always had. She sent him a grateful smile. "Yes, you're right."

"Oh, but the roads are horrible," Summer said. "And some are still closed. Please stay. I know you were hoping Trent would make his decision this weekend but he never makes hasty decisions. He'll want to think on it and get back to you. So you might as well stay and enjoy yourselves, right?"

"I understand about not making any hasty decisions," AJ said. "But —"

"Please?" Summer asked. "We made arrangements for the two of you to join us in our team-building trust exercise workshop."

Darcy's gut clenched. Some of her least favorite words were *team, building, trust,* and *exercise.* "That's very . . . sweet," she said. "Especially since I *love* trust exercises." She slid a look at AJ when he choked on a sip of water. "But we really have to at least try to get home. Right, babe?"

In hindsight, she had no one to blame but herself. If she hadn't added on the ridiculous endearment, AJ would've been on her side.

Instead he smiled. And it was his badass smile, too, the one that usually melted all the bones in her legs. Not so much right now though. Right now that smile struck fear right through her heart.

With his arm still slung around her shoulders, he squeezed, brushing his mouth to her temple. "No worries," he said. "Since I know how much you *love* trust exercises, we'll stay. Just for you. *Babe.*"

Well, shit.

Note to self: Not ready to play with AJ.

FOURTEEN

Ten minutes later Darcy found herself in a ballroom with fifty of Trent's employees and some of their friends and family as well. They were all divided into pairs — she with AJ, of course — and each twosome stood facing each other.

"Greetings, everyone!" the emcee at the front of the large room said into a microphone. "Now, I want you all to take a look at your partner for the day."

Darcy looked into AJ's eyes and found trouble. Dammit, he was enjoying this.

"Take a good look," the emcee said. "Because this might not be the partner you win with." He grinned. "Yeah, you'll have a chance to switch. So if the boss paired you up, or if you're with your work teammate and you don't want to be, or if your significant other sucks at games . . . or maybe you simply like change, no worries. Things are going to get interesting."

This didn't sound interesting to Darcy at all. It sounded terrifying. The only thing worse than having to do this with AJ would be having to do this with a perfect stranger.

"Now, I'm going to ask you to answer some questions," the emcee said. "To start, keep in mind that not everyone will have to answer every question — it's just the luck of the draw. Hope you're feeling lucky. Oh, and one final thing: The winning pair gets a thousand bucks."

The room *ooh'd* and *aah'd* — Darcy included. Her half of a thousand bucks would make a nice chunk that she could use to buy service dogs and also help Zoe get ahead of the house expenses for a change.

"Ready to get going?" the emcee asked. "Good. You're already facing your partner, right? Reach out to put your palms to your partner's."

AJ held up his hands and Darcy set hers against them. His were much bigger than hers, warm and callused, and gave her a little shiver.

Okay, maybe not so little.

"Lean toward each other," the emcee said.

They both leaned in, their faces close enough that she could see the gold flecks in those hazel eyes dance. Close enough that if she wanted to, she could press her jaw to his scruffy one. Close enough to catch the scent of his skin, which somehow made her . . . ache.

She decided to attribute this stupid phenomenon to sleeping with him, which, FYI, had felt more intimate than . . . sex. But being in bed with a man all night long had most definitely brought back memories of sex. Granted, they were distant memories. In any case, she told herself this was all just a simple biological response, nothing more.

If only he hadn't kissed her.

But the truth was, she couldn't one hundred percent blame him for that. And them being here, doing this, that was all on her.

"Lean even closer," the emcee said. He paused while everyone did this. "Move your feet farther back. A little farther . . . Good. Now even more."

Some groaning from the room. Some laughing. Definite discussion.

AJ didn't speak, just moved his feet farther away and leaned into Darcy.

She did the same, perfectly aware that he was taking on all of her weight and yet — clearly in deference to her disabilities — keeping most of his own on himself. "I can do this," she whispered.

"You *are* doing this," he said, refusing to

admit he was handicapping her.

Next to them Summer was laughing as she and Trent worked on their balance. On the other side of them, two guys leaned on each other, laughing a bit, goofing off. One of them fell and hit the floor, much to the delight of his partner.

"Someone's thinking about his hot date this weekend," the emcee said. "Concentrate, people. There's a thousand bucks on the line here. Now everyone move a little bit farther back, and . . . hold it. Good."

Good? Darcy was on the balls of her feet, balanced only because AJ had her balanced. She was breathing heavy, sweating, and he stood there looking utterly at ease.

"Stare into each other's eyes," the emcee said, "and know that the person you're looking at is all that's keeping you from faceplanting." He paused and chuckled, the diabolical bastard. "Now's probably not a good time to air out any dirty laundry, like who left the printer out of paper, or the toilet seat up, or who's a bed hog."

AJ arched a brow at Darcy, silently reminding her which of them was the bed hog. She couldn't help it; she laughed.

His gaze dropped to her mouth, which suddenly had trouble dragging air into her lungs.

"So of course that's why we're going to do exactly that," the emcee said. "While you're dependent on each other for not hitting your face on the floor, one of you is going to admit your deepest fear."

Everyone stared at their partners. No one spoke. Darcy's heart pounded. "I don't have fears," she said.

AJ smiled.

The emcee said, "If you're having problems figuring out who's going to answer this round, let me help. Most people's gut reaction is that they don't have any fears to admit."

AJ smirked at Darcy.

She rolled her eyes.

"So . . . youngest first," the emcee said, and half the people in the room protested.

Darcy included. "Age racist," she muttered.

AJ just waited.

"Fine," she said. "I'm afraid of spiders."

He shook his head. "No, you're not. I caught you just last week saving Ariana from one in her locker and I watched you carry the thing outside rather than kill it."

"Because hello," she said. "I'm afraid of them."

"Seriously. You are such a liar."

"Hey, maybe I'm afraid of killing them."

"Try again."

"Whatever," she muttered and sighed. "Fine. Maybe I'm afraid of everything, you ever think of that? Maybe I'm just one big coward."

AJ tipped his head back and laughed, his white teeth flashing against that dark jaw, his eyes lit, all the while keeping his balance with annoying ease.

"I don't know why that's so funny," she griped, looking away because looking right at him laughing was like being in a candy shop. So tempting.

And so bad for you.

"I'm pretty sure you're not supposed to laugh at my fears," she said.

When his fingers gently squeezed hers, she looked up and was startled to find his expression now serious, eyes warm. "You're not afraid of much," he said. "But there is one thing and it's not spiders."

Again her heart pounded. "You don't know."

"I do."

"You *don't.*"

"Alright, then tell me," he said.

"Oh, no. I don't need half of a thousand bucks *that* much."

"I'll double it if you tell me," he said.

She narrowed her eyes. "You'd pay me a

second grand just to hear me say my biggest fear?"

"Think about it," he said. "More dogs."

She stared at him. "That's hard to resist."

"I am," he agreed.

This made her smile but it faded quick. "I don't like that I can be bought," she said quietly.

"For a cause," he said just as quietly. "And we can all be bought for our cause, Darcy."

"You admitting your fears, Youngest?" the emcee called out. "Because you've got two minutes left."

Darcy only needed two seconds. She closed her eyes. "My biggest fear is . . ." Her lips tightened, not allowing the words to escape. Which was silly; they were just words.

"You're afraid of love," AJ said.

Her eyes flew open and she stared at him. His gaze dared her to contradict him.

She blew out a breath. "Well, that's not true at all," she said. "I love plenty. I love Wyatt, for instance. Zoe. Xander. Oreo."

"If you're not afraid of love, then what?" he asked, his eyes daring her to say it.

She'd known him for years, though not like she had the past eleven months. Since then he'd had his hands all over her in a healing capacity, and as of yesterday in an elevator in a *not* healing capacity. He knew her better than just about anyone else, and she didn't call his bluff because she'd bet he *did* know the truth about her deepest fear. "Okay, so it's not love I'm afraid of," she admitted. "I can love, just like anyone else." She paused, her gaze caught in his. "I'm afraid of what happens once you do love. And when that person stops loving you back."

"Abandonment," he said.

She shrugged, looking away.

"Neglect. Being discarded."

"I didn't ask for synonyms," she said, getting pissy.

He squeezed her fingers again until she tipped her head back to meet his gaze. He was utterly serious, so much so that it stole her breath.

"You're right, Darcy. You have people in your life who you love and who love you. But you should also know that those people would never stop loving you back."

"Never say never," she said as lightly as she could.

He opened his mouth to say something but she'd never know what, because the emcee spoke.

"Time's up," the guy said. "But don't move. There's one more thing."

219

Darcy's leg buckled. "Crap —"

AJ caught her, holding on to her just until she found her balance and righted herself.

If he'd been the one to slip she'd never have been able to catch him. They'd have both gone down in a heap.

"Okay, everyone," the emcee said in a way-too-jovial tone that made Darcy want to smack him. "Now you all have a choice. Stay with the partner you have or switch. Hold your position unless you're switching partners on my count of three."

Darcy felt a bead of sweat trickle between her breasts. The horror of being possibly dumped and made to switch made her pulse race with anxiety.

"One . . ." the emcee said.

AJ shifted and Darcy sucked in a breath, trying like hell to look like the kind of partner he couldn't possibly live without. But her muscles were already protesting and quivering and she didn't know how much longer she could do this. "I don't blame you," she said to AJ. "There's a thousand bucks on the line here, so . . ."

"Two . . ."

Oh God. She closed her eyes, unable to take the suspense.

"Three!" the emcee called out. "Incredible, folks. This is a first. No one, not a single one of you, went looking to switch partners. Nice."

Darcy's eyes flew open.

AJ released her hands and stepped back. He was watching her, his eyes narrowed slightly as if it bugged the shit out of him that she'd expected him to want to change partners.

"Is this a pity stay?" she asked. "It's because I just admitted to being a big puss about being discarded, right? Well, you can just forget it. I won't have you stick around just because —"

"Darcy," he said. "There's no such thing as a pity stay. There's a pity fuck, but not a pity stay."

She narrowed her eyes. "So you hereby solemnly swear that you aren't feeling sorry for me?" she demanded.

"I feel a lot of things for you, Darcy, but sorry isn't one of them."

"Okay, back in position, everyone!" the emcee said. "Back to leaning on your partner. Ready?"

"You've got to be kidding me," she muttered and put her hands to AJ's.

"This time one of you has to admit something to your partner," the emcee said. "Something you've been holding on to. It can be as simple as, 'I know that you're the one who ate my precious lunch out of the office fridge,' or as complicated as admitting a feeling that you've held back."

Oh, God. This was dumb. Beyond dumb.

"Whoops," the emcee said. "I almost forgot to tell you which one of you has to make the admission." He laughed gleefully, clearly thoroughly enjoying himself. "The shorter of the two of you. Go."

AJ cocked his head at her, waiting, a smug smile on his face.

"Hey," she said. "If I was back to my old self, I'd be wearing my high-heel boots today and then we'd be the same height. And that would mean a tie and as a gentleman, you'd take your turn at this stupid gig."

"Never claimed to be a gentleman." He flashed a heart-stopping grin. "And even in your fuck-me boots, I'm taller than you. But nice try."

She closed her eyes and wracked her brain for an easy admission that wouldn't hurt too much.

I've got a serious case of hot-for-you.

Nope. No way.

I feel really badly that I lied to Trent.

Yeah, she really should say that, but it wasn't a conversation she wanted to have with Trent and Summer only three yards away.

I know I've done everything in my power to be a bitch to you, but it's to hide the fact that I really like you.

Yeah, that one was perfect . . . if she'd been in *middle school.* Good Lord.

"We going to do this any time today?" AJ asked.

Actually, maybe she didn't like him as much as she thought. But she did want him. Bad. She flashed him her own badass smile and — screw it — she kissed him.

Take that!

AJ stilled for a single beat and then his fingers entangled with hers and he squeezed her hands as he tilted his head and deepened the kiss.

She'd meant for it to be just a peck but clearly he had other ideas. He swept his tongue to hers and then retreated, and damn if her own tongue didn't follow, demanding more. But he pulled free, his eyes hot and also amused.

Lifting her head to glare at him, she forgot what they were doing and once again her arms collapsed. She gasped, perfectly aware she was going down and on her face, but . . . she didn't.

Again AJ caught her, his arms encircling

her, her feet dangling above the ground.

"Aw, don't they look so sweet together?" Darcy heard Summer whisper to Trent. And AJ grinned down at Darcy because they both knew he was about as sweet as a hungry mountain lion.

FIFTEEN

The second hour of the workshop wasn't nearly as much fun as having Darcy kiss him, AJ thought. Or kissing her back until she'd gasped in surprise and stared at him like she'd never seen him before.

Nope. Nothing near as good.

Up next was the obstacle course, which was a "minefield" with chairs, balls, cones, boxes, and other objects that were potential obstacles and could trip someone up.

The catch? Every round consisted of someone being blindfolded, to be led around by the other's voice alone.

Upon receiving these directions, Darcy turned to AJ with a wide-eyed look of such heartbreaking, genuine panic at the thought of being blindfolded, he volunteered.

Fucking sucker, Wyatt would've said.

It wasn't until they'd been divided up among several hotel boardrooms for their turn that the rest of the exercise came out.

If the one doing the vocal guiding got the other through the obstacle course in less than five minutes each, they got to ask a question of their partner.

It was like some big game of Truth or Dare, but with both truth *and* dare.

And of course AJ was up first.

Trent clapped a hand on his shoulder. "Good luck, man." He and Summer were to go right after AJ and Darcy, with Summer being the blindfolded one.

"Guess we know who the most trusting ones are, don't we," Summer murmured to AJ with a low laugh.

Darcy had given him a look of surprise, like she hadn't realized he trusted her.

How the hell could she be surprised? But then again she didn't have a lot of experience with trust. Given away by her parents over and over again, often separated from her siblings without any communication allowed, then later as an adult wanderlusting all over the planet on her own, she'd rarely let anyone in, much less allowed herself the luxury of trust.

They were given a blindfold. Darcy met his gaze and then moved behind him, her arms coming around him. *You are not having sex with her,* he reminded himself. *Not unless she strips naked and throws you to the bed and* —

No. Under *no* circumstances were they having sex. Period. He couldn't, not without getting his heart involved. Even though there was already an entire section of his heart with her name engraved on it.

Darcy's body brushed his and he stilled in order to catch every single second of it.

"You okay?" she asked.

"Yes." No . . .

She settled the blindfold against his eyes, during which time her hair brushed his jaw and her scent filled his head. He actually caught himself trying to inhale her whole.

"Don't get any ideas," she murmured in his ear.

Too late. He had all sorts of ideas. "About?"

"About doing this to me."

With his eyes covered, his other senses kicked into gear, like the feel of her mouth so close to his ear, her breasts pressing into his back. "Turnabout *is* fair play," he said, voice low and husky even to his own ears.

She laughed but her voice was just as low and husky as his. "Maybe if you're *very* lucky."

Damn. She was only teasing him, he knew this, but . . . *damn.*

She led him into the boardroom, shutting

the door behind them. She was told to climb up the platform and call out directions to her partner from there.

"The first station's about six feet," Darcy said. "But there're boxes right in front of you, haphazardly stacked. If you even brush them, they're going over. Take a big step to the right."

He took a big step and crashed into what felt like netting.

"Sorry!" she gasped. "I meant my right, your left!"

He corrected and she said, "Good. Now you've got to go up and over what looks like one of the things that construction workers use for their saw."

"A sawhorse?"

"Yeah," she said. "That. Go over it because you can't go around without knocking over a set of foam bricks."

AJ felt out in front of him, gauged the height and swung a leg over.

"Duck low," she said.

He crouched.

"Crawl forward five feet to the first station."

His hands hit something that felt an awful lot like snakes. His fears hadn't yet played into this whole trust-building game they'd been playing all morning, but they were about to. Logically he knew damn well he wasn't crawling through a pile of snakes, but the mind was a funny thing and his instantly rebelled. "What the hell is this?"

"Four more feet," she said. "Hurry, there's only one minute left and I want to get to ask my question!"

He was starting to sweat. "Darcy —"

"Yeah? Hey," she said, her voice suddenly soft. "AJ? You okay?"

"Peachy. Next move."

"Okay," she said, gentle but firm, as if she knew. "You're almost there. It's almost over. Just stretch out in front of you. You'll feel the platform. Pull yourself up on it. You just need to move forward a few feet, that's all."

He sucked in a breath and surged forward and up onto the platform. On his knees, he gulped air in like he'd been running a marathon.

A set of arms came around him and squeezed. "You rocked it," Darcy said in his ear. "You're all done."

Ripping off the blindfold, he stared down into the large kiddie pool he'd just climbed out of.

Filled with rubber snakes.

"Jesus," he breathed.

Darcy, on her knees facing him, was running her hands up and down his back, her eyes worried. "You're not peachy at all."

"Sure I am," he said, swiping the sweat from his brow. "I've never been better."

He'd dislodged her arms from him but she didn't move away, just kept looking into his face. "So . . . snakes, huh?"

He shuddered. "Little bit."

Without another word she offered him one of the two bottles of water that had been waiting for them on the platform.

He gulped it down.

"I'm sorry," she said softly. "I didn't know."

"Ask your question."

"It can wait."

"Just ask your damn question," he said.

"Alright." She met his gaze. "Who's Kayla?"

Darcy let herself into her hotel room, plopped down on the bed, and stared at the ceiling.

They'd finished the trust workshop but hadn't won. She couldn't be surprised. After she'd asked her question, she and AJ had sat on that first platform staring at each other long enough to fall into last place going into the second round.

She'd had to prompt him again about her

question and he'd answered with one of his own.

"How do you know about Kayla?" he asked.

"You said her name last night. In your sleep."

And that had been the last thing they'd said to each other because someone in the next boardroom over chose that moment to have an anxiety attack in their "snake" pit and had to be taken out on a stretcher.

AJ had checked the roads on his phone and showed her the app. "The summit's closed, even to four-wheel-drive vehicles with chains."

Just her luck. Karma was a bitch.

They'd lunched with a large group, including Trent and Summer. And then Trent and AJ had gone to the gym while Summer and Darcy had hit the spa and had mani-pedis while looking out the sixteen-foot-high windows as the snow continued to dump out of the sky in lines so heavy it looked like a cartoon of a storm.

They'd all had a drink and hors d'oeuvres in the bar and then Summer had claimed exhaustion. Trent had taken her upstairs, leaving AJ and Darcy free to hit their own rooms.

Alone.

Which was fine. Great. Darcy blew out a sigh and looked out her window.

White.

As in a complete whiteout.

Which meant another night here . . .

She pulled out her phone and texted Xander: Not going to make it back for tonight's poker game.

His reply was immediate: WTF?

Look out the window, she texted back. Mother Nature's on a rampage.

Not here, he responded.

Perfect, she thought. The storm was only exactly right over her head. There had to be an analogy in there somewhere . . .

And then another text came in from Xander: So you're sleeping with him.

She nearly choked on her gum. After staring at the words for a moment, she thumbed: Wow. Really?

He was quick to reply: Hey, if I'd taken you off to some "conference" I'd be making up lines about being snowed in, too. And I'd make sure we had only one room. And you'd be in my bed, sleeping with me.

She stared at her phone. He'd had plenty of chances to try and sleep with her this past year. He'd never made his desire for her a secret but nor had he pushed. Not once.

It was because of her. She knew this. She'd held back. She loved him, she really did. But she also knew that while he loved her back, he happened to love a lot of women. They flocked to him and he enjoyed it. Thrived on it. She'd never be his one and only.

Not that she wanted to be someone's one and only. Because she didn't.

But it was more than that. She'd watched Xander work his way through women like some men worked their way through new tires, and she realized that he had the same problem she did.

He didn't love himself enough to really love anyone else. That, and then there was the biggie — she knew in her heart of hearts that she wasn't going to ever be *in* love with him.

She debated on what to say and finally settled for: Cocky much?

Nice evasion of the question.

She blew out a breath. She owed him answers. She texted: There's nothing to say. Nothing's going on between AJ and me.

That she wanted there to be was none of his business.

Xander didn't respond.

She was still staring at her phone when

the wind kicked up, battering at her windows.

Raising the hair on her arms.

The night of her accident the weather had been like this. *Just* like this.

The wind hit again and her room creaked, and this time she shivered and wrapped her arms around herself on the bed, staring out the windows into the dark, black night.

When the lamp at her bedside flickered and nearly went out, she jumped up and strode straight to the minibar. She could almost hear AJ's horror, but she'd just have to owe him for it.

The lights flickered again and she gasped out loud. Maybe she'd just pay AJ back right now, she thought, and, grabbing her wallet and the bottle, she headed out the door.

The elevator was empty, for which she was grateful. So was the hallway on his floor. At his door, she knocked once and stared down at her feet.

Bare.

What the hell was wrong with her?

The door opened and she lifted her head and sucked in a breath. AJ wore a pair of black sweatpants and nothing else except a whole lot of testosterone. She tried to swallow but her mouth was too dry.

"You okay?" he asked.

"Yes." No. "Maybe."

He leaned on the doorjamb, arms crossed over his broad chest, feet casually crossed, watching her. "Miss me?"

"In your dreams."

A slight smile appeared at the corners of his mouth. "Yeah. You missed me."

"You fit you and that big head of yours in that room okay?"

His smile spread. "Come in and see for yourself."

She contemplated her options. If she left now, she'd look like an idiot. If she stayed, she'd have to admit that she'd manufactured a reason for being here.

She felt his fingertips under her chin as he pulled her gaze up to his. She knew he was waiting on her to speak, but something was wrong with her and she'd lost her words. Scratch that. She knew exactly what was wrong with her.

It was called lust.

And she had it bad, too, possibly even a terminal case. Forget it, she decided. Forget this, and she whirled away to go.

Sixteen

"Turning tail?" AJ asked Darcy. "That's unlike you."

"Not turning tail," she answered. "A *tactical* retreat."

"Also unlike you."

Yeah, but she definitely needed a retreat here. With a sigh, she turned back to him. "I came because . . ." Crap. Why had she come? What had been her excuse again? "I owe you money," she remembered.

"For?"

She waved the bottle of scotch. "They restocked my room."

"So you're here to . . . pay me," he said, his voice carrying more than a whisper of disbelief.

"Yep." She was sounding more and more lame but her ego wasn't ready to give up the façade. "And also I thought you might be thirsty after all that exercising we got in today."

His mouth twitched. "Did you just refer to the trust workshop as exercise?"

"Yes," she said. "It hurt my brain the way real exercise hurts my body, so it makes sense in my head."

Just as she said this, a heavy wind battered the hotel, making it creak and — she would swear to this — sway. Going still as stone, she stared over AJ's shoulder at the window in his room and the black night beyond.

She felt his hand slip around her elbow and pull her in. He shut the door behind her, bolted it, and then gestured for her to precede him the rest of the way into the room.

The only light came from the muted TV. The blue glow cast over the room, illuminating the bed, which was mussed up. The pillows had been shoved up against the headboard like maybe he'd been sitting up.

Also unable to sleep.

She headed straight over there and sat on a corner of the mattress. "Scotch or . . ." She eyed the two bottles in her hand. "Scotch?"

Not answering, he sat at her side and met her gaze.

"Don't judge me," she said.

He reached for one of the bottles, opened

it, and handed it back to her. Then he took the other, opened that one as well, and clicked it to hers in a toast. "Never," he said.

"*Never*'s a pretty strong word."

"Never," he said again.

Okay. She could deal with that. They clicked bottles again and tossed back. The storm continued to rage outside, making her heart pound. To distract herself, she spoke the first thing on her mind. "So," she said.

"So."

"You ever going to answer the question I won?"

And just like that his face closed up. "Not going there."

"Not going there?" she repeated.

"That's what I said."

She stared at him, more than a little stunned. "Seriously? My life's an open book to you. You brought me here to be an open book for you."

"Doesn't mean mine's open to you."

This was such an unexpected hit that she had to work at sucking in enough air for her lungs. Not that it beat back the pain. Shaking her head, she stood and headed to the door.

"Darcy."

Nope. They were done here. She shut the

door behind her — not quite a slam, in deference to the others on the floor, but definitely a statement.

Out in the hall she took one step before she realized she'd left her wallet — with her hotel keycard — back in his room with her liquor.

Dammit.

The only thing worse than being a drama queen was being a stupid drama queen. Note to self: Think through your next temper tantrum.

With great reluctance she turned back. She lifted her hand to bang on AJ's door just as he opened it. She nearly knocked right on his nose.

He held out her wallet, but not the scotch. Whatever. She snatched her wallet without making eye contact and bolted for the elevator.

A huge gust of wind must have hit the building because the lights in the hallway flickered. She turned from the elevator and hit the stairwell instead, unwilling to be stuck in the elevator if the power went out.

Plus, she really needed to be on the move.

The stairs were hell on her tenuous balance and bare feet but somehow she got to her floor and into her room, where she lurched/limped into the bathroom.

She turned on the hot water, stripped naked, and stepped into the shower. Her first order of business was to stand in there until the hot water ran out or until her life improved, whichever came second.

As the water rained down on her she sighed in humiliation, hating that AJ knew so much about her, knew *everything* about her, including her fears.

Hated.

Especially because apparently she wasn't good enough or important enough to get to know his fears in return.

It was like being naked in public.

Worse. Because it was AJ, and because somehow over the past two days she'd sensed a change in their relationship. She'd actually thought . . .

Damn.

She'd thought maybe she was falling for him.

And that he was falling back.

So stupid — and clearly it couldn't be further from the truth. Not only was he not falling at all, he'd just pushed her away.

He might as well have sent her packing to Switzerland.

She sank to the floor of the shower and brought her legs into her chest and dropped her head to her knees. Oh how she hated when she did stupid stuff that left her feeling open and exposed and vulnerable. She was usually much more careful. But somehow between opening up to Summer and spending the night next to AJ, she'd let down her defenses.

At least in here she couldn't hear the storm. She didn't have to slide into that big bed all alone and hide under the covers like a scared little kid. All she had to do was stay in here until morning —

She shrieked when the curtain was suddenly yanked aside.

AJ reached in and turned off the water and hauled her out of the shower.

"Hey!" She squirmed and kicked and shoved but it was all ineffective against a grimly determined AJ.

Wrapping her in a towel with clinical efficiency, he backed her to the wall. "Stop," he said when she tried to knee him in the family jewels. "Jesus, just stop a second."

When she didn't, he leaned into her.

"What the —"

Ignoring her, he gripped her hands and slid a powerful thigh between hers, pinning her in place so that she could do little more than suck in air.

"You're going to have to kill me," she snarled at him. "Because if you let me go,

241

I'm going to kick your ass."

His eyes sparked an equal temper but his voice was quiet, calm, and controlled. "I'm trying to apologize."

"Yeah, well, you have a hell of a way of doing it. Read the handbook," she snapped. "You forgot the flowers and ass-kissing."

His jaw was tight, the muscles bunching. "If I let go, will you listen?" he asked.

"Hell no."

"That's what I thought." Gripping both her wrists in one hand, he yanked them above her head. With his free hand he cupped her face and forced it up so that she met his gaze.

Wet, naked, and furious, she was still staring at him, sending him the sharpest daggers she could, when he lowered his head and kissed her.

Seventeen

Darcy heard a soft, needy moan and realized it was hers as AJ held her prisoner against the wall and pillaged.

She let him.

Not only did she let him, she strained for more.

AJ's big body always ran hotter than most, and she'd never been more grateful in that moment. Naked and wet and up against his fully clothed self, she should have been fighting him down and dirty to get free after what he'd said.

Instead she wanted to get down and dirty.

He fisted his hands in her hair and gave her what she wanted, and when his tongue swept against hers, she gave in, pouring every emotion she felt into that kiss. Fury. Hurt. Need.

God, the need.

Breaking away from the kiss, he slid his mouth along her jaw. "Ready to listen?" he said against her ear.

She went still for a single beat before shoving him.

He took a step back. "Come out when you're ready," he said, before turning and walking out of the bathroom.

She resisted the urge to chuck something at his head — not that *that* would help since he had the hardest head of anyone she knew. Closing her eyes, she just breathed a moment, which didn't help. Then she wrapped herself up in the hotel bathrobe hanging off the back of the door and strode out after AJ, ready to brawl.

He stood in front of the windows, hands in his pockets, staring out at the night. His shoulders were squared off and full of tension. He never gave much away, but she'd had a lot of time to study him now and she knew the tells.

He was frustrated and uncharacteristically unsettled.

With a sigh, she came up behind him, catching his gaze in the glass. "I shouldn't have asked about Kayla," she said. "It's none of my business."

He didn't move a single muscle for a long beat, and then he turned to face her. "I was out of line. You were right, you were open to me and I cut you off at the knees when you went looking for the same thing from me. I'm sorry for that."

She nodded. "Thanks. But I meant what I said. It's not my business. And you didn't have to come to my room."

"It's storming."

"Well, yes," she said, surprised at the quick subject change. "It's why we're still here, remember?"

"You're afraid of storms, ever since your accident."

Her first instinct was to deny. Her second was to throw herself at him and beg him to throw her down on the bed and make her forget the storm.

And her life.

Except he'd come here because he'd known she was afraid, which was just another example of how well he knew her and how little he let her know him. Which in turn reminded her that she was hurt and pissed, a bad combination for her. "I'm fine," she said.

But she must have looked longingly at the minibar because he let out a low laugh and pulled not one, not two, but *four* mini bottles of scotch from his sweatshirt pocket.

Right then and there she nearly told him she loved him. In fact, she might have done just that if a heavy gust of wind hadn't rattled the windows. "I know I can't live my life being afraid of storms and driving on the highway," she said. "But damn."

He handed her one of the scotches. The wind kicked up and she trembled enough to nearly spill. To avoid that, she tipped the bottle back and downed it.

"Easy." AJ took the empty out of her hand and set it on the nightstand next to his. He pulled the heavy curtains over the window and turned on a few lights and the TV. He flipped through the channels until he found an old repeat of *Friends.*

"Thanks," she said, and climbed onto the bed. "But that's not going to be enough to distract me." She held out a hand for bottle number two.

He opened another one for each of them and clinked his bottle to hers.

"What are we toasting to?" she asked.

"Getting the hell out of Dodge soon."

"I'll second that."

AJ sat on the bed, his long legs stretched out in front of him as he took a long pull on his scotch. "Okay. So you asked about Kayla."

"Forget it."

"I can't make you face your fears and not face something myself," he said. "Kayla was my fiancée."

Her heart skipped a beat. How was it she hadn't known this? Granted, until recently she'd been gallivanting across the globe writing for various travel sites and paying absolutely no attention to anything or anyone but herself. "Your . . . fiancée."

"Yeah." He stared down at the empty bottle in his fingers. "She was beautiful. Flawless, actually. She dreamed of getting out of the military and becoming a model. She had a big, supportive family and was always the center of attention. She was loved, happy. We were happy, too, stationed overseas together. She was a ship mechanic. Five years ago we had an onboard fire in the engine room where she worked."

"Oh my God," she whispered.

"She lived, though she was injured. Not all that badly when it came right down to it, not compared to the other two with her. They both died of their injuries. Kayla suffered second-degree burns to her hands and face, that was all, but she scarred pretty badly. She couldn't handle it. In her eyes she was no longer beautiful, and even though she still had her life and family and friends, all of whom adored her, it wasn't enough. She couldn't cope because she thought she was no longer desirable, not to a modeling agency, not to the people who

247

loved her, and not to me."

Darcy tried to put herself in Kayla's shoes but she couldn't. She'd always looked at her scars as battle trophies, was even proud of them in a weird way.

"She changed," AJ said. "She turned angry, withdrawn. Bitter."

Darcy wondered how she herself must look to him, a guy who'd been engaged to perfection, and she cringed. "What happened?"

He'd been staring sightlessly at the TV but his gaze tracked to her. "She wouldn't talk to me, wouldn't see me. She completely shut me out. Shut everyone out," he said. "I took a leave to try to help her. I dragged her to counseling, forced her into rehab when she got addicted to her painkillers. It took two years to bring her back to the land of the living, and I was with her for every minute of it."

"She recovered," Darcy said.

"She went through the motions, but in the end she wasn't strong enough to beat it. I couldn't fix her, and that . . . that sucked."

Yeah. Darcy could only imagine how tough that had been, fighting so hard for her, and yet in return she hadn't fought for him.

And maybe that was why he'd always

pushed her so hard in PT, why he wouldn't allow anyone to give up on their own healing.

"No matter what I did," he said, "she still couldn't come around and let herself love again. She felt no passion, no desire."

"Because of the scars."

"That's what she'd tell you." He shook his head. "But the truth of it has nothing to do with that. She let the scars destroy her, and me while she was at it. She'd been pampered and adored all her life and she'd never had to develop a single life skill. She'd had everything handed to her and she didn't know the meaning of the will to survive, much less how to be a warm, giving person when there was even the slightest bit of a hurdle to overcome or any sort of controversy to face."

Which had never been the case for him. He'd had to work hard for everything in his life and he'd been successful because of it, giving back to so many. And here he was, six hours from home trying to secure grants to help even more. "She should have tried," she said. "For you."

"I certainly wanted her to. But she'd never been broken before and had no way to come back from it."

Darcy looked at him. "I think it's okay to

be a *little* broken."

The very corners of his mouth turned up into a small smile. "Only a little?"

She smiled. "Or a lot. Either way, I'm pretty damn good at holding pieces together if you ever need help. Just wanted you to know that."

"I'm not broken," he said, like any alpha male, not willing to show a weakness.

"I think you're one of the strongest people I've ever met," she said quietly.

"Muscles don't mean shit when it comes to living life."

She shook her head and crawled across the vast expanse of the bed to kneel at his side. She put a hand on his chest. Beneath her palm she could feel the slow, steady beat of his heart. "Inside," she said. "You're strong inside. Kayla was weak, AJ. You need someone who can weather whatever comes along."

On her knees as she was, she was taller than him, so he had to look up at her. "Like someone who's fierce and loving with those she lets in, even though she can count those people on one hand?" he asked. "Someone who'd drop everything just because I need her for the weekend, someone who'd defend me to her brother, someone who cares enough to use her own money to pay for emotional support dogs and give them to people in need? Someone who has some seriously out-of-control hair at the moment and is terrified of storms even though she's the biggest storm in my life?"

His words robbed her of her own but she didn't know how to respond anyway. She sat back on her heels. "You shouldn't say things like that. It's like a game that I don't have the rules for."

"Have I ever played you?" he asked, wrapping his fingers around her wrist so she couldn't further retreat.

No. No, he hadn't ever played her. He was stoic and stubborn as a mule and he thought he was always right. But there wasn't an ounce of duplicity in his big, perfect body.

A bolt of lightning lit everything in the room in bold relief, including the fact that AJ watched her as carefully as she watched him, crowding her space while he did so, making her feel important to him.

His eyes had changed, she realized as the ensuing thunder shook the hotel.

They'd . . . heated.

And that heat in turn did something to her. It melted something deep inside, like the block of ice she'd settled around her heart a long time ago.

"Come here, Darcy."

Why the hell was that quietly uttered command the sexiest thing she'd ever heard? She had no idea. And as a rule, she didn't do "come here." She didn't do commands period.

And yet she swallowed hard and said, "I'm right here."

"No, you're not."

She scooted a little closer, but then unsure, stopped. Held her breath.

With his free hand he crooked his finger at her and she closed the distance.

He let go of her to open his arms and she crawled onto his lap.

His arms came around her, a hand sliding up her back to the nape of her neck, bringing her mouth to his. He locked his lips on hers, kissing her senseless before pulling free only enough to meet her gaze, his own dark and searching.

"I want you," she said, answering his unspoken question.

"Be sure, Darcy. A few minutes ago you wanted to kick my ass."

"I still want to kick your ass."

He smiled. "And?"

"And . . . up until a few minutes ago I didn't know we had the serious hots for each other."

His hands skimmed down to cup her ass

and rock her against a most impressive erection. "Liar."

"Okay, so up until a few minutes ago I was *pretending* I didn't know we had the hots for each other."

"You're as bad a pretender as you are a liar," he said.

"You really going to piss me off right now?"

He laughed low in his throat and it was an incredibly sexy sound. "I think it's a safe bet to say yes," he said. "Yes, I'm going to piss you off. It's what I do best."

Brushing her mouth along his delicious rough jaw, she whispered, "Surely there are some other things you do even better."

He let out a slow, sure smile, and on the menu of AJ smiles it was the appetizer and the main entrée *and* the dessert all in one. "As a matter of fact, there are," he said, toppling her to her back on the bed and coming down over the top of her.

Eighteen

AJ wasn't surprised when Darcy rolled them both across the bed so that *she* was on top, braced above him on her arms, smiling triumphantly into his face. He wanted to yank her down and crush his mouth to hers, but she looked so sexy bending low to give him little nibbles here and there. Finally, when he couldn't take it anymore, he fisted his hands in her hair and held her still.

"Careful," he said. "I don't want you to hurt yourself."

"I'm not hurting right now."

"Let's keep it that way."

Breath warm against his face, she sighed, slowly rocking her hips against his, ripping a groan from him as he let her tease both herself and him. When her robe slipped open, giving him peekaboo hints of her gorgeous body, he swore roughly. "Kiss me."

Breathing labored but clearly pleased with herself, she flashed him a smile as her hands slid up his shoulders. One curled around the back of his neck to hold him to her as she slowly, finally, deepened the kiss, giving him her mouth.

He let her dictate the pace for as long as he could take it, which wasn't all that long. Needing her under him, naked, buck wild with his name on her lips, he took over, rolling them again, pinning her to the bed.

"Hmm," she said, sounding like she might be pleased.

Entangling his hands in hers, he pulled them up over her head. "Wrap your legs around me."

"Feeling dominant?" she murmured, even as she did what he'd asked and wrapped her mile-long legs around his hips.

He nipped her lower lip. "Feeling something," he said, and kissed her hard, letting himself get more than a little lost in her. He'd never get over the shock of this, how fast she could wind him up and take him to a place he hadn't been in a damned long time.

If ever.

When they were both breathless he lifted his mouth a fraction of an inch and stared down at her, assessing, making sure she wasn't hurting, that she was still into this. One never knew with Darcy. She could be over it. She could be pissed off. She could be anything.

Definitely she wasn't hurting. Her eyes were glazed, her mouth slightly open as if she needed it that way just to drag air into her lungs.

Just as aroused and shocked as he, he saw, and felt slightly mollified.

Again he lowered his mouth to hers, wanting inside her, wanting a hell of a lot more than that, too. He wanted to possess her heart, body, and soul . . . Pretty fucking terrifying considering that she didn't tend to do heart, body, and soul for anyone.

"AJ." That was it, just his name as she tore at the shirt he'd thrown on to chase her back to her room, pulling it out of where it had been half tucked into his sweatpants.

Her hands were icy on his hot skin. "Cold?" he asked.

"No." She let out a low laugh. "Nervous."

And hell if that didn't turn him on all the more. He smiled down at her. "Cute," he said, using the same adjective she'd used for him.

She snorted while her hands were very busy trying to get into his sweats. He liked where this was going, a lot. To help her get there, he pulled off his shirt and skimmed his hands down the front of her robe to jerk it open.

"Damn," he said. "You're beautiful."

She flushed. It was the sweetest, hottest thing. "You've seen it all before. You —" She broke off on a shuddering moan when he lowered his mouth to a breast, and then again when he sucked on the tight tip, trapping it against his tongue.

Beneath him she wriggled and panted. Music to his ears. Palming her thighs, he pressed them open and slid down until he was at eye level with heaven on earth.

"AJ —" she choked out.

"*So* beautiful," he said, and slipped his hands beneath her, cupping her ass, holding her still for him.

She cried out with the first stroke of his tongue, but he wouldn't let her rush him, not now that he finally had her right as he'd been fantasizing about. He'd had a great time in those fantasies — and there'd been many — but not a single one compared to Darcy in the flesh. Taking his time, he gave her a taste of her own medicine, teasing her until it was her turn to swear at him. He licked and sucked while she writhed helplessly against his mouth.

"Please," she gasped. "Damn you, AJ, *please*."

"Aw. Since you asked so sweetly," he said, and took her completely apart.

When she finally stopped shuddering and quivering, she relaxed her hold on his hair with a low apologetic murmur. Eyes still closed, she sighed. "I came."

It was her tone of utter surprise that had him lifting his head to look at her.

She took in his silence and opened her eyes. "Sorry," she said. "Ignore me, I say the stupidest stuff in the aftermath."

"You say stupid stuff never," he said. "You've never had an orgasm before?"

Her face flamed. "Don't be ridiculous. Of course I have." She closed her eyes again. "Just not in a long time."

"How long?"

"Since before my accident." She kept her eyes closed. "Look, it's no big deal. After the crash I felt like such shit for so long, and completely energyless. And then when I finally started to feel better, I . . . couldn't." She shrugged. "I tried, it just didn't happen."

"Tried how?"

She didn't respond.

"Darcy."

She blew out a breath. "I figured I'd take myself out for a test drive before I slept with anyone, okay? But I couldn't rev my own

258

engines. Figured that was that."

"Did you tell your doctor?" he asked.

"No. And damn," she said on a sigh. "Do you always talk this much during sex?" She reached between them and untied his sweats. Sliding her hand inside, she wrapped her fingers around him, hummed her pleasure, and then gave him a slow, eyes-rolling-in-the-back-of-his-head stroke.

"Why are you still wearing clothes?" she asked, and nipped his chin.

He hadn't the foggiest. He moved to kick them off and she helped, using her feet, although mostly that just succeeded in tangling them up together. The sweats got caught on his running shoes. She got a leg cramp.

She was laughing and he was swearing like a sailor when they finally were both naked.

"Now," she whispered, her hands skimming down his back to his ass.

Yeah. They were on the same wavelength. And that's when he remembered. "I don't have a condom."

She stared at him for a beat, the wheels clearly turning. "Okay, we can work with this," she said. "I'm on the pill to keep my cycle regular, and you . . . maybe just had a physical?"

"Six months ago," he said. "I'm clean."

"Well then, I trust you."

She trusted him. That was even better than having her sprawled naked beneath him.

Darcy swallowed hard as AJ's eyes raked down her body, sending sparks to her every single good spot, of which there were so many more than she remembered.

She understood his need to look. She had the same need because with all that hard muscle and warm, tanned skin he was a visceral delight for the eyes. She could look all day.

But he leaned in close, blocking her view, his mouth hovering over hers. When she traced his bottom lip with her tongue, she tasted herself.

His lips curved in a sinful smile and she trembled. Only he could make her tremble with just one look. And that mouth. Good lord, that mouth.

Putting it to her ear, he whispered, "You're hot when you come. I'm going to make you do it again." He sank his teeth lightly into her earlobe. "And then again."

She whimpered as his mouth bypassed her lips and skimmed her throat. Her eyes fluttered closed and she bit her bottom lip as the dark velvet sound of his voice reverberated through her, seducing her with ease. He was a man of few words, but he had a way of making the most of the ones he used, that was for sure. "So what's taking you so long?" she asked.

He laughed low in his throat and the sound went through her like a sinful promise as he stroked his fingertips along her body, leaving a trail of fire in their wake that she felt all the way to her toes.

"Look at me," he said.

She opened her eyes and looked into his, which were dark and heavy lidded with desire, and her stomach clenched as she caught something new as well. Need, for *her*. It was raw and unspoken, but as apparent as the beat of her own heart.

His hands slid south and she felt the jolt of electricity as he teased her, rubbing himself between her legs until she whimpered again. "AJ." She wrapped her legs around his waist, positioning him right where she needed him the most, and arched her back, shamelessly grinding her hips into his.

He stilled her hips with his hands. "Wait for it."

"But I'm not good at waiting."

"No kidding." Lowering his mouth to hers, he kissed her into a boneless, quivering mess as he slid home.

He stilled, like maybe she was the best thing he'd felt in a long time. That was all she could take in because he began to move, pulling back and then slowly pushing in again, holding her captive with the delicious glide of his every thrust. Her toes were already curling when she moaned and pushed up with her hips, grinding into him for more, panting with need.

"Killing me," he murmured, his voice a sexy rasp.

"But not a bad way to go though, right?" she managed.

His laugh was rough and she took some pride in reducing him to speechlessness.

When he moved again, he hooked his elbow beneath her knee, forcing it wide so he could go even deeper, and the laughter backed up in both their throats.

"Tell me you're still okay," he rasped out.

"More than," she promised, and cried out as he took her right out of herself and splintered her into a million pieces.

For the second time.

She brought him along with her this time. When they were done and still breathing against each other like lunatics, his arms tight around her, his face pressed into her throat as if he couldn't get enough of her scent, his hands slowly stroked her back together again.

When Darcy managed to stir she had no idea how much time had gone by. "Wow," she murmured, and tried to extract herself.

He stroked a hand down her back and settled it on her ass, obstructing her escape. He didn't speak but for some reason she really needed him to, if only to hear his voice and know by the tremor in it that he was even half as shaken as she.

Because honestly, *wow* didn't come close to a good enough exclamation for what they'd just done. *Holy shit* didn't cover it, either.

You're screwed? Yeah, maybe that covered it.

And still AJ said nothing.

"I mean *really* wow," she said, testing.

More silence, and she came up on an elbow to look into his face, finding him smiling smugly. *"What?"* she demanded.

"I thought maybe you were going to try to tell me that was pretend, too."

She narrowed her eyes and opened her mouth to blast him, but he easily tucked her beneath him and slid back inside of her.

She gasped, quivered, and clutched at him, already halfway to her next orgasm.

"God."
　"Nope, just me."

Nineteen

AJ opened his eyes when Darcy slipped out of his arms and vanished into the bathroom. The clock's blue glow said two oh five a.m. At two oh six he heard the shower come on.

Maybe he should go in there. He was most excellent in the shower. Before he could move there came the click of the bathroom door lock sliding into place.

Nope. She didn't want company.

He blew out a sigh and stared up at the ceiling. He had no idea how things were supposed to go back to normal now that he knew how she kissed, knew the sexy little sounds she made when she came.

They'd fit together like she'd been made for him, and he also wasn't sure how this one night was going to be enough, not when he was already thinking of having her back in his arms, her mouth hot on his again, her body writhing beneath him, all warm, soft curves.

And no matter what she was in that shower telling herself, he hadn't been alone in this. There'd been gut-churning need in her eyes, in the way she'd clutched at him, in her voice when she'd cried out his name.

She'd been just as blown away by this as he was.

He'd known the lust was there between them, but there was something more too, something beyond the desire.

But damn. If he was falling in love with her, he didn't want to know it. After Kayla he'd decided it would be a cold day in hell before he went there again, down the road of demoralizing devastation.

The shower was still on. She was probably in there turning to a prune, overthinking everything. Hell, maybe she was plotting out her escape.

He should save her the effort and give her some space, though he felt reluctant to leave her alone with the storm still raging on.

He'd leave it up to her, but he got up and pulled on his clothes just in case. He was tying his shoes when the bathroom door finally opened.

Steam emerged first.

And then Darcy, wrapped in a towel that was tucked between her breasts and barely covered the very tops of her thighs.

His mouth watered, which was ridiculous. He'd just had her, every single inch of her, and while it had been . . . amazing, it should've satisfied his hunger for her.

It hadn't.

Her wet hair was loose, dripping from the ends, down her shoulders and chest.

Her expression was unreadable, her body language achingly unsure.

"You leaving?" she asked.

"Whatever you want."

She paused and he got the feeling she was battling with some inner demon. "What I want is to not sleep alone," she said, and glanced at the window. "Not tonight."

His heart tightened at the admission that had undoubtedly cost her.

"The wind gives me bad dreams," she said quietly.

Ah, hell. "I'm not going anywhere," he said.

"I don't normally think about the night of the accident, but this weekend . . ." She drifted off but he knew.

This weekend she'd thought of it plenty. She'd had to, thanks to him bringing her here. With a low sound of regret, he moved back to the bed. "Come on."

She hesitated and then came close.

He kicked off his shoes and then tugged

his shirt back off over his head. He slipped it over hers and then reached beneath to slip off her towel. He nudged her onto the bed and beneath the covers, and slid in after her.

"You just tucked me in," she murmured sleepily.

"Tell anyone and die. Do we need to talk about it, Darcy?"

"What is it with you and all the talking?" She yawned. "You must've dated some real high estrogen levels." She shook her head. "No, we don't have to talk about it. I'm not big on the talking."

He smiled. "Yeah, you're more the screaming sort."

"Hey! I most definitely didn't scream."

"Close enough," he said.

She smacked him and he laughed. "I wonder if anyone's in the rooms on either side of us."

"I was *not* that loud." She paused and slid him a look. "And at least I wasn't needy."

"Needy?"

" 'Come here. Wrap your legs around me. Kiss me. Open your eyes. Do this. Do that,' " she said in a low voice, clearly imitating him. "Needy *and* bossy."

He grinned. "Admit it. You like it when I'm bossy."

"Hmm. Maybe just a little bit." Her eyes had been drifting shut but they flared open again. "And if you tell anyone that, I'll . . . *something,*" she vowed. "I don't know what yet but it'll hurt, I can guarantee that."

He laughed. "Who am I going to tell, your brother? He'd kill me dead and then bring me back to life just to kill me again."

"No," she said. "I'd make sure he knew I instigated and jumped your bones."

"You'd protect me, huh?"

"Well, it seems only fair," she said, snuggling into him. "Since I pretty much *did* jump your bones."

He shook his head. "We jumped together." He ran a finger along her jaw. "And while we're on this topic, I don't want you trying to protect me, ever. I'm not ashamed or sorry about what happened here."

"I'm not, either. And I can protect myself as well." She turned her head and caught his finger in her teeth, making him laugh.

"So . . ." she said. "We're back to what happens in Boise stays in Boise."

"Maybe we should define exactly what it is that happened in Boise."

"Wild monkey sex?"

"I do like the sound of that," he said. "And my reputation could probably use the boost."

She grinned and then yawned again, and he flipped off the light and hauled her into him. He kissed her once, softly, ordered himself to not go for more, and then he flipped her so that she faced away from him, her back to his chest. Spooning her, he entwined his fingers with hers at her chest. "Okay?"

She nodded and yawned some more, relaxing into him. He could feel every single inch of her sweet, curvy body, and because *that* was going to have a quick effect on him, he did his best to keep his hips back.

But she foiled him by snuggling in with a quick little butt wriggle that just about slayed him. Even more so when she wrapped her free hand around his arm, holding him to her.

Intimate comfort.

He just wasn't sure who was comforting who. "I'm sorry about the dreams," he said quietly.

"I just feel so stupid that after all this time I still get them."

"I get them sometimes, too. There's nothing to be ashamed of. We all have things that haunt us."

"What haunts you, AJ?"

When something happened to someone he loved . . . "Things out of my control," he

270

said. "Like my mom and her RA. Kayla and her accident." He cut himself off before saying, *You.*

"You do like your control," she said mildly. "And micromanaging."

"I don't micromanage," he said, and she laughed.

He stared at her.

"Oh," she said, appearing to bite back her amusement with great effort. "You're serious."

"I don't micromanage," he said, as though saying it out loud again would make it true. "Not all the time."

She looked as if maybe she was trying to not laugh again. "Okay," she said agreeably. "But you totally do. And there's nothing wrong with that. You've got a lot to take care of. Problem is that you can do all the right things but bad things might still happen."

No shit.

"That night of my accident, I wasn't being reckless or crazy. The storm came up quick and the car in front of me got all squirrely and I had to swerve to avoid hitting it. Then my car got away from me. *That's* what I dream about. Being stuck in my car. The flames —" She shuddered. "It's always the same as what really happened except I don't get out. And I can feel myself suffocating, running out of air . . ."

"I never heard about the other car," he said.

She shrugged. "It vanished into the night. I'm sure they had no idea I crashed, it was so dark."

He loved that she didn't whine about how the accident wasn't her fault. And he knew if she had been in the wrong, she would have taken responsibility for her actions. She owned up to her own mistakes, her own behavior. He loved that about Darcy. Then there was the way she'd told him about her nightmares to make him feel better. It touched him, deeply.

He might have told her so but he was having a flashback of her mangled car after her wreck, and then Darcy in the hospital, in so much pain. He'd spent months and months helping her out with that, until the pain had mostly retreated and she'd looked at him with temper instead.

Infinitely better.

"I'll never forget the sight of your wreck," he said. "We went out there the next day, Wyatt and I."

She turned her head and sought out his gaze. "You did?"

His arms tightened and he buried his face

in the back of her neck and wild hair, unwilling to let her see his expression of remembered horror. "We saw the scrap of metal, all that was left of your car, and I couldn't believe you'd survived." He shook his head. "It was a miracle."

"I know," she whispered, and slid out of the bed, heading in the dark to the mini fridge. "When I dream, it's the regrets that get me more than anything else," she said, pulling out two bottles of water.

He rose and accepted the bottle she held out to him. "What is it you regret?" he asked.

"Wasting so much time and energy being mad at my parents and how we were raised," she said. She hopped up onto the low-lying dresser next to the fridge and drank deeply. "The truth is, I always had a roof over my head and food and clothing, more than plenty of people."

AJ leaned a hip against the dresser and wished there was more light so he could better see her face. "It's okay to be mad at them."

"I'm the one who got into trouble in the first place," she said. "And when they sent me away, I'd get into even more. My own doing, all of it. It was only when they refused to help me when I needed it, or even to call Wyatt and Zoe to do so instead, that it got pretty rough, but at least I'm here to tell the tale, right? And at least I learned to fend for myself."

"It's okay to be mad at them," he repeated, hating them all over again. "What happened at school?"

She shrugged. "The usual. I screwed up. Though the time I landed in Switzerland's equivalent of juvie for stealing some girl's wallet, *that* I didn't do." Her laugh was short and she took another long drink of water. "I'd never steal from someone, but hey, who was going to believe me if my own parents didn't."

"They let you stay in jail?" he asked in disbelief.

"Yeah." She shuddered and hugged her water bottle to her chest. "And trust me — every single story you've ever heard about evil headmistresses and their enjoyment of torturing the bad girls? All true."

"How long?" he asked, trying not to let his anger for her show.

She slanted him a quick glance, so clearly he hadn't been all that successful at hiding it. "Three months," she said.

Jesus. "They hurt you?"

"It was a long time ago," she said, clearly regretting her decision to tell him the story that he knew for damn sure neither Wyatt nor Zoe knew.

God, she'd been so alone. No wonder she'd grown up and gone on to wander the world for a living. It was all she knew. "It doesn't matter how long ago it was," he said. "It shouldn't have happened. You were innocent."

"Maybe that time, but there were plenty of other things I got away with, so it all equaled itself out."

He didn't believe that. And he didn't know how to get rid of the temper now pulsing through him. He wanted to go back and vindicate the girl she'd once been, and he felt helpless that he couldn't. She amazed him, she really did. All she'd been through and yet she showed no visible weaknesses. She was good at making people believe she was okay. Real good.

Too good.

She'd been taught the hard way not to depend on those around her, not to trust love, and worse, to be ashamed of any need for it. "I'd really like to strangle your mom and dad," he said as mildly as he could.

"Lots of people suck at being parents," she said. "And the bottom line is I made it out alive in spite of myself."

"Hell yeah, you did," he said. "And you've

chosen to really live, too, not just survive."

Maybe it was the dark and the forced intimacy. Maybe he'd finally gotten inside the real Darcy, but she kept talking. He hung on every word.

"I have a lot I want to do," she said. "I want to start a website where people in need of emotional support dogs can register, and I'll do my best to get them what they need. I want to work with trainers and breeders willing to donate dogs, or maybe I can get grants like you're doing to fund PT for those in need. I don't want someone to lose out on getting a dog just because there's no money for it. Or for a service dog to have to go to a shelter because his job no longer works out."

His chest constricted. He knew damn well she saw herself as a throwaway, just like one of those dogs. "I want to help you with that."

"No." She softened her voice. "You've helped me so much already, AJ. More than I even knew. I can do this."

He understood that. He'd always felt he needed to prove himself, too. To his father. To the military. The big difference was he'd always had someone at his back.

His grandparents. Friends. And even his dad, as hard on AJ as he'd been.

Darcy had Wyatt and Zoe, but she didn't

often let even them in.

But she'd let AJ, at least tonight.

Still, he had no grand illusions. Sex did not equal a relationship, not when it came to Darcy. But it was a start.

To remind her, he took the now empty bottle from her and set it aside, along with his, and then he took something else. Her mouth. He needed this, needed her, and he liked to think she needed him just as much, at least in the moment. When his tongue stroked hers she moaned, a deliciously help-less sound as she clutched at him.

He stepped between her legs, happy to note that the height of the dresser was perfect. He nudged the hem of her T-shirt northward.

"Again?" she murmured.

"Always. Lift up, Darcy."

She did and he swept the shirt over her head. She wrapped her arms around his neck and leaned in until her lips barely touched his. "What's gotten into you to-night?"

"Actually," he said, "the question is, what's going to get into you?" He slid his hand between her thighs, causing her to dig her fingers into his biceps.

"Wait," she gasped.

Damn. He took his mouth and hands off

her body, waiting to see if there was a *stop* to go with that *wait*. If there was, he'd take it like a man and not cry.

Probably.

"What's wrong?" he asked.

"Nothing." Her hand made its way down the front of his sweats and got a handful of him. "I just think we should take this to the bed."

"Now who's bossy?" Scooping her up, he turned and tossed her to the bed. "What else have you got?"

She came up on her elbows and smiled a badass smile. "Strip."

"Whatever you say."

"Really?" she asked. "You'd do whatever I said?"

"In this bed," he clarified with a laugh.

"I can work with that," she said.

Darcy woke with a start at the sound of the low groan of pain.

Not hers.

Disoriented in the dark hotel room, she sat up, whipping around when the sound came again from the body thrashing in the bed next to her.

"AJ?" Leaning over him, she set a hand on his shoulder. "You okay?"

Before she could blink he'd moved and

was on her, pressing his hard body flat to hers, pinning her to the mattress. Using a knee he forced her legs apart as he jerked her hands up over her head, holding her utterly immobile.

Neither of them moved.

Not that she could . . .

The only sound in the room was AJ's labored breathing, like he'd just run a marathon.

A nightmare, she thought, her heart squeezing with empathy as he lifted his head. She could feel the weight of his stare in the early dawn's light, could hear his breathing still sowing in and out of his lungs. His body felt like a furnace, heat blasting from it. "AJ," she said softly, wanting to ground him. "It's just me."

He jerked back from her and came up on his knees.

Freed, she leaned over and turned on the bedside lamp. As it illuminated the room she caught the image of him kneeling there in absolutely nothing but his glory, his ripped body damp with sweat as his chest heaved.

"You okay?" she asked quietly.

Instead of answering, he shoved off the bed and strode into the bathroom.

And hit the lock.

"Right," she said shakily, not enjoying being on the other side of the closed door. "You're fine."

The shower came on. He stayed in there for thirty long minutes, which she knew because she watched the clock tick the minutes over.

When AJ finally turned off the water, she cut the light, knowing from experience that having a witness to your nightmare sucked.

The last time she'd had one hadn't been all that long ago, and she'd woken up screaming like a banshee, drenched in sweat, cowering in her bed like she was still trapped in her burning car. She hadn't been able to stop screaming until Zoe had crawled onto the bed with her, gathered her close, and held on tight, stroking her hair for an hour before she'd been able to relax.

But AJ lived alone. Who gathered him into their arms and held on tight until the memories faded?

The bathroom door opened, and for a brief moment he was outlined in bold relief from the bathroom light behind him.

Until he clicked it off.

She strained to listen for him but he could be silent as a cat when he wanted to be. "AJ?" she whispered.

He didn't answer but she could hear him

now, clothing rustling. He was dressing to leave.

She got that. Her first instinct was always to run like hell, too, because that's what she did when she got scared.

And she was scared.

To the bone. She was scared because she was feeling things, *big* things, *deep* things, and she'd never been good at any of them. What they'd shared this weekend went beyond her scope of experience and she had no idea how to handle it all.

Yeah, she'd most definitely be running if it hadn't been for one fact — he needed her.

She'd never been needed before. "AJ?"

Instead of answering, he headed for the door.

Yep. He was leaving.

"It's nearly dawn," he said. "You'll be fine now. We can leave whenever you want."

Since the only words she had clogging her throat were *please* and *don't,* she kept her mouth shut tight, holding herself taut until the door clicked quietly behind him.

She stared at it, stunned. She hadn't taken one important fact into account. AJ didn't want to be tied down any more than she did. Good to know. Clearly they'd had their roll between the sheets and it had been good.

Hell, it had been great.

And he'd given her back something she hadn't realized she'd been ready for — intimacy. She'd never forget and she'd always be beholden to him for that, but . . . it was done now.

So done.

And because it was, she needed to find a way to seal off the feelings and sensations he'd awakened in her. Because if she didn't care, she couldn't lose. She'd learned that a long time ago and it was the gift that kept on giving.

That decided, she slipped out of the bed and turned on every single light before curling up into the chair in the corner to wait for dawn.

TWENTY

They were both quiet on the way home. Normal for AJ, who liked to relax into a driving zone and enjoy the quiet anyway. But definitely not normal for Darcy, who he doubted could find a zone to save her life.

Twice he stopped for her to stretch her legs and twice he asked if she wanted to drive, hoping to goad her out of her own head.

She'd declined with a polite shake of her head and an unspoken *fuck you.*

And then she'd sat there in painted-on black jeans, kick-ass boots, and a Lynyrd Skynyrd tank, attitude personified.

When he pulled up in front of her house she slipped into her sweater and was out of the truck before it came to a full stop, her long legs striding away from him as fast as they would take her.

"Darcy —" He didn't know what to say. Sorry I left your room so abruptly, I needed to process what the hell happened between us? No. Way too pussy. "I —"

It didn't matter because she was out.

He threw the truck into park and started to get out to go after her — to say what, he still had no idea. All he knew was that he wasn't done with this, with her.

Except apparently he was.

Because a guy rose from the bottom step of the porch where he'd been sitting, clearly waiting for her.

Xander.

Darcy dropped her duffel bag and walked right into his arms.

AJ did his best not to react, swallowing the growl that rose in his throat as he peeled out of there like the hounds of hell were on his heels.

Clearly there was no need to worry about her. She was like a cat with nine lives. No matter what happened to her, no matter what she went through, she landed on her feet.

"You're an idiot," he said out loud.

When Xander went to lower Darcy to the ground, she winced in anticipation of the bolt of agony she knew would shoot up her legs per usual when she first put all her weight on them. But Xander was slow and careful, sweetly so.

"Okay?" he asked, hands still on her. "You don't look okay. What happened?"

What happened? She'd gotten into the whole pretending to be in love with AJ thing, that's what. And it had felt good. Right. And in turn, she'd felt . . . happy.

And it had scared the shit out of her, and when she got scared, she tended to self-destruct. "Nothing."

"Bullshit."

Darcy turned from him and stared down the street where AJ's truck had vanished.

He hadn't been able to drive away fast enough.

Xander tugged lightly on a strand of her hair, waiting for her to look at him. "Do I need to kill him?" he asked seriously.

He was tall but lanky as a bean pole, and a good wind could knock him over. So she choked out a laugh and then to her horror, burst into tears.

"Oh shit," Xander said, looking pained as he pulled her back into him. "Darcy, please don't cry."

"I'm not," she said soggily. "I never cry." And yet the waterworks continued.

"Shit," he said again with more feeling this time, and sank back to the steps with her, holding her close while she bawled into his chest.

"It's just allergies," she finally managed to say.

"Right. Allergies."

Behind them the front door opened and Zoe stood there looking stunned to see Darcy curled into a ball against Xander. "What happened?" she demanded. "What's wrong?"

"I don't know," Xander said in utter male confusion. "But I know it's AJ's fault."

Zoe sank to the step next to them and put her hand on Darcy's back. "Talk to me."

But Darcy couldn't talk. Because what could she possibly say? She'd finally started to feel again, for a man who'd been there, bought the T-shirt, and was over it?

"Soon as she dries up," Xander said over Darcy's head, "I'm going over there to kick his ass."

"Yeah?" Zoe asked. "You might want to eat a cheeseburger first."

Xander flipped her off and she rolled her eyes. "Get in line," she said and stroked Darcy's hair. "Do we need to call in the Coast Guard?"

That was Zoe. Pragmatic. Steady as a rock.

Suspicious.

And to be fair, it wasn't Zoe's fault. She'd

grown up a child of the world and then she'd nearly married a felon with a talent for telling really good fibs. So yeah, Zoe kept a pretty big chip on her shoulder, along with a damn tough hide that no mortal man had been able to break through in ages. She also had a hell of a bullshit meter, hard-earned.

Darcy sat up and scrubbed at her eyes. "Nothing's wrong, I'm just tired."

"Yeah?" Zoe asked, clearly not buying it. "Because the last time you cried was when you found out there wasn't an Easter Bunny."

"Well, that was pretty traumatic," Darcy said in her defense. "Who was going to bring me candy?"

"You know damn well it was always me and Wyatt leaving you the candy."

This was true. When they'd been traveling the world with their parents they'd never celebrated any American holiday. They'd never celebrated any holiday.

So naturally whenever they'd been here in Sunshine with their grandparents, they'd gone overboard. And when their grandparents had died within two years of each other a decade ago, Wyatt and Zoe had kept up the tradition as often as they were all together.

Which hadn't been all that often.

Until recently.

"What's this about AJ needing his ass kicked?" Zoe asked her.

"He doesn't. If anyone needs their ass kicked, it's me. At the very least I need my head examined for agreeing to go with him in the first place."

"You two have a fight?" Zoe asked.

Darcy shrugged and dropped eye contact. The one person she'd never been able to lie to was her nosy-ass sister. "Nothing more than the usual."

"Hmm," Zoe said, which she uttered whenever she was thinking something she wasn't ready to say out loud. Zoe then slid a glance at Xander before coming back to Darcy.

Yep. Whatever she had to say couldn't be said in front of Xander.

Confirming that, Zoe stood up and headed to the front door.

"Hey," Xander said after her. "You're not going to get out of her what happened?"

"No," Zoe said.

"Why not?"

"Hello, have you met her?" Zoe asked. "She never talks until she's ready. Darcy, honey, I need your help in here."

"Doing what?" Zoe didn't need help, ever.

"Rearranging the stock cabinet," Zoe

288

answered. "You know, where we keep all of our feminine hygiene products like tampons and panty liners. Xander, you're welcome to come in and help if you'd like."

Xander paled. "Uh . . ." He looked like he'd rather have his nuts surgically removed. Without drugs. "Can't, sorry."

Darcy snorted and stood up, carefully stretching to avoid any cramping in her legs. "Go home, Xander. Sorry I cried and snotted all over your shirt. I'm just really tired, that's all."

He stood with her. "Something happened," he insisted.

"I'm fine," she said.

"Darcy —"

"Honest. I'm just exhausted and I need a hot soak." She cupped his face and smiled up into it, letting him see that she really was okay.

"You're not lying, right?" he asked warily. "This isn't one of those things you women do, where you pretend to be okay when you're not?"

"We don't do that," Darcy said.

"Are you kidding? You were *born* to do that."

"Okay, true," she said. "But really, I'm fine."

He brushed a soft kiss across her lips and

touched her face. "Dinner?"

"Can't. I have to help Zoe with the thing."

"Yeah," Zoe said. "The tampon thing."

"Never mind," he said, scrambling for his keys to make his escape.

When he drove off, Darcy looked at Zoe with a laugh. "That was mean."

"Hey, if he can't handle the heat then he has no business getting so close to the fire. And you're definitely fire."

"He means well," Darcy said.

"You sure about that?"

"Yes," Darcy said firmly. "He's my best friend. He'd do anything for me."

"Whatever you say."

"You don't think he cares about me?"

"Oh, I know he does," Zoe said. "Just not as your best friend."

Darcy blew out a breath. "He'll get there."

"Just don't be disappointed if he doesn't."

"He will," Darcy insisted. He had to; she didn't know what she would do without him.

"Honey, I mean this in the most loving way," Zoe said. "But don't be naïve, it's not like you. Men don't do the best-friend thing. They do the sex thing. And some of them do the sex thing really really well. But being friends with a woman with no possibility of benefits?" She shook her head.

"Not in their genetic makeup."

"That's harsh," Darcy said.

"It's truth," Zoe said, and held the front door open for her.

They hit the kitchen together, where Zoe poured tea and added a healthy dollop of whiskey into each.

"Nice," Darcy said, and lifted her cup. "What are we drinking to?"

"You tell me," Zoe said.

"Nothing to tell."

Zoe added another dollop of whiskey to Darcy's cup of tea and Darcy laughed. "You think that's going to work?"

But Zoe wasn't playing. She didn't smile. She reached across the kitchen table for Darcy's hand. "Listen to me, okay? I've known AJ a long time. He's one of the best men I know. He's strong, both inside and out. He's resourceful, smart, and steady as a rock."

"Sounds like you're trying to sell me a dog."

"AJ isn't exactly a puppy," Zoe said.

No kidding.

"I'd trust him with my life," her sister went on. "And I'd trust him with yours."

"But?" Darcy asked. "Because I definitely sense a *but* at the end of that sentence."

"But he's a man. And I've seen the way

he looks at you."

"Oh yeah?" Darcy asked. "Like he's watching the circus?"

"Like you're his next meal."

Well, hell if that didn't shut Darcy up. She *had* been his meal. And she'd loved every single second of it.

"So are you going to tell me what's going on?" Zoe asked.

"Like I told Xander, I'm just tired."

"Yeah?"

"Yeah."

"I've known you a long time, too," Zoe said. "And as luck would have it, you're one of the best women I know."

Darcy snorted but Zoe squeezed her fingers. "You are," she said fiercely. "You're strong inside and out, just like him. And also resourceful and smart."

"But not steady as a rock?" Darcy asked.

Zoe laughed softly.

Darcy did, too. "Okay," she said. "I admit, steady as a rock is a stretch."

"Tell me what happened," Zoe said. "You two had a moment?"

"Yes." Darcy paused. "Several." She sighed, and at Zoe's quiet patience, said the rest. "I slept with him."

So much for what happened in Boise stayed in Boise.

Zoe went brows up and then she added a third healthy dollop to their cups.

"The thought of AJ and me together makes you drink?" Darcy asked.

"The thought of keeping you both alive for the ride is making me drink."

"The ride?"

"The dance. The leap off the cliff. The trip to the moon."

Now it was Darcy's turn to blink. "I know you're speaking English but . . ."

"Love," Zoe said. "You're going to fall in love with him."

At that, Darcy stopped being amused by this little by-play. "Don't be ridiculous. Sex isn't love. We were having some fun, that's all."

"Yeah? So fun is why you sobbed on the porch like your puppy just got run over?"

Darcy let out a breath. "Okay, so maybe for a little bit there last night I gave some thought to letting it be more than fun." And it hadn't been when he'd had his tongue halfway down her throat and his hands all over her, either. Nope, it had been when he'd fallen asleep with his arms wrapped tight around her.

"And then what happened?" Zoe asked.

"I woke up."

Zoe's eyes filled with worry. Well, *more*

293

worry. "Are you scared of love, Darcy?"

"Hell yeah," she said. "Join me, won't you?"

"Oh, I'm terrified of it. But I think I'm supposed to tell you that love can be good."

"Yeah? Based on what?"

This stumped Zoe for a beat, then she brightened. "Based on *The Heat* and *21* and *22 Jump Street.*"

Zoe loved buddy-cop flicks, thought of them as love stories. "How about something real-life-based?" Darcy asked.

"Fine," Zoe said. "For all the damage our parents did, they're still together. And Wyatt's in love with Emily and planning on marrying her. It could happen to us, too."

"Yeah, well, you first," Darcy said and finished off her tea. "And if it works out for you, *then* we'll talk."

"I think you're afraid of rejection, not love. You're afraid you're going to put yourself out there and you'll be the only one."

Hard to argue with the truth. Especially when it had already happened.

TWENTY-ONE

When AJ got to the gym and saw Wyatt already there working out, he nearly turned around again. But it was too late; Wyatt nodded at him.

"You get the money guy on the hook?" Wyatt asked.

"He's thinking it over, said he'd get back to me soon."

"So it was good?"

"Great," AJ said.

"Getting snowed in with a cranky Darcy was great?" Wyatt asked in disbelief.

"Well, not that part." Just the part where he'd been buried deep inside her with her legs wrapped around him, his name on her lips . . .

"What part, then?" Wyatt wanted to know. "Where you got stuck spending two nights together?"

AJ nearly dropped the weights on his own face. When he righted himself, Wyatt was watching him with narrowed eyes.

Definitely not the time to be thinking how his sister's curly hair looked streaming out across his pillow, her naked curves sprawled across the sheets. Shit. *Redirect, soldier.* "What?"

"You tell me what," Wyatt said.

AJ opened his mouth just as Wyatt's phone went off. "Emily," Wyatt said, and answered with a goofy smile. "Hey, sweetness — Yeah?" Wyatt's voice lowered to a deep timbre. "Tell me more . . ." His eyes glazed over. "I'll be right there."

Saved by the sexy, horny fiancée . . .

Since it was Darcy's turn to cook dinner, she did as she always did. She went and grabbed takeout. Tonight was Thai, and after she paid, she walked back to her car, head down while she texted with a new S&R dog breeder who'd been referred to her by Adam. He had a five-year-old Siberian husky with a bad knee. The dog needed to retire from the physical demands of S&R work but would make a great therapy dog due to his sweet, patient temperament.

Darcy texted that she'd buy him and find him a great home. She hit send and looked up, stopping short.

The sight of AJ leaning casually against

296

her driver's-side door made her heart skip a beat. When she got closer, he pulled something out of his pocket.

Cash.

And all the warm fuzzies along with the heat she'd started to feel went ice-cold. She was way too tired to be on her game enough to deal with him. "What are you doing?" she asked.

"Paying you for the trip."

"No, you're not. And move," she said. "You're in my way."

He didn't move. "Take the money, Darcy."

"No. I told you I wouldn't take payment after you did all that physical therapy pro bono. Now go away. I need to sit down."

He moved instantly and opened the door for her. She slid in behind the wheel, grateful to sit since her legs had started to tremble.

AJ crouched in the space between the opened door and the driver's seat, one hand on her steering wheel, the other on the back of her seat. It was a possessive stance and also a protective one, and her brain didn't know how to process it.

"What's wrong with taking the money?" he asked.

"Oh, please. I owed you a favor and we both know it. Just as we both know that me talking to Trent and Summer doesn't come close to settling the score between us. Especially after —" Nope, she couldn't say it, couldn't go there.

AJ leaned in and gave a quick twist of her keys, turning off her car. Then he turned her face to him and she was surprised to find that his rare, almost nonexistent temper had kicked in.

"A deal is a deal," he said. "I never go back on my word. And as for you owing me for your treatment, listen carefully because I'm only going to say this once. What we give each other? There's no tab."

"Exactly. So forget paying me. I'm not taking your money, not after we —" He arched a brow and she broke off. "You know," she said.

"I do," he agreed. "Do you?"

She put her hands to his chest and gave a little shove. He didn't budge. "Dammit, AJ, I need to go."

"I see what you're doing with the dogs, helping people."

"Yeah? So?"

"So you're getting involved, Darcy. Invested in Sunshine. You want all of us to think you're just blowing through, that you're stuck here only until you're good enough to fly the coup. But you know what

I think?"

"Way too much of yourself, for one . . ."

"I think you're enjoying having a home base for once," he said, eyes serious. And still pissed. "I think you like having family, friends, people to care about — and in return, people who care about you. Yeah, I think you're getting into it, feeling good. And maybe even happy. And since that probably scares the shit out of you, you're one inch from destroying it all."

Oh how she hated that he was right. About all of it. "You don't know what you're talking about."

"Don't I?" he asked softly. "Are you telling me you aren't chomping at the bit to get the hell out of here?"

"I never intended to stay in Sunshine and make roots."

"But you did," he said. "Can you really just uproot now and go?"

"Absolutely."

"Worst. Liar. Ever," he said. He slid a hand to the nape of her neck, pulled her in, and kissed her.

And that was the thing about AJ. He could make her feel so many things. Angry. Frustrated. And in the case of right now, like the most incredibly sexy, fascinating woman on the entire planet. With words, a look, or even a single touch he could erase all the doubt in her mind and reinstate any confidence she'd ever lost. She'd never imagined a man being able to make her feel that way, but here he was. Ready, willing, and able.

The question was — was she ready, willing, and able?

She was trembling when he pulled back, and this time it had nothing to do with exhaustion. He stared at her and then gave her one last kiss and walked away.

When she turned forward to turn her car on again, she found the cash was in her lap.

She couldn't sleep that night. At all. She was dead tired and achy, too, but her brain wouldn't stop racing.

She was going to have no trouble finding a home for the husky, she had a lot of people on her waiting list. She thought about Ronan, AJ's PTSD patient, who she knew desperately needed a dog's help out in public, navigating crowds and social situations. She'd call him tomorrow.

Just before dawn Darcy gave up. She could take something to knock her out, but it wasn't a foggy oblivion she wanted. No, she wanted a different type of oblivion altogether, one that involved a hard body and talented hands, both of which belonged to the one man who'd ever made her want to go back for seconds.

And thirds.

She took a shower, dressed, and then tiptoed past Zoe's bedroom door, stilling with a grimace when Zoe called out to her.

"You okay?"

Darcy rolled her eyes and took a step back to the doorway. "Great."

Zoe's nightstand lamp went on and she sat up in bed looking sleepy.

"Didn't mean to wake you," Darcy said. "I'm just going out for some Gummy Bears."

"At . . ." Zoe squinted at the clock. "Four thirty in the morning?"

"Hey, I don't have control over my cravings."

"Uh-huh. You do know that Gummy Bears aren't what you really want, right?"

Darcy did her best to look innocent. She wasn't ready to discuss what she wanted — which was to jump AJ's bones.

"Is the pain that bad?"

"No. Well, I mean, yes, sometimes, but not as bad as you think. Honest, Z, I'm okay. I'll be back in a little bit."

"Want me to drive you?"

"No," she said quickly. Too quickly, because Zoe went still and stared at her thoughtfully. "I'm fine in town."

The highways were still another story entirely.

"I'll take a rack of chocolate donuts," Zoe said. "Unless, of course, you're not really going for goodies but to AJ's house."

Darcy blinked. "That's . . . ridiculous." Wow, AJ was right, she was a terrible liar.

"Just tell me this," Zoe said. "Did you shave your legs?"

She totally had and she knew where this was going, but she played dumb. "What does that have to do with anything?"

"You know damn well what," Zoe said. "If you shaved your legs, you're not going for junk food. You've got other . . . expectations."

"I do have expectations. For you to mind your own damn business."

Zoe laughed and flipped off her light.

Darcy was nearly halfway down the hallway when Zoe called out, "Tell him hi for me."

Darcy pulled up to AJ's house, which was lit from within.

He was up.

His place was an old farmhouse, which he'd restored and updated. The front yard wasn't large but the back of the property butted right up to the river. Off to the side was a fenced-in pen where Sergeant, AJ's horse, grazed. Actually, Sergeant was his father's horse but AJ had taken over care of the aging animal for him.

Two huge cats — Thor and Stark, left to AJ by his superhero-loving grandma when she'd passed away — sat perched at attention on the front porch, eyes narrowed in feline suspicion, watching Darcy approach as the sky lightened.

And then there was AJ himself, too, in jeans and a hoodie sweatshirt, working a shovel in the horse pen, his body moving with easy grace. Like the cats, he stopped to watch her approach. Unlike the cats, his eyes weren't narrowed, but warm and curious, making her heart leap into her throat.

She hadn't the foggiest idea what she thought she was doing. In fact . . . yeah. This was really a terrible idea, and shaking her head at herself, she turned back to her car. She was reaching for the door when AJ caught her by the wrist and turned her to face him.

His eyes were still warm and curious, and now also assessing. "Hey."

"Hey," she said. Look at her all casual, like she hadn't come here for a booty call.

"If you're here to give me back the money,

forget it," he said.

"No."

He studied her. "Same goes if you're here to fight with me. I'm not in the mood."

She shook her head again. "I'd love to fight with you but I'm too tired." As for what she *had* come for . . . "Look, I've gotta go get Zoe donuts. And I want Gummy Bears."

He grimaced at her breakfast choice. "So your car drove you here by accident?"

"Yes!"

"To . . . yell at me?" he guessed.

"Not exactly."

"Then what?"

She pulled her lower lip between her teeth, and he smiled. "You want me."

God help her, she did. But her legs were feeling a little shaky and she needed to sit down right now. So she did, right there on the grass lining his driveway, where she let out a huge, wide yawn.

Before she could even register his movements, he was in front of her, on his knees, cupping her face and looking into her eyes. "You're in pain and you haven't slept."

"No. Not since . . ." When she'd been with him in the hotel room. She looked away. "No."

The next thing she knew she was in his

arms and he was striding toward his house, his long legs eating up the distance with no effort at all.

"What are you doing?" she asked as her arms went around his neck. For balance, she told herself, and not because of the entire body tingle he'd created by the strongman act. "I can walk."

He didn't answer, just shouldered his way into his house, kicked the door closed, and kept going.

"AJ, put me down."

"How about you just pretend to enjoy being carried off to my bed. You know, the same way you *pretend* to enjoy my kisses."

His bed? "Um —"

"Talk later."

Oh boy. She didn't know whether to be aroused or nervous.

In his bedroom, he let her slide slowly down his body.

Both, she decided. Aroused *and* nervous. She was still standing there thinking that when he tugged off her sweater and took in the fact that she wore nothing beneath it.

"Laundry day," she said.

He worked her jeans open and tugged them to her thighs, grinning at her lack of panties. "I love laundry day," he said, and pushed her jeans to the floor.

She opened her mouth to say something sexy-kitteny but yawned instead. Damn.

Before she could try again he'd nudged her — not all that gently, either — onto his bed.

Anticipation gripped her. Maybe they couldn't get along to save each other's lives, but they could have this. And his bed was perfect, big and warm and cushy . . . She lay back, watching as AJ stripped quickly and efficiently.

Hmm. Definitely way more aroused than nervous now, her eyeballs soaked up the sight of his gorgeous bod. She opened her mouth to say so but another wide yawn racked her. "Sorry," she murmured.

He crawled onto the bed and kissed her. Then he flipped her away from him.

Okaaaaay. She preferred her wild monkey sex — when she could get it — face-to-face but she didn't really have any limits, at least none that she knew about, so —

AJ slid a corded forearm around her hips and hauled her back into him, her spine to his front.

More yum. In this position she could feel his hard chest, his powerful thighs . . . and everything in between.

He pinned her in place with one of his legs over hers and a deliciously muscled arm holding her still as he nuzzled his mouth at the nape of her neck. "Close your eyes."

She shivered in anticipation. "Do we get to skip a condom this time, too?" she asked hopefully. "Cuz I don't have one."

"Shh." He possessively palmed a breast, lazily stroking his thumb over her nipple.

"That feels good," she whispered.

His body shook as he laughed at her. "Darcy, shut up and close your eyes."

"But I'm not tired anymore. Or mad." She added a butt wriggle against his erection to prove it. "And neither are you."

"Close 'em."

"Okay," she grumbled, "but I hope this means you're about to do something really kinky."

He was laughing again and she closed her eyes and sighed. "I really do like the sound of your laugh," she whispered, and that was the last thing she remembered.

At some point — the muted light coming through the window suggested six-ish — she woke up draped all over AJ's warm, hard, gorgeous body and heard herself moan.

Still asleep, he pulled her in closer and brushed his mouth to her forehead.

Nice, but not what she was looking for. She rolled over on top of him and then it was his turn to groan as his hands slid to the curve of her ass and squeezed.

Needing more, needing him, all of him, Darcy straddled his hips and sheathed him inside of her.

"Darcy." AJ's voice was sleep-roughened and so sexy she nearly came from the rough timbre alone. "I've got to get up and get to work —"

"No going. Only coming for you." And then she started a slow grind, having to close her eyes as the hunger and desire rose up and began to overtake her as it always did with him.

AJ laced his fingers through hers and straightened his arms up above his head. This forced her lower, stretching her out over the top of him so that he could take her mouth with his. "You're going to come, too," he said against her lips. "In fact, you're going to come first." Having effortlessly wrestled control from her, he playfully tortured her with every stroke of his tongue and his body.

But she wasn't done yet. Maybe he was the stronger, badder one, but she still had some moves, and she rocked her hips, taking him deeper. He sucked in a breath as he met her with a thrust of his own, over and over again, each sending a hard jolt of pleasure pulsing out from her core.

The low burn started at her toes and worked its way north. Slipping his hands from hers, AJ grabbed her hips, moving her in a rhythm that made them both moan as they stared at each other. Her eyes never left his as they rode together to climax.

After, she fell forward onto his chest, boneless, sated as she tried to catch her breath, smiling as his hand settled possessively on her ass. She managed to lift her head and blow her hair from her face. "Sorry to keep you," she said, not sorry at all.

He flashed a sexy grin. "Believe me when I say this — *any*time."

When she woke up six hours later — *six hours!!* — she was alone and had a note pinned to her pillow right next to where she'd been drooling.

HEY, SLEEPING BEAUTY, I TOOK YOU OFF THE SCHEDULE TODAY. STAY IN BED. SLEEP. RELAX. THERE'S FOOD IN THE KITCHEN THAT ISN'T GUMMY BEARS. HELP YOURSELF. LOVE, AJ.

She stared at the note for a full five minutes before she spoke out loud in shock.

"*Love,* AJ?" she asked the room.

The room didn't have an opinion on the matter.

Well, she thought with a calming breath, there were all kinds of love, right? She loved Zoe and Wyatt, for instance. She loved Adam and the entire gang at Belle Haven. She loved dogs. She loved Xander. Hell, she even loved her distant parents. She loved Gummy Bears. She loved Christmas. Okay, more accurately she loved presents. She loved the beach.

AJ loved a lot of things and people, too, so really, the note meant nothing.

But still, she stared at the words for another few minutes. So did he love her the way he loved healthy food? The way he loved her brother? The way he loved . . . Ariana?

At that thought she grinded her back teeth together. She didn't want him to love her in the same way he loved Ariana.

Which didn't make this any more clear to her.

Her stomach rumbled so loud she had no choice but to follow its demand that she hit the kitchen. She looked inside AJ's refrigerator with the same expression she'd face a veggie smoothie — gag. Indeed, there were a lot of veggies, and she resigned herself to eating twigs and berries for breakfast.

But hold on a minute.

There was a brown bakery bag with her name on it. Be still her beating heart. "Please be brownies," she whispered, and peeked inside.

Not brownies, but a banana nut granola muffin. She slathered it in butter and nuked it. "Here goes nothing," she said, and took a bite. And then she moaned out loud and stared in surprise at the muffin. "Okay," she told it. "I owe you an apology."

And very possibly she owed AJ a lot more than that. She texted him a thank-you and got an immediate response.

For?

For everything, she could have replied, because he always knew. How did he always know? She had no idea but decided on something more specific: For the bed, the sleep, the food . . .

She could have also said the orgasms but refrained. The man had skills, but he knew he had skills. No sense in stroking his ego any more than she already had.

His reply took fifteen minutes, which told her he was with a client. And then when the response came, she laughed out loud.

You owe me.

Oh so now we're keeping tabs? she texted back.

Never, came his startlingly simple and devastatingly revealing answer. And then right on the heels of that text came another. No hoops to jump through, either.

She stared at her stupid phone, feeling her stupid heart do a stupid squeeze as she thumbed her reply: That's good because I don't exactly excel at hoop jumping.

His answer caused her first laugh of the day: It's okay, you excel in other areas.

TWENTY-TWO

The next day Darcy was scheduled to work at Belle Haven. She spent the morning at the front desk and the afternoon with Adam in his office.

Adam was a good teacher but he was crap at paperwork for his training classes and cert workshops. Once she'd gotten him all straightened out, she told him about the new husky she needed to pick up.

"You really need that website," Adam said.

"I know. I was thinking something like CareDogs.com or TherapyDogsRescue .com," she said. "And people in need of a dog can learn more about what I'm doing and how to get on my list."

They worked on a design for a few hours before Adam drove her out to pick up and then deliver the husky to his new owner, Ronan. And damn. She knew it wasn't brain surgery or solving hunger or world peace, but she felt . . .

Of value.

The minute she thought it, the tightness in her chest spread and she realized it was warmth. She felt good about herself.

And . . . happy.

She was chipping away at her bad karma one dog at a time.

Back at Belle Haven, Wyatt was waiting for them. He gave Darcy a hug and . . .

A key to Belle Haven. She stared at the key, and then back to her brother and Adam.

"You're a part of us here," Adam said. "And this key proves it. It's also so that when your brother forgets his key, which he does weekly, he can call you to save him so Emily and I don't have to make fun of him. Here's your office." He opened a door.

"What? An office?" She stared inside. "Um, a supply closet?"

"We're going to fix it up," he said, waving a dismissive hand at the racks of dusty shelves. "Use your imagination for now."

Her chest tightened. "Really?"

"Yeah. CareDogs.com needs a center of command, don't you think? And there's no better place than Belle Haven for that."

She threw herself first at Wyatt and then Adam, hugging the big badass tight. Adam sighed at the display of affection and awkwardly patted her back. Wyatt, well used to her mercurial moods, took the hug with barely a grimace.

When she pulled free, they had an audience. Dell and his wife, Jade, were standing there beaming.

"You're an official part of our team now," Jade said.

Darcy had spent most of her life living purposely on her own team, telling herself she didn't need anyone. But the thought of being part of the team here at Belle Haven gave her a warm glow normally reserved for her rescues and Gummy Bears. "Thank you," she managed. "You won't be sorry."

"Of course we won't," Adam said. "Especially if you keep your hugs to any member of the team but me."

That night Darcy was sitting up in bed staring down at the blank Word doc on her laptop, trying to figure out something to write about. She missed writing about her adventures, but getting out into the world to have a new adventure wasn't going to happen.

She was still waiting for inspiration to strike, and also wondering how she was going to sleep . . . and what AJ might be doing . . . when her bedroom door opened and the man himself slipped into her room.

She stared at him. "What are you doing?"

"Playing Sandman." He toed off his shoes and stripped down to black boxer briefs, which were sitting dangerously low on his hips, before climbing into bed with her.

"Is this about what I owe you?" she asked hopefully, setting aside her laptop.

"No. No tabs, remember?"

"Damn," she said with heartfelt disappointment.

He laughed — God she really loved his laugh — and tugged back the covers to look at her. He laughed again as he took in her nightie, which featured Queen Elsa from *Frozen.*

What could she say, she loved the woman's 'tude.

AJ tucked her into the same position they'd been last night.

"You keep getting my hopes up," she said as he reached past her to turn off the light.

He bit down lightly over the back of her neck. "Soon."

Her entire body broke out in anticipatory goose bumps. *"When?"*

"When your sister isn't right down the hall."

She sighed. "So why are you here if not for all the orgasms?"

"To tell you that Trent left me a message.

He's coming up the day after tomorrow to seal the deal."

"Oh, AJ," she breathed, clutching his arm to her chest. "That's wonderful."

"It is, and I owe it all to you."

"No tabs," she whispered, and fell asleep with him holding her tight.

When she woke up, she was once again stunned and startled to realize she'd slept the night through.

And her Sandman was long gone . . .

Dammit. She was hot and achy *all* the time and he seemed so easily able to resist her. *What did that mean?* She called him.

"Hey," he said, sounding distracted.

"Hey yourself. What's with the repeated vanishing act?"

"Had work."

She waited for more. It didn't come. "You sure it's just work?"

He paused, and when he spoke he sounded baffled. "What else would it be?"

"Gee, AJ, I don't know, seeing as you're a word miser."

Silence, and she rolled her eyes. "You know what? Never mind."

"Darcy —"

"No, forget it," she said. "I won't beg for crumbs, not even from you. So do us both a favor and don't play Sandman tonight." And then she punched END so hard she broke a nail.

Luckily she was scheduled for a shift at Belle Haven and not the wellness center, and as she sat at the desk manning the front reception area with Peanut the Mouthy Parrot at her elbow and Bean the Grumpy Cat asleep on her printer, she did her best not to replay that conversation over and over in her head. The one-sided conversation.

"Men suck," she said.

Peanut bobbed her head in agreement. "Men suck."

"Oh shit," Darcy said and stared at the parrot. "No, Peanut, that was my bad, okay? We can't use that word here."

Again Peanut bobbed her head.

Whew, Darcy thought, and smiled at the woman who walked in the front door with her cat for their appointment. "Hello," she said in greeting. "Just have a seat."

"Shit!" Peanut screeched just as the woman sat.

She leapt up as if there'd been a cobra on her chair. "What? What's wrong?"

Darcy realized that the woman thought she'd yelled shit. Damn Peanut for being an incredible imitation artist. "I'm sorry, our parrot is feeling naughty today." She turned to Peanut. "Puppies, rainbows, kittens." She waited for Peanut to repeat any of that.

Peanut said nothing.

"Cupcakes, cookies, pies," Darcy said.

"Men suck," Peanut said.

Darcy thunked her head on her desk.

It was going to be one of those days. And even worse, she couldn't help but notice that love was definitely in the air here in Sunshine.

For one thing, Dell kept cornering Jade in his office every chance he got.

And Darcy's own brother did the same to Emily. Even hard-ass Brady, ex–special ops and helicopter pilot-for-hire, softened whenever Lilah, the love of his life, came through the offices.

And then there was Gertie, the hundred-pound Saint Bernard that belonged to Dell and Jade. She was in love with Bruiser, a six-pound Chihuahua, currently recouping from having his nuts surgically removed.

Gertie didn't care. She lay outside of Bruiser's crate sighing forlornly, thumping her heavy tail whenever Bruiser woke up from a nap and lifted his tiny head.

True love.

"Annoying as sh—" Darcy started to say, breaking off with a guilty look at Peanut.

"Boner," Peanut yelled cheerfully.

The woman waiting stood and walked out.

"I so did *not* teach you that one," Darcy said.

Peanut whistled and made Bean jump and fall off the printer.

The cat immediately employed Kitty Logic, which was to ignore any embarrassing situation — like falling off the printer — by redirecting. She redirected by lifting a leg to groom her Lady Town.

"Nice tactic," Darcy said. "But it totally happened."

Bean gave her a dirty look that suggested maybe Darcy should put her shoes back on before something bad happened inside of them.

Darcy bent beneath her desk to grab the shoes she'd kicked off and went into the storage closet — soon to be her office! — for paper to refill her printer, and found Adam in there pressing Holly up against the metal shelving unit, his hands up her pretty sweater.

"Okay, really?" Darcy asked, tossing up her hands. "All the romance around here is giving me serious heartburn. I'm out."

Adam stopped massaging Holly's tonsils with his tongue and grinned. "Sorry. I'll make it up to you."

"How? By bleaching the memories from

my brain?"

"Better," he said. "I've got another dog for you. Raisin, a one-year-old golden retriever from a long line of therapy dogs. She passed all the classes and testing with the rest of her litter, but she can't be sold."

"Why?"

"She only has three legs. And the owner doesn't want to ruin his rep by selling her — I know," he said when he saw Darcy about to lose her collective shit. "I know. But his shortsightedness is *your* gain. He's willing to let her go for two hundred and seventy-five bucks. I told him to consider her sold. I'll cover you on this one."

Her throat tightened at the generosity. "I want her, absolutely. And I have just the right someone for her, too. But I've got the money for this one."

"You win the lottery?"

"Ha. And no, or I'd be on a deserted island with an endlessly charged Nook and an equally endless supply of Gummy Bears. When can I get her?"

"Today."

She grinned and he returned it.

"You're pretty damn cute when you stop snarling," he said. "Anyone ever tell you that?"

She thought of AJ and stopped smiling.

"No." She turned to leave but stopped when Adam said her name. She glanced back.

"Whoever he is," Adam said, eyes serious now, "I'll be happy to kick his ass for you."

"I'll keep that in mind, thanks."

Two hours later she'd taken possession of one gorgeous, sweet, warm, lovable three-legged Raisin. Darcy spent some time at Belle Haven with the dog, out back in the wide open space between horse pens, walking through the wild grass together.

Even handicapped as she was, Raisin had no problem keeping up. She had no problem handling any command Darcy gave her. And every time she praised her, Raisin slid in a boneless heap of love to the ground to have her belly rubbed.

"You're possibly the sweetest thing I've ever seen," she said.

Raisin smiled up at her in demure agreement.

When Darcy left Belle Haven, the dog curled up trustingly in the backseat of her car. She'd texted Xander for Tyson's whereabouts and got the reply that they were both at the wellness center.

She'd been doing her damnedest to avoid thinking of AJ — though she'd have had a lot more luck with attempting to not breathe air — and now if she wanted to see Tyson, she'd probably have to see AJ, too.

Not to mention having both Xander and AJ in the same space right now seemed a little dicey. But if she had to be a grown-up, well, then so did they.

As usual with this time of day, the wellness center parking lot was full. People were working out after work, or in a yoga class with Ariana, or seeing AJ and his other staff. Darcy turned to Raisin. "You wait here while I make sure Tyson's inside. I'll only be a minute."

Raisin licked her hand and settled into her seat, seeming happy to look out the windows.

Darcy went inside. Brittney — Darcy's counterpart on the days Darcy didn't work — was already off for the day. Ariana was there doing something on the computer. She wore yoga pants and a workout tank top that emphasized her lean, willowy, beautiful body. Not a spare ounce on her, no doubt due to the fact that she didn't eat flour, sugar, or anything else processed.

Darcy had tried that for half a day once. It hadn't worked out for her. She'd gotten so irritable and grumpy that Zoe had force-fed her Frosted Flakes for dinner.

"Good afternoon," Ariana said, all lovely and Zen. "How are you today?"

"Fine, thanks," Darcy said. "You?"

Ariana leaned on the counter. "You know that wasn't just a polite question, right? I actually really care about your recovery and how you're feeling."

"Why?" Darcy asked, genuinely curious.

"Well, because I work here and care about all of our patients, and because you work here, too, and that makes us co-workers. And also because of AJ."

Darcy paused. "What about him?"

"Well . . ." Ariana lifted a shoulder. "Clearly something's going on between you two."

Darcy found a laugh. "Sorry, but you're wrong there. I'm looking for Tyson, is he here?"

"Yes, he is." Ariana smiled, the kind of smile that said she was holding back.

"What?"

"Nothing."

"Oh come on," Darcy said. "You're quiet but not shy. Let's hear it."

"I was just wondering if you'd take some advice," Ariana asked.

Darcy hesitated, but who was she kidding, she'd take any advice she could get.

"If you're going for it, then go for it," Ariana said. "Half measures don't work with AJ."

"That's it? That's the sum total of your advice?" Darcy asked. "Go for it?"

"Yes," Ariana said, serene as ever. "And don't blow it."

Darcy stared at her. "Okay, I'll bite. Why do you care if I blow it?"

Ariana just looked at her, and Darcy let out a slow breath. "You want him back."

"I won't step in on you."

"Trust me, there's nothing to step in on," Darcy said. That she wanted there to be was another story entirely.

Ariana's gaze slid to the private patient rooms where AJ walked out in his usual PT uniform of black running sweats and a Sunshine Wellness black T-shirt hugging the body that could make a woman drop to her knees to worship at.

Damn him anyway for being both hotter than sin *and* sex on a stick.

Across the room their eyes met and held. Darcy's knees wobbled.

"Nothing to step in on, my ass," Ariana murmured softly, maybe amused, maybe not as the air seemed to spark between AJ and Darcy.

But Darcy was definitely *not* amused.

TWENTY-THREE

AJ broke off eye contact with Darcy, which was surprisingly difficult, and took in Ariana's gaze. He sensed he'd just missed something between the two very different women — one always so cool and calm no matter the circumstances, the other like a wild, gorgeous tumbleweed blowing through town.

A tumbleweed in a Pink Floyd tank who screamed bad 'tude.

When he'd left her in her bed early that morning fast asleep, she'd been curled up on her side away from him, everything about her calling to him to slip into the bed again: the curve of her hip beneath the sheet, the expanse of her bare back revealing her beautiful tattoo, her out-of-control hair scattered across his pillow.

As business and pleasure mixed uncomfortably in his head, Darcy walked out the front door, moving slowly and stiffly.

She hurt today.

As he remembered that he had staff and clients all around him — something he'd never once had to remind himself of before — he turned to Evan at his side, an active duty marine who'd recently had ACL surgery. AJ had just spent an hour working on his knee, helping him recover some strength. He turned the computer to face him. "I'd like to see you again in a few days," he said to Evan, accessing his schedule.

Darcy came back in the door with a three-legged dog on a leash at her side. She crouched down — with more effort than he liked to see — to love up on the dog. Her head was bent; her beautiful hair fell over her arms and into her own face.

AJ could remember that happening to him, the soft silky curls brushing against the heated skin of his abs and thighs when she'd —

"I'll schedule Evan for you," Ariana said.

Evan offered a fist for Raisin to sniff, which the dog did delicately, her tail mopping the floor as she wagged it with enthusiasm.

"Her name's Raisin," Darcy told the marine, struggling back to her feet.

AJ knew better than to offer a hand but Evan didn't. He helped her up and Darcy smiled at him.

"You need to ice," AJ told her. "I've got a few minutes, I could —"

"I'm fine."

Right. As Ariana made Evan's next appointment, AJ answered some questions for Evan, doing his best to focus while also taking in the tension between Darcy and Ariana.

If Ariana felt it, she didn't let on. She smiled and stroked Raisin, who soaked up the love with more floor sweeping. "I didn't see you on the schedule today," she said to Darcy.

"I don't have a PT appointment."

"You decided to take me up on a yoga class?" Ariana asked. "I've got one starting in twenty minutes. Long, slow, deep stretching. It'd be perfect for you."

"Sorry," Darcy said, "but *perfect* would be a cold, tall beer and a hot beach."

"The class would quiet your mind," Ariana said. "And help you get centered."

"Hmm," Darcy said, which AJ interpreted as her thinking she'd never been particularly centered and didn't see herself starting now.

She glanced at him and then back to Ariana. "So you said Tyson was here?"

She'd done a good job of ignoring AJ. He was impressed. But he raised a brow at her and she rolled her eyes.

"Yeah, yeah," she said. "I'm his least favorite person, blah blah. Old news. I've got something for him."

Everyone looked down at Raisin. Ariana slid a look at AJ. She was surprised, he could tell. Surprised at Darcy's giving nature.

AJ wasn't surprised in the least.

"You got him a therapy dog," Ariana said, her voice much warmer now.

Darcy looked uncomfortable. "It's not a big deal. And it's a surprise. Where is he?"

"It's a beautiful surprise," Ariana said. "And he's out back."

"On the basketball court," AJ added. He handed Evan his exit papers and waited until he'd walked out. "I was with him for an hour," he told her. "And then he and Xander stuck around. They're out there trying to kill each other."

He wasn't surprised when she gave him a barely there nod and walked off, Raisin at her side, the both of them limping in tandem, heads high.

Ariana waited until Darcy was out of hearing range before giving AJ a long look.

"What?"

"You tell me what," she said.

"Nothing to tell."

She laughed at him. "Oh you big, beautiful, stupid man."

"What is that supposed to mean?" he asked.

Ariana made a sound like her head just got a flat tire. "Okay, look, you're my boss and also one of my best friends. And once upon a time you were my lover. So I feel like I've got a right to say this to you — we're never going to sleep together again."

He blinked. "That wasn't what I expected."

"I was good for you," she said. "I know it and you know it. But Darcy's better."

"Also not what I expected."

"I know," she said. "But I do like being unpredictable. And let me just say, I don't know for sure what's going on between the two of you, but I've seen it coming for a long time."

"You could've warned me," he muttered.

She smiled. "Some things are much more fun to watch. And man, last weekend must have been a doozy. But whatever happened, you're different and so is she. So the question is, are you going to do yourself a favor and keep her . . . or let her go like everyone else in your life since Kayla?"

"Ariana —"

"No, let me get this out because I'm only

going to be this gracious once. If I can't have you, then I want this for you. She makes you laugh, AJ. She gives you light. Yes, I'm stupid in lust with you, and yes, I've been hoping we'd have another go at each other sometime, but you're not free, not really. Just do me a favor?"

"What?"

"First, mourn the loss of me just a little bit?" she asked with a smile, making him smile back. "And second — once you mourn me and maybe also lie to me and tell me I ruined you for all other women — *then* let yourself go for it."

"Go for what exactly?"

"Happiness."

TWENTY-FOUR

Darcy found Xander and Tyson indeed in the middle of a vicious game of wheelchair basketball. Xander was greatly handicapped because he sat in Tyson's old chair, not to mention he had no experience in a wheelchair and sucked at it.

Tyson was a pro, of course. A pro who shoved Xander practically into next week to take a shot.

Nothing but net.

Tyson raised his hands in victory and then jabbed his pointer finger at Xander, who'd tipped over in his borrowed chair and lay sprawled on the asphalt. "You suck, bro."

"Nice," Xander said, slowly rising to his feet, hunching over, hands on his knees as he tried to catch his breath. "Real gracious winner, asshole. The game's supposed to be about fun, not who wins."

Tyson flipped him off.

"And that," Xander said, straightening to

jab a finger in his direction. "That right there. Why are you set at pissed off all the time? What did your therapist tell you about that?"

"That you're supposed to hug me." Tyson lifted his arms in a mock request for a hug.

Now Xander flipped his brother off.

"I'm going to tell her you said that," Tyson said.

Darcy stepped onto the court. Raisin hopped alongside her, sitting when Darcy stopped.

The brothers turned to her in unison with varying expressions. Xander's went warm with greeting. Tyson's went cold.

It always did. He hated her, possibly for not being with Xander, possibly just because she was breathing. Granted, ever since he'd gotten home from his third tour of duty he'd hated just about everything, and on lots of days that included the only person he had in life — Xander. So Darcy tried not to take it personally.

But she did. Yet that wasn't why she'd brought him a therapy dog. She knew his therapist had suggested one to help him through his PTSD and his reactions to people in general, along with assisting in the acclimation back to civilian life.

Xander came close, smiled at her and

squatted in front of Raisin. "Hey there," he said. "Who are you?"

"Raisin," Darcy told him. "She's a therapy dog."

Xander looked up at her. "Yeah? For . . . ?"

Darcy looked at Tyson.

Tyson rolled closer and eyed Raisin's three legs. "What happened to her?"

"Birth defect," Darcy said. "Her owner trained her entire litter as service dogs but he can't sell her."

Tyson stared at Raisin.

Raisin stared back.

"You got any tricks?" Tyson asked the dog.

Raisin sneezed.

In Xander's face.

"Ugh," Xander said, and stood up, swiping at his face like he'd been exposed to the plague. "Seriously? Gross."

Tyson nodded in approval at the dog. "Nice," he said. "What else you got?"

Raisin lay down, rolled over, and closed her eyes, playing dead.

"Huh. Not bad," Tyson said. "But can you bring in the chicks?"

Raisin got back to her feet and leaned against Darcy.

Tyson smiled, actually *smiled,* and Darcy was pretty sure it was the first smile she'd ever seen out of him. "Wow," she said. "Your mouth *does* curve up at the ends."

"Jesus," Xander said. "Why do you always have to poke at the bear?"

Tyson met Darcy's gaze, his eyes not quite as cold as they'd been. "And look at that, you're not always a bitch."

"Tyson," Xander said in a low warning voice.

"It's okay," Darcy said to Xander, eyes still on Tyson. "He's right. I'm not always a bitch." She dropped Raisin's leash in Tyson's lap. "And you're not always a bitter, angry asshole."

"Fuck," Xander muttered. "The two of you give me heartburn, you know that?"

"He always was a drama queen," Tyson said to Raisin.

"It's because he loves you," Darcy told him.

"And you," Tyson reminded her. "He loves you, too."

"Seriously," Xander said. "Shut the fuck up."

"I know he does," Darcy told Tyson. "And I love him, too. And because I do, I also love you."

Tyson narrowed his eyes. "You love me," he repeated, heavy on the disbelief.

"Yes. Because *he* loves you — even when you're being an insufferable prick."

Tyson choked out a laugh. "Well, why don't you just tell us how you really feel?"

"I'm about to," Darcy said.

"Okay," Xander said, shifting on his feet. "I think we're done here."

Without taking her eyes off Tyson, Darcy pointed at him to zip it. "You're hurting," she said. "I get that. God, how I get that, Tyson. But by refusing to try to get back to the land of the living, by closing yourself off and depending on Xander for every damn thing every minute of the day, you're making him hurt, too. Do *you* get that?"

Tyson's smile was gone. His jaw was tight, his eyes shuttered. "What, you think I'm a reliant dick for shits and giggles? I can't get around, and I can't handle anyone else near me."

Darcy looked at the hand he'd set on Raisin's back. "Looks like you're handling Raisin just fine."

Raisin lifted her head from where she'd set it on Tyson's leg and licked his hand.

Tyson made a rough noise and lowered his face to look into the dog's eyes. Raisin very sweetly and very politely — and most touching of all, very slowly — leaned in and licked his chin.

Just once.

Then she sat back and seemed to smile.

Tyson stared at her. "She's not afraid of me."

"Well, why should she be?" Darcy asked. "You're injured, not an ogre — at least not in appearance."

Tyson never took his eyes off Raisin. "Aren't you afraid I'll be an asshole to her?"

"I'm more afraid that you'll stop being an asshole all together and I might have to learn to like your sorry ass."

Tyson snorted and finally looked at her. "I can't afford to buy her."

"I'm giving her to you."

"So you feel sorry for me? I'm not a charity case."

Darcy narrowed her eyes. "Raisin was a throwaway. Do you know what that means? It means that her owner took one look at her and decided she was different and therefore not as good as the others. And we both know, being that we're different, too, that that's just complete and utter bullshit. She's *better* than all the others because she had to work doubly hard to do everything. I raised the money and bought her because she deserves to go to someone who gets her, someone who understands, someone who won't treat her like a damn reject because she's different. I thought you were that guy. Am I wrong?"

Tyson studied her for a long beat and then reached down and hauled Raisin up into his lap. Three-legged dog and PTSD man stared into each other's eyes. "You hear that?" Tyson asked the dog. "She's yelling at your new dad. I'm going to teach you to growl at her just a little, show her who's boss around here."

Raisin licked his chin again.

Tyson let out a breath, closed his eyes, and wrapped his arms around Raisin, his expression more peaceful than Darcy had ever seen him. She glanced at Xander, who was staring at his brother like he was someone he hadn't seen in a damn long time, his eyes suspiciously shiny.

Darcy was having the same problem. "I've got a fifty-pound bag of food in my trunk and other supplies," she said. "Like her other food and water bowls and a doggie bed. Be good to her." She turned and walked to her car, with Xander following.

He began to unload the stuff for her but then stopped and looked into her eyes. "You love me?"

"You know I do," she said.

"But you're not *in* love with me."

She met his gaze head-on. She was done with battling the truth, done battling *period*. "I wanted to be," she said quietly. "Do I get

338

points for that?"

He stared at her for a beat, stone-faced. Unmoving. Giving nothing away. "I hate this."

Her heart squeezed at the pain on his face. "Xander —"

"I've loved you for fucking ever, you know that."

He wasn't going to make this easy. She'd known that. But she could make him understand, she *needed* to make him understand, because he meant far too much to her for there to be any other option. She'd just explain exactly how much he meant to her, how important he was to her, and he'd be okay. *They'd* be okay. "I know you've felt things for me," she said carefully. "But I wasn't ready —"

"No," he interrupted grimly. "You weren't. Not before the accident. And not after. I knew that. But I thought you'd get there someday, so I waited. I've been waiting all year, Darcy."

"Xander," she breathed, her heart hurting as much if not more than her leg now. "I never asked you to wait —"

"But you didn't cut me loose, either," he said, pointing at her. "You kept me on the hook —"

"No. Oh hell no, you don't get to say

that." She'd found her own mad and frustration to match his and slapped aside his finger, jabbing her own into his chest. "I told you from the start that we were just friends. I told you that being friends was all I had to offer you. And you're my *best* friend, Xander." Her voice shook. "You're —"

"What changed?" he demanded. "Huh? Tell me, Darcy, what changed that suddenly you're so willing to go there with AJ and not me."

"I'm not going to go there with AJ."

"But you want to."

The shocking truth of that shut her up. So did the pain in his voice. And for the first time she became afraid that she wasn't going to be able to fix this at all, which she couldn't even think about. She didn't want to lose him. Couldn't lose him.

Xander stared at her and then shoved his fingers into his hair and turned away. "Jesus, Darcy. It's true. *Shit.* You know what? The hell with this. I'm over it and the way you hurt everyone you claim to love. The hell with you."

She could scarcely breathe as every single word he'd uttered stabbed her in the gut and heart. "Xander —"

"I don't need you, Darcy. We're done."

"No." She reached out for him. "Xander, no —"

But he threw her hand off, grabbed all of Raisin's supplies, and strode off, leaving her standing there in the parking lot feeling like she'd just been run over.

He'd walked away from her, left her without even looking back, like it had been the easiest thing in the world to do. She'd had it happen before, of course, and she should've been used to it, but he was her best friend and he was gone.

She closed the trunk and then leaned on it until she felt a set of eyes on her.

Tyson sat in his chair at the side of the building, watching her, Raisin at his side.

Darcy blew out a sigh and walked over to him. "If you've got something to add to that, tell me now."

He shook his head. "You're not going to cry, are you?" he asked with the look of a man facing the gallows.

She let out a half laugh, half sob. "I don't cry," she said, but indeed the tears were threatening, blocking her windpipe, sitting on her chest like a two-ton elephant.

Tyson blew out a breath but his eyes were solemn. "Listen, I love the guy," he said. "But he's wrong, dead wrong. He does need you."

But Xander hadn't been wrong at all. She'd been a bad friend to him. She'd deserved everything he'd said, she knew it.

"Also," Tyson said, "I'm sorry for all the shitty things I've said about you."

"I . . . didn't hear you say any shitty things."

"That's because I said them behind your back." Even as he spoke, he reached down for Raisin, pulling her into his lap again, stroking her soft fur.

Raisin stared up at him in adoration. Darcy's heart squeezed and she gave the dog a hug good-bye, cupping her face. "Watch after these two," she said softly. "They mean everything to me."

Raisin panted her agreement, her eyes making the promise.

"Wait," Tyson said to her as she got into her car. "What do I owe you? For all the supplies?"

"Don't skip any more therapy or PT appointments. Do it for Raisin," she said. "She needs you. And maybe be nicer to your brother once in a while."

"So you're really not going to sleep with him?" Tyson asked.

She sighed. "I never was."

"How about me? You ever going to sleep with me?"

She caught the teasing light in his gaze and knew he wanted a smile. She tried but it fell a little short of the mark. "Not even if hell froze over."

He nodded. "I'm sorry we're both such dicks."

Darcy shrugged like it didn't matter, but it did matter. And on top of that, it was getting hard to breathe. An inch from meltdown . . . "I've gotta go," she managed.

Tyson nodded, and then he and Raisin rolled away.

Darcy turned and found AJ watching. Waiting. She had no idea how much he'd seen or heard but given the look in his eyes, it was much more than she'd have liked. "Don't even think about asking me if I'm okay."

"Can I ask if you want to talk about it?"

"No." She didn't want to talk. Not now. Not ever. Ordering her legs to stop shaking and her throat to stop burning, she yanked open her car door. "Gotta go."

TWENTY-FIVE

AJ watched Darcy drive off before he turned and walked through the gym to find Xander, where he was now pumping iron like he had a lot of aggression to work out.

The place had emptied and Xander was the only one there. He met AJ's gaze in the mirror and let the weights drop. "What do you want?"

"You're kidding, right?"

Xander stilled, then shook his head. "We're not doing this, no fucking way."

"You hurt her," AJ said. "On purpose."

"Yeah? Well, she hurt me, too. Now we're even."

"Not even close," AJ said. "Not only did you just jump all over her shit to punish her for not feeling the way you wanted her to, then you went for the jugular and ripped your friendship out from beneath her when you know exactly how much it — *you* — mean to her."

"You eavesdropped?"

"Hard not to, you were yelling."

Xander stood up and made a move to go. "We're not discussing this."

AJ blocked his escape. "Try again."

Xander narrowed his eyes. "Get out of my way."

"You've been there for Darcy through a helluva lot," AJ said. "And you've let her be there for you, and now suddenly you decide to change the rules and betray her when she needs you the most?" He shook his head. "That's bullshit, Xander. Complete bullshit."

"Betray her? I didn't betray her," Xander exploded. "She — She . . ."

"What?" AJ asked. "Told you the truth? Gave you everything she had to give?"

Xander opened his mouth but AJ wasn't done. "Don't even try to justify it. Not to me. I know what happened, Xander. And hell, I even understand it. I understand you. But she doesn't. You know how she grew up, you know how hard it is for her to let people care about her. You claimed to love her but then you screwed with her head and her heart. You gave her your feelings and then added on conditions for those feelings. Even worse, you basically threw her feelings back in her face, pretty much saying she

345

had to love you the way you wanted her to or forget it. What the fuck kind of love is that, Xander?"

In answer, Xander led with his fist. AJ ducked but still got clipped on the jaw. Xander was coming in for punch number two when AJ clocked him.

Xander landed on the mat, hard.

Ariana came running out from the offices, eyes wide with shock. "What in the —" She dropped to her knees at Xander's side and then looked up to AJ. "What did you do?"

When he didn't answer her, she whirled back to Xander, running her hands over him. "Where are you hurt?"

"I'm not." Xander staggered to his feet, holding his eye. "It's nothing."

Ariana rose as well, dividing a horrified look between the two. "You . . . fought? Here?"

"No," Xander said. "It was nothing."

Ariana stared at AJ, knowing he wouldn't lie to her. And he wouldn't. Instead he said nothing.

She blew out a sound of disgust. "You need to take this outside," she said as if she owned the place. "Your negative energy doesn't belong in here." She marched to the entrance, where there was a large drink machine. She pulled a dollar out of her pocket and fed it to the machine, getting a chilled bottle of water for her efforts.

This she brought to Xander. "For your eye," she said. "It's already getting black and blue from the fight you didn't have." She pressed the cold bottle to his face and Xander winced but took ahold of it.

"Thanks," he mumbled.

"You're welcome," she said tightly, very un-Ariana-like, and strode off, leaving the building, steam coming out of her ears.

In her wake, AJ carefully moved his jaw back and forth. Hurt like a bitch but it didn't feel broken.

Xander pulled the bottle away and gingerly touched his eye. "Jesus, you've got a right hook." He turned to make sure Ariana was gone before he spoke again, keeping his voice down as if he might be afraid of her. "And you can fuck off. You of all people don't get to say shit to me about how I treat Darcy, not when we both know which of the two of us is going to end up hurting her — and it isn't me."

And then he stalked out.

AJ locked up and left, too. He went home, where he tripped over Thor and Stark, both of whom had lots of bitching and complaining and caterwauling about how much he'd been gone lately. He showered and told himself he was going to fall into bed and sleep like the dead until dawn.

He did the shower part.

But then he stared at his big, comfy bed, not seeing that but the look of devastation on Darcy's face after Xander had gotten done with her. "Sorry," he told the cats, and grabbed his keys, heading out into the night.

He needed to see Darcy.

She'd come so far this past year, worked so damn hard. She'd fought her way back physically and mentally. She'd given everything she had to the jobs she'd taken on even though they weren't jobs of passion for her. She gave everything to the dogs she rescued, too, just as she gave everything to the few people she let into her life.

Even him.

She'd been there for him in Boise even when she hadn't wanted to be. He'd watched her work her way through the trust exercises with a surprising and touching honesty. Yes, she was still wild, untamable, unpredictable Darcy.

But she was no longer reckless.

Whether she knew it or not, she'd put herself out there, letting some roots take hold. She'd shown more courage in her little pinkie than most people had in their entire body.

He pulled up to the aging Victorian that she shared with Zoe and knocked on the door.

Zoe answered and sighed. "I heard about Xander."

For a beat AJ thought she meant the physical altercation they'd just had, but then he realized she was referring to Xander and Darcy's fight. "I was there," he told her. "Where is she?"

"Not here. She didn't tell me where she was going but I've been stalking her dot on my Find My Friends app. She's at the hot springs. I was just about to send Wyatt after her."

"I'll go."

Zoe looked at him for a long beat as if skeptical of AJ's intentions. "She's hurting."

"I know."

"I want to kick Xander's ass," she said.

"She wouldn't want you to."

Zoe blew out a breath. "He walked away from her — the very worst possible thing he could've done to her." She shook her head. "Promise me you won't do that."

"Never," he vowed.

This had her blinking. Then she narrowed her eyes. "Then why aren't you two together?"

It had all started out so clear to him

exactly why they weren't together, but somewhere along the way he'd forgotten. "It's complicated."

She rolled her eyes in a damn good imitation of Darcy herself. "You know what?" she asked. "I think you're afraid, even though you're the bravest person I know."

The bravest person she knew was almost rendered speechless. "It has nothing to do with being brave," he said. "It's about what's best for Darcy."

She looked baffled at this. "AJ, what could be better for her than you?"

AJ headed to the hot springs, a place Darcy sometimes went to in order to be alone.

But she'd had a lifetime of feeling alone, and he wasn't going to let her feel that way again.

He'd been out here at the hot springs with her before, as a part of her early therapy had involved swimming. They'd done that in a cove on the north side of the springs, protected by trees and rock caves.

Sure enough, her car was there. He parked his truck next to it and walked the quarter of a mile path to the springs.

Steam rose from the water into the night, making it look like another planet. Darcy was sitting on a rock staring up at the moon.

AJ could feel her loneliness from where he stood, and it killed him.

He'd told himself he wasn't interested in love but he'd been talking out his own ass. When it came to Darcy he was interested in everything, and he'd take whatever scraps she'd give him.

"Hey," he said quietly, not wanting to startle her. He had no idea if she'd reveal her emotions to him or not. Retreat or lash out, he never knew with her.

She let her hood fall back from her face, her expression revealing nothing.

Retreat then.

"What happened to your jaw?" she asked, voice quiet. "You've got a bruise."

"Nothing," he said. "It's nothing."

Her eyes showed concern for him but at his words, she turned back to the water. "You were right about something," she said quietly, radiating sadness.

"What's that?"

"I'm good at pushing people away."

He hated that he'd ever said such a thing to her. Hated even more that she believed it. "Darcy —"

"No." She stood, climbed off the rock, and stepped to the water's edge, all without looking at him. "I'm not in the mood to talk. I'm going for a moonlight swim."

"The air's too cold."

"The water will keep me warm." She kicked off her battered sneakers.

"Darcy —"

She stepped into the springs and the water swirled around her ankles. "Mmm, perfect." She stepped out a little bit farther, hands on her hips, in a big old coat that, if AJ wasn't mistaken, was a hand-me-down from Wyatt.

"Xander was out of line," he said. "You don't hurt everyone you love."

"Don't I? Seems like something I'm really good at." She slid out of the coat and tossed it at his feet. Beneath she was in jeans and a sweatshirt. She stripped off both, leaving her in a Rolling Stones tank that had been washed so many times it was sheer, and a pair of pale blue panties so teeny tiny they barely covered her.

Hottest thing he'd ever seen.

Ever.

While he went from zero to sixty in the blink of an eye, he tried to speak normally even though he was suffering severe blood loss to the brain. "This is a bad idea."

"Yes." She tugged an elastic hair band from around her wrist and, reaching up, quickly and easily contained her hair in a knot on top of her head. "I'm often one big, bad idea."

"No, you're not."

"I'm glad you feel that way." And then she pulled off her top. She'd slid her thumbs into the sides of her undies to tug them down when he strode forward and wrapped his hands around her wrist. "Darcy —"

"If you don't want this," she said, "if you don't want me, I *will* hurt you."

He took one of her hands and pressed it against his erection. "Does that feel like I don't want you?"

Humming her approval low in her throat, she let her fingers do the talking, stroking the length of him until the denim nearly cut off his circulation. "How long have you been in this condition?" she asked.

"Around you, I'm always in this condition."

Slowly she shook her head. Denial, because she didn't believe, which was his own fault. He'd fought so that she wouldn't see it. Not his smartest move.

"We going skinny-dipping, Darcy?"

"I'm not sure there's a 'we.' "

He wasn't sure, either, but he knew he wanted there to be. "Try me."

She glanced at him, let her gaze run over him. "You're wearing too many clothes to go skinny-dipping."

He yanked his sweatshirt over his head and tossed it to the shore. Then he kicked off his shoes and socks and shoved down his jeans, leaving him in knit boxers that did nothing at all to hide how much he wanted her.

She stared into his eyes for a long beat and then took a good long look at him in clear appreciation. She smiled, but instead of stepping close, she took a big step back into the water.

And then another.

And then she turned and dove in.

Holy shit. He moved to the edge and stared at where she'd disappeared. One. Two . . . "Goddamnit," he said, and dove in after her.

He caught her around the middle and hauled them both above the surface. It was deep enough here that he had to work to keep afloat. To keep them *both* afloat because she was completely wrapped around him, not helping at all. "You're as crazy as I am," she said, sounding as if she liked that, a lot.

"You've discovered my secret," he managed. "And Jesus, the air's fucking cold."

"You did tell me to ice. I'll use the air."

"Yeah, I told *you* to ice. *I* didn't need to ice."

Her hands slid down his chest and lower, cupping him in her hands. "Aw," she murmured. "Is he going to shrink now?"

"Not with your hands on him."

She gave him a stroke just the way he liked it. "You have my full attention," he said.

"I have this fantasy."

"Okay, now you really have my full attention."

"I fantasize about doing it in the rain," she said, her hands still on him, making it all but impossible to think.

"But this, in the springs," she said, "would be almost as good."

He was starting to get a little breathless, both holding on to her and having to kick to keep them both above water, and then there were her very busy, very naughty hands shoving down his underwear.

"Enjoying yourself?" he asked.

Her eyes were still solemn, still radiating her sadness, but she flashed him a small smile that stopped his heart. "Very much," she said, her hands full of him.

Very full.

"Paybacks are a bitch," he managed.

"Promises, promises." She gave him a nudge and then another, back toward shore. When the water hit his calves, she fought out of his hold and pushed him again. He went down to his ass and she dropped to her knees.

And then she slid between his legs.

The moonlight made her naked form glow like some ethereal being. He could see her image in the water behind her and it was beyond carnal. "Darcy —"

"Shh," she whispered, her hair teasing his abs and thighs as she bent low and slowly dragged hot, openmouthed kisses over chilled skin. Then she ran her tongue up the underside of his length.

He swore, and then again when she sucked him into her mouth.

Barely coherent, things got a little hazy, and in an embarrassingly short amount of time he tightened his grip on her hair to pull her away from him before he exploded. "You've got to stop —"

She didn't. Instead she fought his hold and had her merry way with him.

"Darcy" — Christ, her mouth — "if you keep that up I'm going to — Oh fuck. I'm going to come."

She kept at it and his world spiraled out of control. Somewhere in the midst of the sheer, heart-stopping pleasure, one thing became crystal clear to him. Whatever the hell this was, whatever they managed to give to each other — she owned him.

When he firmly blinked his way back to consciousness, he was flat on his back, half in the water and half out, staring up at the stars and the moon. He had no idea if he was hot or cold or dead or alive.

And then a lovely face suddenly hovered above his, with hair rioting around her face.

"You alive?" she asked.

"I don't know. I can't feel my extremities." He sat up. "But I can feel the rock jabbing me in the ass, so yeah, I must be alive."

She was sitting at his hip wearing nothing but her soaked panties and looking pretty damn smug. "Stand up," he said.

She got to her feet.

Reaching up, he hooked his fingers in the wet cotton and slowly pulled them down, settling on his knees in front of her. He let the material pool at her ankles and slid his hands up the backs of her thighs. "Spread your legs," he said.

She kicked off her panties and did as he asked.

And he just about died and went to heaven. "Damn," he managed, "you are the most beautiful thing I've ever seen."

She shifted as if uncomfortable with the praise. "I don't need fancy words, AJ."

"How about the truth, then? You are

beautiful. And something else — you're not alone. You don't ever have to be alone. Because I'm . . ." Leaning in, he pressed his mouth against a hipbone. ". . . right . . ." And then her other hipbone. ". . . here." He trailed wet, openmouthed kisses across the top of her thighs, stopping to pay special attention in between them. "I came here for you, Darcy. I'll always come for you."

She slid her fingers into his hair and whimpered.

"Say you know it." He cupped her ass and squeezed her cheeks in his palms, tracing his tongue over her hot, wet center. When she didn't speak, he pulled back.

"You came for me," she gasped.

"Yes. And now you're going to come for me."

And not three minutes later his prophetic words became fact as she shuddered in orgasm, panting his name, lost to everything but him.

His chest tightened with satisfaction and so much more he almost couldn't breathe with it as he pulled her down to straddle him, gripping her hips as he pushed upward, seating himself deep inside her, so deep.

She cried out and bent over him, giving him her mouth, her body, and — he hoped — her heart and soul.

Because she certainly was the keeper of his.

TWENTY-SIX

Darcy opened her eyes at the sound of rain beating on her windows — Wait. Not her windows. She was in AJ's bed, alone. She stretched and peered at the clock on his nightstand.

Seven thirty.

Yesterday came back to her in a wave. The fight with Xander and him walking out of her life, which made her heart hurt, physically hurt. She'd tried calling him before she'd gone to the hot springs but he hadn't answered her call. Or her texts. Or her e-mails.

Problem was, she was having a hard time picturing her world without him in it.

Dammit, Xander.

But last night AJ had come for her, needing to see if she was okay. He'd made her okay just by being there. Sure, the skinny-dipping had helped, and then . . . yeah. The *and then* had been pretty fantastic, too.

360

But all she'd needed was him, and that . . . that was the crazy part. Everything about him put her entirely out of her comfort zone.

And yet she couldn't imagine going back to how things had been BB — before Boise.

He'd brought her here afterward. He'd again tried to talk to her about Xander but she'd declined. She didn't know how to talk about Xander.

But then she and AJ had climbed into his big bed and had instead used their time wisely, and she'd fallen asleep on him and slept the night through.

Something that was becoming a habit with him.

There was yet another note pinned to the pillow.

HAD TO GO IN EARLY. TRENT AND SUMMER ARE SHOWING UP TODAY TO MAKE THE DEAL HAPPEN. SEE YOU AT WORK. LOVE, AJ.

Right, today was the big day. She was scheduled to work at the Wellness Center at nine and — Her heart skidded to a stop.
Love, AJ.
What was with the *Love, AJ?*
She stared at the two words once again

scrawled in his usual messy block writing and told herself for the second time that it was nothing more than a figure of speech.

She believed he felt a great deal for her. And she felt a great deal for him as well. It didn't matter whether she was hurting or scared or just in general losing her collective shit, it was AJ she yearned for. AJ's arms around her. AJ's low voice in her ear, steadying her. AJ's belief in her.

He always seemed to just accept her as she was. He wasn't going to ever try to change her. Or send her away when she didn't react as he wanted. He wasn't going to turn his back on her.

Reject her.

It was both wondrous and empowering knowing that he stood at her back no matter what.

Smiling, she tossed back the covers and — in her mind — she leapt to her feet. In reality, she got out of bed like an old lady and carefully stretched to avoid a cramp. "*Really* over that," she said.

She gave herself three minutes in the hot water with AJ's soap.

She could've taken an hour.

Especially if he'd been in here with her. He had a way of making her feel like the most beautiful woman in the world, exquisitely female and desirable and . . . beautiful. With nothing more than a look or a few words, he could take away all her self-doubt in her mind and make her feel good about herself.

But there was something more going on here, something far bigger. For as long as she could remember she'd traveled around experiencing things most people never got to. It had been great, but she'd never really felt entirely secure or particularly safe, not like she did here. With AJ. She hadn't even realized she'd needed to feel either of those things.

"You've got it bad," she muttered, and dried off with his towel, getting another thrill because it was still damp from his body.

The rain had stopped when she walked into the wellness center.

Ariana stood behind the desk looking over her schedule for the day. She glanced over at Darcy, went still for a beat, and then nodded.

"What?"

"It agrees with you."

"What does?"

"Love."

Darcy waited for the panic to hit, but it didn't. "Where is he?"

"In his office. He's —"

"Getting ready for a meeting," Darcy said, heading down the hallway. "I know, thanks." She wanted to catch him alone for a minute before Trent and Summer arrived. Well, okay, she wanted to throw herself at him and kiss him. And then she wanted to tell him that she loved him, too. And then . . . She glanced at her phone, wondering if they had time to pull an Adam and Holly and steal a few moments in a closet —

"So where's your lovely girlfriend?" a woman's voice asked from inside AJ's office. "Or maybe you've made Darcy your fiancée by now?"

Summer, Darcy realized. She and Trent must've already arrived. She couldn't see through the big glass window that opened from AJ's office to the gym because his shutters were closed.

"Trust me." This was Trent. "Making that woman your wife would be the best thing you could ever do for yourself."

Darcy felt the warmth of pleasure at his words. They thought she'd be good for AJ. And she *was,* she told herself. She wasn't like Kayla. She wasn't lost in her own head, unable to love. Not anymore. She made him laugh, made him happy. And damn, that realization felt good. So good.

364

Summer hummed her agreement with Trent. "That's because *I'm* the best thing that ever happened to *you,*" she said.

"You absolutely are," Trent agreed. "AJ, we've had many talks about you. And Darcy, too. You should know, it was mostly your lovely other half that actually sealed the deal for you. It's one thing to know that you're a great physical therapist and philanthropist, but it's another to learn you're a good enough man to catch and hold on to a woman like that. I hope she's around today, I'd like to see her after we get our financial details handled. I want to thank her again for talking to Summer, for being such an important part of our decision."

Darcy glowed a little bit more and took a step to make her presence known but just then AJ spoke and she stopped short.

"I'm glad you were so impressed by her," he said. "She impresses the hell out of me daily. But I've got to be honest with you. We're not a couple, at least not how you think."

Darcy couldn't move. She was rooted to the spot.

"I didn't realize your decision hinged on her," AJ went on. "The truth is, when you saw us in Boise, Darcy was there as a job, as a favor to me."

There was a beat of shocked silence, both in the office and in Darcy's heart.

"But, AJ, I saw you two," Summer said. "I saw how you looked at each other. It was so natural, like it was meant to be."

"I'm sorry," AJ said. "The truth is she wasn't even the patient I wanted you to meet."

Darcy staggered back a step on that one, like he'd slapped her in the face. And though he was simply telling the truth, it felt like a shocking, slicing rejection, the second in as many days. And she actually looked down at herself, because surely with this much pain she was bleeding out all over the floor.

Nope. No blood. She wasn't dying. Yay.

So many things burst through her. Anger. Sadness. Humiliation. All of them racing for the lead.

Anger won.

Before she'd even realized she'd moved, she was on the go, practically running back down the hallway to the front.

Ariana looked up and frowned. "You okay?"

No. No, she wasn't even in the vicinity of okay. She swiped at her eyes, startled to realize she was crying.

You hurt everyone you claim to love,

Xander had said.

It's not what you think between us, AJ had said. She was there as a job . . . She wasn't even the patient I wanted you to meet . . .

Darcy wanted to curl into a ball. She wanted to throw something. "I'm . . ." Her phone rang and she reached for it without thinking.

"Got a dog situation," Johnny said in her ear.

She swiped the last of the tears from her face. That was it, she was not going to shed another single one. She'd been disappointed before, hurt before. She knew how to pick herself up and keep going, it was what she did.

She'd simply do it again.

No one would ever see how AJ's words had affected her. Especially AJ himself. She covered the mouthpiece on her phone and said to Ariana, "I don't feel well." Understatement of the year. "I need a minute and some fresh air."

"Take all the time you need," Ariana said. "I can cover your shift if you need."

That she was being so nice only brought Darcy closer to the brink. "Thanks," she managed and walked outside.

"Define situation," she said to Johnny.

"Four-year-old yellow Lab service dog,"

he said. "His owner went senile and they removed the dog from the home. Two attempts at reassigning him have failed. He's outta here unless you want him."

"Yes," she said immediately, her heart breaking, although she didn't know if it was for herself or for the dog. The fact was that some dogs just couldn't be reassigned as a full-fledged service dog. But she'd bet her last dollar that the Lab would still make a most excellent companion. And if not, she'd find a home for him anyway. "I can come after work —"

"Now or never, sweetheart."

"I can't get a ride out there until after work," she said, knowing everyone in her world was also working today.

"Not my problem," Johnny said. "I'll be here for another forty minutes. If you don't get here before I leave, he's going to the pound."

"You're such an asshole."

"Of course I am. What does that have to do with anything?"

She shook her head. "I have to work, Johnny."

"Well, tell them you're going to be late. The dog's a purebred. He's four hundred bucks."

She grounded her back teeth to powder.

"One hundred."

"Three. And that's final," he said, voice hard and cold. "Forty minutes, Darcy."

And then he disconnected.

"Dammit!" Zoe was on a flight. Wyatt was at work, and at this time of day he'd be in surgeries.

God, she missed Xander, and not just because he might have driven her but because she missed *him*. But hell if she'd beg him to want her in his life.

She tried Adam but he was off the grid.

Crap. Okay, first thing's first. She texted Ariana:

Sorry but I'm going to take you up on your offer if that's okay. Not feeling well. Will be back in a few hours, promise.

Then she got into her car and headed out. She made it all the way to the turnoff to get onto the highway and . . . stopped.

Stared at the onramp.

"You've got this," she whispered. "You're going to make like a Nike commercial and just do it." She put her foot to the accelerator and . . . drove right past the onramp.

She turned around and tried again.

Twice.

On the third pass she slowed to a crawl,

her heart pounding in her throat. Do it, just do it —

Beepbeepbeep came the horn of some crazy person up on her tail. They whipped around, came up even with her and flipped her off, and roared onto the highway.

"Hey!" she yelled after him, sticking her head out the window to return the gesture.

"Excuse me, miss, are you having trouble?"

Darcy turned her head and found an ancient, beat-up truck at her side, windows down, the driver somewhere between ninety and infinity, smiling at her kindly.

"No," she said. "I'm fine."

"Don't let anyone rush you, Sweet Cheeks," he said, and then got onto the highway going *maybe* twenty-five miles an hour.

She laughed at herself — which was better than crying — and made one last attempt. She was sweating buckets and her heart was pounding so loud in her ears she couldn't hear the radio, but she made the turn and got on the damn highway.

"Oh shit." She gulped air. "Okay. Well, I'm on. I'm on the highway."

She had no idea who she was talking to. In any case, she was shaking, and because she was going twenty miles an hour below the speed limit, she also got herself honked at a few more times.

"It's the skinny pedal on the right," some asshole in a Lexus yelled at her.

She would have flipped him off, too, but needed both hands to white-knuckle the wheel. Sucking in a breath, she told herself to think of the dog she was saving. That was the goal. She was a big girl and it had been eleven months and she could do this. It wasn't nighttime and it wasn't storming. The rain hadn't started up again. Everything was *entirely* different than that night, she assured herself.

Over and over.

And then a semitruck came up on her left to pass. Note to self: If a semi can pass you, you're going too slow.

She didn't care. She couldn't bring herself to speed up.

And it was too late anyway. The trucker was hauling a load of live turkeys, and while she stared at them, he honked his displeasure of her speed. She took her eyes off the turkeys to glance at him and her car seemed to catch in his draft.

She tried to steer out of it but she couldn't. In panic, she jerked the wheel to the right.

Her two right tires got caught in a rut on

the side of the road and for a single, terrifying second, she wasn't in control of the car. She heard a horrified cry — her own, she realized — and hit the brakes. But it was too late, her car hydroplaned on the still-wet highway.

"Steer into the swerve!" she yelled at herself. "Steer into the swerve!"

So she steered into the swerve. And right into the ditch, where her front end nose-dived and hit the embankment hard.

The airbag deployed and punched her in the face.

She came to fighting the now deflating airbag. When she managed to get out of the car, she shook her head. Her vision was blurry and when she tried to blink past that, she realized her face was wet. Oh hell no. She was *not* crying again. But when she swiped an arm over her face, she realized that was true. She wasn't crying.

She was bleeding.

Call for help. That's what she needed to do.

Her head hurt as she staggered around her car to the passenger side to look for her purse. She found it on the floor, contents scattered. She shuffled through a dog leash, a bottle of aspirin, another of her prescription meds that she still hadn't touched, a

tampon, her favorite berry lip gloss —
There. There was her phone, way beneath
the seat, and by the time she straightened,
little black dots danced across her vision.

Sitting down hard, blinking past the dots,
she stared at her car. Worried about all the
movies she'd seen where cars exploded after
impact, she moved to what she thought
might be a safe distance and sat on a rock
to catch her breath.

Very few cars went by. None stopped. Just
as well, as she'd also seen a lot of movies
where the lone girl on the side of the road
meets up with a psycho dude with a ma-
chete.

Second note to self: Stop watching scary
movies.

She needed to call for roadside assistance
in a minute and get towed out of the ditch.

And maybe the guy would also tow her
straight to a new life . . .

TWENTY-SEVEN

AJ was still talking with Trent and Summer about the terms of their partnership when Ariana texted:

Can you come up here a minute?

AJ stood up from his desk. "Excuse me, I'll be right back."

Trent looked at his watch. "We've got a lunch meeting with some business associates who might be interested in giving grants as well. Time is money, AJ."

"I realize that. I only need a minute." He went out to the front desk and found Ariana looking harried. She was on the phone and the computer, and two people were waiting to talk to her. "Where's Darcy?" he asked.

She covered the mouthpiece on the phone. "Sick."

AJ helped the two people waiting at the counter and then waited for Ariana to get off the phone. "She's sick?"

She shrugged. "She was here for a few minutes. She went down the hall and then came back looking ill, saying she needed a minute. I offered to take her shift and she said she'd be back in a few hours. You screw something up?"

"I didn't even see her."

"Well, she definitely went down there."

AJ turned and looked at the hallway as if that was going to help him.

Ariana sighed. "The two of you are driving me to chocolate." She yanked open a drawer and pulled out a candy bar. "You see this? I stole it from Darcy's stash. Like, seriously, stole it. And I think it's messing with my karma, so you need to get this right with her so I can get back to my zen."

Trent strode up, looking pissed. "AJ, we need to talk."

"Yes, in a minute." Unable to set aside his bad feeling on this, AJ pulled out his cell and called Darcy. She picked up on the third ring but didn't speak.

He frowned. "Darcy?"

"Yeah."

He could barely hear her so he turned up the volume as far as it would go. "You okay?"

There was a long pause. "I called in sick,"

she finally said.

"I know. Do you need anything?"

"No thanks. I'll be fine."

And then she disconnected.

AJ frowned and stared at his phone. She hadn't sounded fine. She'd sounded . . . upset.

The last he knew, she'd been in his bed practically purring. And not sick.

What was he missing?

He started with what he knew. He knew he'd slept with her last night, and though she hadn't wanted to talk about Xander, they'd managed to exhaust each other out pretty good. He'd left her with a smile on her face, he knew that much. She'd come to work. She'd gone down the hallway to see him but hadn't. And then she'd left sick.

Why? What could have happened? Maybe the Xander thing had hit her this morning harder than yesterday. He called her back but this time she sent him right to voice mail, and a bad feeling settled in his gut.

"I'm thinking if you're having to run your own front desk," Trent said, "I misjudged your business prowess."

AJ turned to him. "I've got no problem taking a turn up front when I'm needed. But that's not what this is." He called Darcy's house line with both Ariana and

Trent staring at him; one with worry and the other with irritation.

No answer.

"You think there's a problem?" Ariana asked.

"I don't know." AJ called Wyatt next. "Where's Darcy?" he asked when Wyatt picked up.

Wyatt paused. "Hang on a sec."

AJ could hear him giving directions on how to catch something coming out of a birth canal. Clearly the guy was hands deep, literally, at Belle Haven.

Then he was back. "What's the matter?"

"I don't know," AJ said. "Probably nothing. You know where she is?"

"She isn't there?"

"She left. Said she was sick."

"What am I missing?" Wyatt asked.

"I wish I knew."

Another pause. "Is this thing going to end badly?" Wyatt finally asked, sounding pained. "And before you answer, you should know, you're like a brother to me, but if this goes south and she gets hurt, I'm going to kick your ass into next week."

"Okay, great, thanks for the help," AJ said and disconnected. Ignoring Trent's long, impatient sigh, he tried Zoe. He got no answer, which meant she was probably in the air. Just as well. Wyatt had just threatened to beat the shit out of him but Zoe wouldn't give him any warning at all; she'd cut off his nuts, feed them to the squirrels, and then let him bleed out slowly.

He stared at his phone.

"What now?" Ariana asked.

AJ accessed his contacts and scrolled down to the X's.

Ariana blew out a breath. "Maybe I should clear your schedule for an hour."

"*I'm* on his schedule," Trent said. "And I came all the way from Boise for this. I thought you were serious about my offer, AJ."

"I am," AJ said. "But not as serious as I am about making sure Darcy is okay. If you've got a problem with that, you're free to go. I understand the consequences but I have to do this."

Ariana sucked in a breath.

Temper lit in Trent's eyes. Clearly he wasn't a man used to waiting on others. "If I leave, that's it," he said. "I won't be kept waiting."

"Then it's best if you leave," AJ said without hesitation.

Trent met his gaze, swore, and then turned on his heel and headed back down the hallway, presumably to get Summer.

"Oh, AJ," Ariana whispered as he hit Xander's contact.

"What the fuck do you want?" Xander said in lieu of greeting. "I'm in the middle of a tat."

"You with her?" AJ asked, watching as Trent led Summer out the front door and out of his life without looking back.

"You mean Darcy?" Xander asked.

"No, the fucking Tooth Fairy."

There was a beat of dead air. "Huh," Xander said slowly. "This doesn't make sense."

"What doesn't?"

"My Find My Friends app says she's out on Highway 64, fifteen miles from town. Shit. She must be heading to Johnny's for another dog. Wait — No, her dot is still. She's not moving. Why is she on the highway not moving?"

Any answer AJ could come up with made his gut hurt like hell. He disconnected from Xander and strode out of the wellness center. On a good day with no traffic the trip would've taken him twenty minutes.

He made it in ten.

She'd driven into a ditch, and at the sight of her piece-of-shit car leaning at an angle with its two right wheels buried into the edge of the muddy ditch, his heart just about stopped.

He threw his truck into park and ran toward the car, having to drop to his knees to peek into the passenger window. The driver-side airbag had deployed. It had mostly deflated but the blood spatter had his heart kicking back into gear. "Darcy!"

"Here."

Still on his knees in the mud, he whipped around and found her sitting on a rock about ten yards away. Pale as a ghost, a gash over her left eye, she was as still as the stone beneath her, as if it hurt to move even a single inch.

At her side in an instant, he crouched and ran his hands carefully down her arms and legs, searching for broken bones.

"I'm not hurt," she said.

Since she had blood running down one side of her face, he ignored her assessment, until with a sound of annoyance she pushed his hands away. Conceding the body search, he checked her pulse, not liking how fast she was breathing.

"I'm fine," she gasped, not looking anywhere even in the vicinity of fine.

"You're starting to hyperventilate and your pulse is way too high," he said. "It's a miracle you're even conscious."

She smiled grimly. "I'm a very determined

individual when I want to be."

"Gee, that's brand-new information about you." He pulled out his phone.

"No!" she said. "*No* ambulance."

"Darcy —"

Her eyes flashed. "I mean it, AJ."

"I've got to at least call Kel and have your car taken care of."

She tried to stare him down, but she clearly had a hell of a headache because she reached up to hold on to her head like she was trying to keep it on her shoulders. "I want you to go away," she said.

Yeah, he was getting that loud and clear.

"Actually," she said. "I want to tell you where to go. Which is straight to hell."

He was getting that, too. What he wasn't getting was why. Maybe Xander hurting her had made her decide to hate all men? Which, with Darcy, was entirely likely. He called Kel while she glared at him, and then he reached out to brush the hair from her face, wanting to better see her injury.

She smacked his hand away twice but he had grim determination on his side. She had an inch-long gash along with a nice goose egg. "This needs to be checked out."

"No hospital," she repeated, her voice even shakier now. "I've got a dog to rescue."

"We'll get the dog after we get you

checked out, I promise," he said.

"You don't want to know what I think of you and your promises right now."

"Actually, I do. But my wants are going to have to wait until you're not bleeding everywhere." Very carefully he went to pull her into his lap, but she resisted.

"Don't touch me."

He ignored that and tried again, as she was weaving like she might fall over. "Darcy," he said gently. "It's going to be okay."

"No." She swallowed hard. "It's not." Her tone said nothing was ever going to be okay again. Then she shocked the hell out of him by bursting into gut-wrenching tears like her heart had been utterly decimated.

Feeling his own heart crack in two, he gathered her in as carefully as he could and held on to her as she sobbed all over him. He was pretty sure she'd lost a gallon of fluids and also that she'd just wiped her nose on his shirt when she finally lifted her face, narrowing her eyes at the sheriff SUV coming down the highway toward them, followed by a tow truck.

"Kel's going to take care of your car," AJ told her. "I'm going to take care of you." He lifted her chin. "And after that, we're going to talk."

"No, we're not."

"Is this about what happened with Xander?" he asked.

"No."

"Then talk to me."

"Right," she said. "Because *that* always works out so well for us."

He studied her a minute. "It would if you'd tell me what's really going on here."

"No need," she said. "I've got it all figured out now."

"Care to share with the class?"

"The 'Love, AJ' thing that you do on your notes," she said. "It confused me at first, but I get it. They're just words, like . . . 'have a nice day.' "

What the hell? It took him a minute to figure out what she was even talking about, but once he did he felt like a first-class ass for not making sure she'd understood. "Those aren't just words," he said. "Not to me."

The temper and pain in her gaze was shoved aside to make room for wary uncertainty.

"Darcy," he said slowly, willing her to hear him. "When I say 'I love you,' it means I love who you are. I love what you do, how you live your life, your incredible passion and your strength. It means I've seen the best and worst of you, that I know who you are down to the bone and there's nothing — *nothing* — you could do or say to change how I feel about you. I love you, Darcy. Just the way you are."

"And you love Wyatt and Zoe and Ariana and your patients and your dad and your grandparents . . ."

"Love doesn't really have a full-up capacity," he said. "You can spread it around, you know that, right?"

She hugged herself and looked away. "Yeah."

But he knew she didn't. Unfortunately he didn't get to press because Kel was there. And as AJ had done earlier, he crouched in front of Darcy.

"Hey, honey. Rough morning, huh?"

She managed for the sheriff what she hadn't for AJ — a smile. "I thought maybe you were bored and needed some field action," she said.

"Always a giver," Kel responded. "Listen, don't worry about your car, we'll get it home for you. I'll contact your brother and sister to meet you at the hospital."

"Not necessary," she said. "I'm not going to the hospital."

Kel removed his ball cap, scrubbed a hand over his closely cropped dark hair, and shoved the hat back on his head. "Do you remember that time you got into that bar fight with Zoe and I let you both go with just a warning and you said you owed me a favor?"

She narrowed her eyes. "That was like six years ago," she said.

"Yeah," he said. "Is there a statute of limitations on favors for friends?"

She blew out a sigh. "No."

He smiled. "So we understand each other."

"Fine," she said. "But I'm not going to the hospital with *him.*"

No question who the *him* was.

Kel looked at AJ and then met Darcy's gaze. "Patient's choice. I'll call an ambulance."

"Dammit." Darcy got to her feet and started toward AJ's truck, but she wobbled and stopped short, hands out in front of her like she was walking a tightrope.

"AJ," Kel warned.

"I've got her."

But when he got close, she pointed at him. "Don't you dare —"

Tired of this and over her anger that he didn't understand, AJ simply scooped her up and carried her to his truck.

She sighed and set her head very carefully

down onto his shoulder. "I really hate that it was you who came for me."

"Because . . . ?"

"You know damn well why."

"My mind-reading powers have never really kicked in."

She glared at him.

"Though I don't need to read your mind for that look."

"Just put me down, I'm fine."

"Not yet, you're not," he said, and set her down in the passenger seat of his truck, pulling the seat belt across her to buckle her in. "But you will be, in spite of yourself."

Kel stopped him before he could shut the door. He leaned in and looked at Darcy. "I want to hear you say you're good with going to the hospital with AJ."

Darcy's gaze slid to AJ and then back to Kel. "Feeling guilty for making me take a ride with the guy?" she asked.

"I don't do guilt. Yes or no, Darcy?"

She closed her eyes again and turned her head away from the both of them. "Yes."

TWENTY-EIGHT

Darcy drifted off with AJ's *I love you* on repeat in her mind. She knew better than to misread the words or let herself pretend even for a moment that it was the kind of love she felt for him and wanted him to feel in return.

Not even for a second . . .

She knew she'd have to get to a place where it was okay, and she would. But not today with a jackhammer in her head and a pity party for one on tap.

Maybe tomorrow.

She woke when she was lifted into a pair of strong arms and hugged tightly to a muscled chest. For a moment she let herself snuggle in close because when she was in AJ's arms like this, she felt as though nothing could touch or hurt her.

We're not a couple . . .

Dammit.

"Put me down," she said.

He didn't, and with her head still on his shoulder, eyes closed — trying not to toss her cookies — she felt the vibrations rumble in sync with his voice as he spoke to the nurse at the ER station.

Then they were on the move again. When he set her down, paper crinkled beneath her and the smell of disinfectant and the faint beeping of monitors made her sigh. "I'm fine," she said. "Why isn't anyone listening to me?" She opened her eyes to peer directly into AJ's concerned hazel ones.

"I always listen to you," he said. "I just don't always agree with you."

Too weak to argue anymore, she closed her eyes again. She kept them closed as they stitched her up, though she let up on her AJ moratorium enough to allow him to hold her hand through the process. For *his* sake, of course.

When the final verdict came — mild concussion — she was discharged with a prescription of pain meds that she turned down.

AJ was watching her, and she lifted a shoulder as if it was no big deal.

"Was that hard?" he asked.

"It's getting easier. This time I only want to cry a little."

He gathered her things but she shook her

head. "I don't want to go with you."

AJ made a point of looking around. He was the only one there.

She grated her teeth. "I'll wait for Wyatt or Zoe." To prove it, she texted them both, telling them whoever could get to her first, she'd appreciate a ride. Zoe was still on a flight and Wyatt in surgeries but one of them would be here soon, she was sure of it.

AJ had gone still, very still. When he spoke, his voice was dangerously low. "You'd rather wait in the hospital — which you hate being in — than get a ride home with me."

"That's right," she said as cool as she could manage. "Thanks for the rescue. And for all the good times, too."

"Thanks for the good times?" he repeated. "Are you kidding me? What the hell's going on?"

"What's going on is that I started to think maybe the whole love thing was a better deal than I'd given it credit for. But Xander walking away reminded me that I can't count on anyone but myself."

"Bullshit."

"It's not," she said. "Look at Kayla. You thought you could bet on her, but you couldn't. I'm more like her than you think. I'm not someone you can bet on either, trust me."

"I do trust you," he said. "Which is why this whole thing is utter bullshit."

"Knock knock," Emily said at the door. Wyatt's fiancée was wearing a white doctor's coat and a stethoscope with a tiny stuffed kangaroo on it. "I got here as fast as I could. Wyatt sent me. He's almost done with surgery and is meeting us at the house." She looked back and forth between Darcy and AJ. "Did I interrupt something?"

"Yes," AJ said.

"No," Darcy said at the same time, and moved to leave. "Get me out of this place."

"Darcy," AJ said quietly behind her. "We're not done."

But they were.

At home, Darcy peeled out of her sweater and kicked off her shoes on the way to her bed.

Oreo was already there, the bed hog.

"Move over," she told him.

He didn't.

She simply crawled onto the bed next to him, set her head by his big fat one on the pillow, and accepted a face lick from chin to forehead. "Thanks," she whispered.

Oreo sniffed at her stitches.

"You're a good boy. You're the best boy, the best in the whole wide world."

She got another lick for that compliment, and then she crashed. She woke God knew how much later when Wyatt sat on the bed.

"Name and serial number," he said.

"Go away."

"Nice to meet you, Ms. Go Away. I'm here to make sure your brain isn't set to shuffle. Recite the alphabet, please."

"B-I-T-E and M-E," she spelled out.

"Sorry, not even close to correct."

She flipped him off and he nodded. "Getting closer."

With a groan she covered her head with her pillow. "Seriously? Go away."

He pulled the pillow off. "Bitchy," he noted. "So you *are* okay."

It was his tone that reached her. "More okay than you," she said, and relented. He was in scrubs, which meant he'd come straight from work. She squeezed his hand. "You can stop worrying about me."

"Sure I can. Any second now," he said dryly, but his eyes were dark and serious. "You took another five years off my life."

"I'm sorry. I was trying to be independent. You know, like I used to be, in the old days?"

He laughed softly at that and his face cleared of a lot of the stress. "And just like the old days, your crazy streak is still intact."

"Hey," she said. "Independent, not crazy."

"In this case, same thing. Now tell me why you were trying to go it alone? Why do you still think you have to?"

"I knew you were busy at work."

"If you'd called and said you needed me, I'd have been there." Temper flashed in his eyes. "*Anyone* would've been there. I get that a lot of you not believing it is on our parents, but at some point you've gotta open your eyes, Darcy, and realize that pushing away everyone who cares about you on the off chance they might hurt you is stupid and selfish."

"Selfish," she repeated slowly, working her way up to her own mad. Which hurt her mother-effing head, thank you very much. "How in the hell is me trying to figure out my own shit without bothering anyone selfish?" she asked.

"Because you don't *have* to fucking figure it out on your own! We're a fucking family."

Wyatt rarely swore and usually only if sorely provoked. But that's what Darcy did best, provoke. And she'd always been pretty proud of that fact, too, but at the moment she felt nothing but ashamed of it. "I know, Wy-Ty," she murmured, using her childhood nickname for him, knowing it would soften him. Blatantly manipulative, but hey, she was the baby sister and manipulating him was her job. "I'm working on it."

He relented, sighing deeply, shoving his fingers into his hair. "Shit, Darce."

"I know," she said again, more softly.

"Just let us in," he said. "Me and Zoe, that's all we're asking, okay? She's out there blaming herself for not being around when you called. You know she's like a mother bear when it comes to you."

A small smile curved her lips. "So are you."

"True." He pointed at her. "But if you tell anyone I said that, I'll find a way to cut you off from Gummy Bears."

"Hey," she said. "No need to get hasty."

"AJ's beside himself over what happened to you," he said. "Do you have any idea how much he cares about you?"

AJ did care about her, she knew that. He just didn't care about her in the way she wanted him to.

Which wasn't his fault. She knew that.

"I know I drive him crazy," she said. "I drive all of you crazy. I also know I'm not easy to care about."

"Hold up," he said. "I'm trying to cut you a break since you hit that hard head of yours, but you're flat-out wrong. You're *easy* to care about, goddamnit, and anyone who says otherwise —"

"Mom, Dad, every teacher I've ever had, Xander, AJ —"

"Mom and Dad were wrong," he said fiercely. "And Xander's got his head up his ass right now. But AJ? No. I don't believe that. You haven't seen him, Darce. He's a mess over this, over you. You're strong, one of the strongest women I know, and that makes it hard for you to let others in, but it's worth it, I promise you."

She got that he was talking about Emily and how he'd found love with her and also a home base for the first time in his life.

Darcy hadn't been the only one her parents had screwed up. They'd done a number on both her siblings as well. But Wyatt was right. She *was* strong, strong enough to let someone in. She just needed that someone to *want* in.

And to not break anything while they were there. And also to not ever let go . . .

But she could no more force AJ to love her than she could force herself to love Xander. "I'm not sure it's in the cards for me," she admitted. "Love."

"You're wrong about that, too," he said. "But because you're a Stubborn-Ass Stone, I know you won't believe it until it hits you in the face. Get some more sleep." He rose and brushed a kiss to her forehead. "Love you, Darce."

"Love you, too," she murmured. "You big, obnoxious oaf."

"See? How hard was that to say?"

She smiled but froze as she remembered. "Wyatt, there's a dog at Johnny's . . ."

"Rest now," he said at her door. "Dog later." He closed the door behind him so she couldn't argue with him.

"Dammit." She rolled over to get out of the bed and the room spun. She closed her eyes for a minute and woke up a short time later when Zoe came in and made her sit up to drink some tea and eat a piece of toast.

"Eat," Zoe said.

Darcy ate some toast, trying to remember what was bothering her.

"Do me a favor?" Zoe asked before Darcy could remember.

"What?"

"Don't blow off what you feel for AJ like you blow off all your other feelings."

Darcy choked on her toast. "I don't —"

"You do. Promise me."

She stared into Zoe's solemn eyes. "I'm not blowing off anything, but he doesn't feel the same for me."

Zoe frowned. "He tell you that?"

"No, but —"

"Promise me."

Darcy blew out a sigh. "You're more stubborn than Wyatt."

"That's right. And you're more stubborn than both of us put together. This isn't about AJ's feelings for you, which, by the way, you're wrong about. This is about you and your heart, and for once learning to trust it." Zoe leaned over her and tucked her in. "Now go back to sleep and let that hard head of yours repair itself. When you wake up, maybe your heart will do the leading for once."

But that was the problem. Darcy didn't know how to lead with her heart.

The next time she opened her eyes she could tell by the fading light that it was late afternoon. She'd slept the day away. She stretched and sat up, and then went still at the realization that someone was sitting on the bed at her hip.

AJ.

"Why are you here?" she asked.

"Take a guess." Pinning her in with a hand at either hip, he leaned in and looked her over. "Better," he said.

"I'm fine. I just needed a nap." Or a break from her life. Pick one . . . "I think I made things perfectly clear at the hospital," she said.

"Your car is in town for repairs," he said, completely ignoring her statement. "The damage isn't bad."

"The dog —"

AJ patted his thigh and a dog's head and torso appeared, his front paws resting on AJ's leg. "This is Chance," AJ said.

"Oh," she breathed, feeling gratitude nearly choke her. "Oh, he's beautiful."

"Handsome," AJ said. "Beautiful is too girly. Good boy, Chance. Lie down."

The dog lay back down on the floor.

Darcy blew out a sigh, not wanting to soften toward AJ, but she couldn't help it. "You went and got him for me."

"Not me. Xander."

Xander stood from the chair in the corner of her room and she couldn't breathe. Just couldn't breathe. She was so happy to see him that she lost all her words, too. Plus, she was afraid to say anything and scare him away.

But he wasn't going anywhere. He walked around to the other side of the bed, sat, and took her hand in his before finally meeting her gaze. "Hey."

"Hey," she managed around her tight throat. "Why do you have a black eye?"

Xander's gaze went to AJ and then back to Darcy. He let out a low laugh. "I walked into a door."

Darcy looked at AJ, too, at the shadow of a bruise still on his jaw, and felt her own jaw drop. "You hit him?" she asked AJ. "Are you kidding me?"

"Actually, I took the first swing," Xander admitted.

She stared at both of them. "You two brawled?"

"Only for a minute," Xander said. "He kicked my ass with the return punch. And I deserved it."

Darcy squeezed his fingers, hating the image of the two of them hitting each other. "Not that I'm not happy to see you, because I'm ecstatic, but . . ."

"Why am I here?" he asked.

She smiled. "Yeah. You were holding on to a really good mad at me, I know that much. Don't tell me that my stupidity today made you soft."

Xander's eyes went suspiciously shiny and he shook his head. "I'm here because what happened to you today made me realize something."

"That I should stay off the road?"

"No. That I'm an asshole."

She choked out a laugh. God, she'd missed him. "No, you're not," she said. "You know, I've always wondered what it'd be like to have two guys in bed with me. It's not quite what I thought it'd be."

Xander choked out a laugh and brought their joined hands to his chest, not taking his gaze off of her.

"What, did I break my face and no one told me?" she asked, trying to pull free. "Get me a mirror —"

"No. You're gorgeous," he said. "But I once promised I'd never hurt you. And then I did. I'm so sorry, Darcy. So fucking sorry."

"It's okay. I understand —" She tried to shift so that she could hug him but pain sliced through her head.

"Just be still," AJ said quietly. "I know it's not your strong suit, but try."

"Okay," she whispered. "Being still." She squeezed Xander's fingers again. "You got the dog for me."

"Yeah. Because AJ called me and asked me for help. He'd have gone himself but he wanted to stay with you, even though it meant letting that moneybags dick leave town without signing the deal."

"Xander," AJ said in soft warning, but it was too late.

Darcy stared at AJ. "Wait — What?"

"Yeah," Xander said. "Ariana said he walked away from a meeting to go find you. Which, by the way, was exactly what he was supposed to do, put you first. He always does and I never did."

Darcy felt overwhelmed and confused. Part of that was her concussion but it was also because it just didn't compute. AJ had walked away from the deal with Trent and Summer?

For her?

Why? Why would he do such a thing when the deal had been what he'd wanted, needed, so badly? Slowly and carefully, she turned her head to look at him, but he was giving nothing away. "Tell me you didn't lose the deal with Trent because of me," she said.

AJ shook his head. "I didn't lose the deal because of you."

She let out a breath of relief. "Okay, good, because —"

"I lost the deal because of *me.* Trent thought his time was more valuable than your safety. He was dead wrong."

"I'll call them," she said, patting around for her phone. Unable to find it, she started patting down AJ for his. Never mind that she'd thought she wasn't speaking to him and now she wasn't so sure — she had to fix this. She wouldn't ruin this deal for him, couldn't take it if she did. "I'll call them

right now. Maybe they're still in the area
—"

"Darcy," he said gently, catching her
hands. "It's been eight hours. They're gone."

"Are you sure?"

He looked at her for a long beat, as if assessing her ability to handle the truth. "I
got an unhappy text, let's put it that way,"
he said. "It's over. But it's okay."

"How?" she demanded. "How is it okay?"

"There are other people out there willing
to get involved. I'll find them."

She dropped her head to his chest. "Dammit, AJ. Why did you do it? You didn't have
to come for me. And you didn't have to stay.
I kicked you out."

"It didn't take." He slid his fingers into
her hair, carefully avoiding her stitches, and
tilted her head up so that she stared into his
eyes. "And yeah, I did have to stay with you.
And you already know why, but I'll keep
telling you until it sinks in."

She felt Xander start to get up from the
bed and caught his hand. "You're leaving?"

He glanced at AJ and nodded. "But I'll
come back later if you want."

"I want," she said. "You do know that
you're one of the most important people in
my life, right? I need you to know that,
Xander."

He slid a quick look at AJ and then came back to Darcy. "I do know it. And ditto, babe."

"So . . . we're going to be okay?" she asked, her heart hitching. She wasn't good at this, at asking for what she wanted. But she wanted him in her life.

"We already are," he said, his eyes still very serious, his mouth slightly curved. He leaned in and touched his lips to hers softly, giving a small smirk at the low growl that came from the other side of the bed. "I've got a client waiting," he told her and stood. "But I could bring dinner."

"Pizza?"

"Naturally."

Darcy felt more than saw AJ's grimace, but her stomach growled with excitement. "Pepperoni," she said. "Extra cheese."

Xander nodded and headed to the door.

"And soda," she called after him before she lay back and closed her eyes. "Not going to comment on my menu choices?" she asked AJ.

"No."

"Are you being gentle for the crazy lady?"

He slid her a look. "Have I ever gotten mad at you for your menu choices? Have I ever given you any impression I want you to be anything other than what you are?"

"And what am I?" she asked softly.

"Perfect."

She snorted and he smiled. "Okay," he said, "perfect to me."

Her heart stopped just as it had when he'd said "I love you" with such ease — but there was something far more important than her own feelings right now. "AJ, the grant money —" She didn't know if she could live with that, with what he'd done for her.

"It doesn't matter," he said. "None of that matters."

She met his gaze. "What *does* matter?"

"I'll give you one guess."

Twenty-Nine

Darcy hated that she felt so weak and pathetic that tears threatened at AJ's words. Again.

"Do you need a hint?" he asked. "Or my shirt to wipe your nose on again?"

Words failed her so she went with her usual fallback. She flipped him off.

He smiled. "Aw," he said, and grabbed her hand. "You're number one in my book, too."

She choked out a laugh. How the hell could he do that, make her laugh when she wanted to strangle him? She had no idea. And how could he make her laugh at all? But he always could, no matter what was happening. "I distinctly remember dumping you at the hospital," she said. "Why won't you stay dumped?"

"Stubbornness. According to the captain, I was born with more than my fair share.

Tell me what happened today," he said softly.

"You saw what happened."

"You got on the highway."

She let all her air out with a single whoosh. "Yeah. And then a big, stupid truck carrying live turkeys passed me and I panicked and swerved. It was all me. *Again.*" She rolled over and buried her face in the pillow. Which, by the way, hurt her head. It was really hard to be a proper drama queen with a concussion.

AJ slid down into the bed to lie with her and carefully turned her to face him. "You got on the highway."

"Didn't I just say so?" she asked, hands on his chest to hold him back. "I think I've got blood matted in my hair."

"You did it," he said, his arms inexorable steel. "You overcame."

"Yeah. For Chance."

Hearing his name, the dog popped back up and jumped on the bed. He turned in a circle — three times — and very carefully plopped himself down by Darcy, setting his big head on her legs.

Her heart melted. "You're a good boy," she said softly.

AJ stroked the dog, his eyes still on Darcy. "You took a step past just surviving life; you took your first step toward living it."

His eyes revealed so much. Pride in her, for one. And affection. And that light she'd seen a few times before, the one that had made her fall for him. "Well, not my *first* step," she said, wondering if he'd know what she meant.

His eyes warmed. He knew.

"But an important one," he said. "Do you need aspirin or anything for the pain?"

Confused at the subject change, she said, "No."

"Water?"

"No."

"Good. Talk time."

Her stomach was suddenly filled with butterflies. "Wait. I might need something, after all."

"Too late," he said. "Now I want to know why I'm dumped."

She opened her mouth and then closed it.

"Oh, come on," he said. "You love to fight. Let's have it."

Admit that she'd fallen for him and had gotten upset and mad and hurt because she was alone in it? That made her no better than Xander. "I was having a bad day."

"A bad day made you tear out of work like the hounds of hell were on your heels?" he asked.

"I told Ariana I was sick."

He stared at her for a long beat. "You're holding back."

And he wasn't, which just about killed her. She gave him a smile and gave a very small — and careful — head shake, like *Who me? I'm not holding back anything, and especially not the fact that I've fallen in love with you . . .*

"Listen," she said. "I'm pretty tired so . . ."

He shook his head. "Lame," he said. "I've seen you lie much better than that. Try again."

"Let's try you leaving."

"Sure," he said and leaned over her, caging her in with a hand on either side of her hips.

"What are you —"

"It's called a good-bye kiss," he said, and covered her mouth with his.

The kiss fried her brain cells — the ones she had left, anyway. There was nothing gentle or soft or careful about it, either. No, he was fierce and determined and definitely making a statement.

She stared at him when he pulled back, completely thrown off her game — which had become the new norm around him. "Since when do we kiss good-bye?"

"Since you decreed we were a couple."

"That was pretend," she managed to say.

"And we've never kissed good-bye."

"We do now," he said, and leaned in and kissed her again, slower this time, sweeter, a kiss so achingly tender that she actually forgot her hurt and anger entirely. Hell, she forgot everything and let out a low moan while simultaneously trying to get closer. Finally, when she was a puddle of need and desire, he lifted his head and stared at her.

"Yeah," he murmured, rasping his thumb over her wet lower lip. "*Much* better. Now talk to me."

That was the last thing she wanted to do. Willing to set everything aside for a good-bye orgasm, she rocked the neediest part of her to the neediest — and, well, look at that — also the hardest part of him. "I've got a better idea."

AJ cupped her face and stroked her hair back to smile into her eyes. It was his sexy smile, his wanna-get-seriously-dirty smile, but he held her off. "You're hurt. I'm not taking advantage of that."

"No problem," she said. "I'll take advantage of you."

"Talk first," AJ said with great difficulty.

"Are you kidding me?" Darcy asked. "You're a guy, you're not supposed to turn down sex. It's not programmed into your genetic code."

"I know but —" He hissed in a breath when she leaned forward and licked his Adam's apple. "Something's wrong," he managed. "And that's what couples do to figure their shit out, they talk."

She jerked back. "But we're not a couple."

"Because you dumped me."

"Because I heard you," she said.

"Heard me what?"

"You telling Trent and Summer that we weren't together, that it wasn't like that between us. That I wasn't even the patient you wanted them to meet."

Her voice was light, casual even, but AJ heard the hurt behind the words as it finally sank into his thick skull what the problem was. "This morning," he said slowly. "That's what sent you running."

She looked away.

Shit. He really was an idiot. "Okay, first of all," he said, "when you told Trent we were together, you were just messing with me, remember?"

"Oh, I remember."

He went still briefly at the odd tone to her voice. "You told him that only because you were mad at me."

"Annoyed," she corrected.

"Whatever the reason," he said, "you let

him think we were in love. It wasn't true then, not even close, and I couldn't let them continue to think otherwise, not after I realized their decision to fund my grant had been based on the lie."

"No, you're right," she said with a calm voice that he didn't think boded well for him. "You're absolutely right. We weren't a couple, not by any stretch of the imagination. We were just two people who had sex during a storm in a hotel room. It happens."

He narrowed his eyes. "Not to me."

She shrugged. "The point is, we aren't a couple."

"Weren't," he corrected. "But that changed."

"I don't think so."

"Really?" he asked. "Then what do you call the rest of that weekend? Or the nights since?"

"Animal magnetism," she said. "But don't worry, it'll pass. In fact, I think it's already passing."

"If that's true, then what is this conversation about? If you're over me, what does it matter what I told Trent?"

"I have no idea," she said coolly. "You were the one who wanted to talk, not me." She turned away, lying facing the wall, her hands tucked beneath her cheek. "I'm go-

410

ing back to sleep now. Let yourself out."

"Not yet." He rolled her back to face him, and what he saw in her gaze made his heart plummet into the pit of his stomach.

Her eyes were hollow, devastated. And it hit him with a punch a thousand times more solid than Xander's. "You thought I was throwing you away," he said.

Darcy felt the humiliation burn her cheeks and she closed her eyes. "Never mind, okay? Forget it, forget all of it. We're good."

He narrowed his eyes. "That's exactly what you told Xander."

"So what?" she asked. "Xander and I are just friends, too."

"We're not just friends," he said, something dark and dangerous in his voice, something that tightened her chest and made her head ache. "Darcy, look at me."

She rolled to her back and stared up at him.

"We've *never* been just friends," he said, his voice low and burning with intensity. "I love you, Darcy."

"And yet you told Trent we weren't together."

"Because you didn't love me. I'd never rush you, not with this."

She stared at him. "You really have no idea

how I feel?"

"I've hoped," he said. "But you've never told me, and you've been really good at keeping your feelings to yourself."

"I slept with you," she whispered.

"I have no illusions about that equaling love. But in case I've never been clear, let me be crystal on this one thing. I love you, unconditionally. I want you in my life, but this is your choice, Darcy. It always was. And when you make that choice, I hope you'll let me know which way the cards fell."

She nearly choked on all the emotion clogging her throat. Oh, how she wanted to believe it, all of it. But her head hurt and she couldn't think. She closed her eyes. "I'm sorry. I'm really tired now."

"I know," he said. "Rest."

She nodded and forced her breathing to even out. Not easy when her chest felt like it might be caving in.

But somewhere between pretending to sleep and waiting for him to leave, she really did get sucked into dreamland.

THIRTY

A week later AJ was at the wellness center working with Tyson.

Tyson lay flat on his back with his legs bent, a yoga ball beneath his knees, which he slowly and painfully worked side to side, sweating like crazy.

Raisin sat at his hip, watching with infinite patience.

AJ himself had no patience. Zero. He'd been in a viciously bad mood all week and everyone in his life was over him.

Especially the one person who mattered the most.

He hadn't heard from her, not a single word. He was starting to believe that it was truly over.

Tyson swiped sweat from his eyes.

"Need a break?" AJ asked.

"No."

AJ appreciated the sentiment, since some might say *he* needed a break. In fact, Ariana had told him so just this morning — while sporting a new tattoo, a small phoenix rising from the back of her shoulder.

Xander's work.

Rumor had it they'd been out twice. AJ didn't care. Didn't care about shit.

Wyatt and Zoe had kept him up-to-date on Darcy, which was a doubled-edged sword for him. He knew that she was fine, recovering, almost back to her usual self.

The self that didn't need anyone or anybody, him obviously included.

She was writing again. She'd been on the town's website that morning with a new gig reporting in on adventures within the state of Idaho. Her first article had been "How to Road Trip the Back Roads to Boise," although he couldn't help but notice she'd left out the creative use of a mini iPad to punk your travel mate.

He'd also heard she'd been to work at Belle Haven in her new office.

What he didn't know was if she missed him. He figured the answer to that was a big fat no or she'd have shown her face.

The front door opened. Trent held it wide for Summer, who walked in ahead of . . .

Darcy?

She wore a long, flowery skirt, a denim jacket, and some kick-ass boots. Her hair

414

was loose and wild, a pair of big sunglasses blocking her eyes.

Until she shoved them to the top of her head, surveyed the large open room, and found him. She said something to Trent and Summer and, her eyes still locked on AJ's, cocked her head toward his office.

Nodding, he turned to Tyson. "Give me a minute."

"Take a bunch of minutes," Tyson gasped, flopping to his back on the mat. "Take *all* the minutes."

AJ strode across the floor and met the three of them in the hallway outside his office. He greeted Trent with a handshake and tried to offer the same to Summer but she threw herself at him and hugged him tight.

Darcy took a purposeful step back out of his reach.

Not knowing what to make of this, of any of it, he untangled himself from Summer and opened his office door to let everyone in. "What's going on?"

"We're here to apologize for questioning your judgment and behavior," Summer said.

Trent nodded. "She's right. I had no right to do that. We'd like to back your grant program, if you'll still have us."

AJ hadn't taken his eyes off Darcy. He forced himself to do so now and met Trent's gaze. "What changed?"

"It wasn't your behavior that was the problem," Summer said for him, taking Trent's hand. "It was ours, right, baby?"

"I'm impatient," Trent said. "And more than a little spoiled, to be honest. I thought my presence should've been the most important thing to you that day, but I was wrong. Very wrong. I didn't see that until Darcy came to visit and reminded me that love trumps work."

Darcy still didn't speak but there was lots going on in her eyes. Too bad AJ didn't trust himself to read any of it. "You went to see them?" he asked her.

She nodded.

"She drove herself," Summer said, smiling at Darcy proudly. "She said it was her first time on the highway since her accident."

"It was the first *successful* time," Darcy corrected. "And you saw me when I answered. You know that I was a complete wreck when I got to your place."

"Not a complete wreck," Summer said.

"It took me an entire day," Darcy said wryly. "I stopped at every gas station and rest stop, and two malls along the way."

AJ was undone. "Darcy."

"Wait, is that where you got those amazing boots?" Summer asked. "Totally jealous of those."

Trent reached a hand out to AJ. "Hope you can forgive us. We believe in you. We want to work with you."

"Even though my patients might come first?" AJ asked.

"Especially if your patients come first," Trent said. "In fact, I'll insist on it."

AJ nodded and they shook hands. Trent looked at Darcy, and then back to AJ. "I think we'll go get settled in at the inn for the night and give you two some alone time."

AJ didn't say anything until Trent had guided Summer out of his office and shut the door.

"You got on the highway days after what happened?" he asked Darcy.

She nodded, eyes full of things he was almost afraid to read. "I couldn't stand that I'd screwed up your deal for you," she said softly.

"You got on the highway after what happened," he repeated, unbearably moved. "For me."

"Yes."

"Why?"

"I just kept thinking about how my brain didn't want to believe that you could have deep feelings for me, but my gut and heart said you could, that I was worth those feelings and I could trust them. That I could trust you."

"You can," he said. "Always."

"It's starting to sink in." She moved to his wall where over the years he'd pinned pics of his patients and clients. She studied them for a long moment before speaking again. "You're driven to help people." She paused and turned to look at him. "It's one of the things that draws me to you."

"Do you want to know what draws me to you?" he asked.

She hesitated. "I'm still accepting that you're drawn to me at all."

He let out a low laugh and pulled her in. "Everything," he said, pressing his face into her hair. God, he'd missed the scent of her. "Everything draws me in, from your unstoppable spirit to how you use your voice to stand up for those who can't stand up for themselves, to the way you throw yourself — literally heart, body and soul — into everything that matters to you."

"You matter to me," she said, voice firm and strong.

"Finally," he breathed, squeezing her tight. "You get it."

Her arms wound around his neck. "I'm not a throwaway."

"No. And you never were. *Never,*" he said fiercely. "Your parents didn't know what to do with you, and that was on them, Darcy. But Wyatt and Zoe would go to the ends of the earth for you. Xander, too. Even Tyson. Everyone you pull into your orbit falls for you." He pulled back to look into her eyes. "Everyone," he repeated, hoping she was following along and believing.

"And you?" she asked, as if half afraid of his answer.

"I fell a long time ago."

She stared up at him. "You were already in love with me when we went to Boise."

"Yes."

She let out a breath as if she'd been holding it in too long. "I don't want to be just friends, AJ. I know I said that's all I wanted, but I lied. And I know that's a mystery to you because you always say what you mean and you don't make mistakes with things like this. Or make mistakes period. But I do. Sometimes I say stuff in the moment that later I realize was just a knee-jerk reaction, not to mention shortsighted and stupid."

"I've made plenty of mistakes when it comes to you," he said.

"Not like me," she said. "But I'm done screwing things up."

"I like where this is going. But don't do this unless you're sure, Darcy. I never intended to give my heart again."

She cupped his face and kissed his rough jaw. "I've never been more sure about anything in my life. It's you who should be thinking this over. People would say I'm a pretty shitty bet."

"I don't care what people say. What do *you* say?"

She laughed low in her throat. "I say I'm so far out of my league I can't even see the league." She flashed a smile. "But I always did like to try new things, not to mention prove people wrong."

Damn, he'd missed that smile.

She sucked in a breath, letting it out with slow exaggeration. "I know I said I don't need love, but I've discovered I want it. I want you, AJ, if you'll still have me. I . . . I love you." Looking like maybe she felt light-headed, she dropped her head low and put her hands on her knees, sucking in a harsh breath. "Holy cow."

It was probably wrong to be grinning at her panic attack. After all, she'd put her heart on the line, maybe for the first time ever, but he couldn't help it. Swamped with feelings for her, he stroked a hand down her back. "You okay?"

"Jury's still out on that one."

"Just keep breathing. It gets easier."

"Good," she said and gulped in some more air.

He was still smiling. "I've waited a long time for this."

She lifted her head. "For me to nearly pass out?"

He smiled into her eyes. "For you."

"I have no idea why you're grinning. This isn't going to be easy."

He laughed. He laughed so long and hard that she narrowed her eyes and went hands on hips. "Maybe you want to explain why that's so funny you're practically busting a gut."

He hauled her back into him where she belonged and held her still while she squirmed. "One thing you'd never be, Darcy, is easy. But I don't want easy. I want you. Any way I can get you."

She stared at him and then her mouth curved, too. "I can think of quite a few ways," she murmured.

God, he'd missed her. "Can any of them be executed in an office with a window that opens to the main floor?"

She turned her head and stared at the glass where, yep, he had his shades up today and everyone in the place was watching like it was their job. Trent and Summer. Ariana. Tyson. And, damn, Zoe had stopped by. Darcy waved at them all and . . .

Shut the shades.

Darcy saw the lock on AJ's door and hit that, too, with great satisfaction. "That should keep everyone out," she said, and made her way back to AJ, standing there so big, bad, and effortlessly sexy. She fisted her hands in his shirt and tugged him in. "I've got a question."

"Anything," he said.

Her heart took a good, hard leap at that. "How strong is your desk?"

She had the pleasure of seeing the surprise flash across his face, quickly followed by heat as his eyes darkened. "Strong enough," he said in a voice that took her halfway to orgasm. "But I'm not taking you on my desk when the building's full of nosy-ass people."

"You're not?" she asked, disappointed.

"No." He pushed her up against the desk and then lifted her onto it, pushing her legs open to stand in between them.

Mmm . . . She locked her ankles around his hips, letting out a little humming sound of sheer arousal.

AJ groaned and rocked against her, sliding his hands up from her knees to beneath her skirt.

Darcy got hopeful, really hopeful, even more so when he pushed her hem higher and then higher still, intimately exposing her to his heated hazel eyes.

He took in her bikini panties with the words *Rock On* across her crotch and smiled. "Damn, you're distracting."

"Good," she said. "Take 'em off, AJ."

"Not yet."

"When?" she asked.

"Later." He gathered her very busy hands from where they'd been trying to get into his pants and entwined their fingers together. "I want a promise from you."

"Absolutely," she said, leaning in to kiss his jaw. "I promise to take your undies off, too."

He slid his fingers into her hair and pulled her head back, his eyes smiling, his mouth serious. "Not that."

"Sounds serious," she said carefully.

"It is."

She bit her lower lip, her heart starting to pound. "Are you going to ask me to go steady? Because I've got to tell you, up until this point, I've not been all that good at keeping people happy."

"I'll keep myself happy," he said. "You don't have to do anything different or be anyone different, ever." He kissed her softly. "But maybe you could tell me you love me, again, just every once in a while."

She felt her heart melt. "I will. I love you, AJ," she said softly. "Truth is, I've always loved you. I just thought maybe someone else would be better for you."

"There's no one better for me than you."

She'd never been so grateful that he was just as stubborn as she. "There's something I realized after you walked away from a very important business deal to help me," she said. "Which, by the way, was stupid."

He smiled at her vehemence and kissed her again. "So you love me because I'm stupid?"

"Yes. I realized that you can't live without me." She smiled when he laughed. She was never going to get tired of his laugh. "And that I cared for you more than I ever thought possible. And —"

He stopped her for another hard, long kiss. "And?" he pressed after they broke apart to breathe.

She blinked, mind empty. "I don't remember."

His smile was pretty damn smug. "Maybe we should take this to my place."

"Yes, please." She grabbed his hand and backed to the door, tugging him with her.

She pulled it open, turned to go out, and stopped short.

Everyone had moved closer but no one closer than Zoe, who had her ear against the glass. "Okay," she said, "I know this looks like *maybe* I was trying to eavesdrop."

Darcy crossed her arms over her chest. "Actually, it looks like you were most definitely eavesdropping."

"Yes, well, it's just that I wanted this for you both so much," Zoe said. "You two are together for real now, right?"

AJ pulled Darcy in and gave her a kiss that chased away anyone's doubts. "For as long as she'll have me," he said.

"How long will that be?" Zoe asked Darcy.

Everyone else looked at Darcy, too.

Normally being the center of attention like this would give her hives, but all she felt was . . . love. "For as long as he'll have me," she said, mirroring AJ's words.

"Which will be for as long as I live and breathe," he responded.

Her heart swelled against her ribs. "I can work with that."

EPILOGUE

Five months later . . .

Darcy watched Wyatt toast his wife-to-be, grinning from ear to ear, staring at her like she was the best thing that had ever happened to him.

Emily appeared to melt.

So did Darcy. They were at the couple's co-ed bridal party. "So sweet," she said as Emily wrapped her arms around Wyatt's neck, pulling him down for another kiss.

"Yeah," AJ said. "It all seems to come down to the last person you think of each night. That's where your heart is. Emily's his heart." He met Darcy's gaze. "And you're mine."

Every time he said something like that to her, she marveled at how lucky she was to have him. "I've never known Wyatt to look so happy before."

"It looks good on him." AJ pulled Darcy into his arms. "You're looking pretty happy yourself."

"It's the goofy-ass smile," she said. "I see it when I look in the mirror in the mornings but I can't seem to get rid of it."

He grinned. "You're welcome."

They were in Emily's backyard. It was sunset, the sky a brilliant kaleidoscope of colors as a storm rolled in. Thunder rumbled and Darcy looked up. "I hope we get rain soon. I want to dance in it."

Even as she said it, the sky opened up. Around them everyone grabbed their drinks and belongings and made a beeline for the house.

AJ tried to pull Darcy inside as well but she resisted, laughing as the rain soaked through her clothes, plastering them to her like a second skin.

So what if she was starting to shiver and looked like a drowned rat? She twirled in a circle and did a hip-shaking boogie just because she could. As a bonus, she didn't fall on her ass.

AJ stood there watching her dance in the rain, lips curved, those hazel eyes lit with affection and heat. Still apparently baffled by her love of being in the rain, he nevertheless always indulged her. The rain pelted at him, too, soaking his shirt, defining his sexy build.

Sometimes in moments like these Darcy just stared at him, unable to believe he was all hers. But he was, for as long as she wanted him. He'd promised, and AJ never broke a promise. He was sharing his bed and his life with her, and just thinking about it had love swamping her. "You're getting wet."

"No shit," he said on a rough laugh. "It's raining." Reaching out, he stroked a strand of hair from her temple. "You've got some good moves."

"I do," she agreed.

"So do I." And he started doing some sort of ridiculous white boy boogie that made her toss back her head and laugh.

And then she was scooped close, up against his chest. He shook his head down at her, showering her with the water from his hair. "You laughing at my moves?"

"Yes," she said, still grinning.

"I have more."

"Let's see 'em."

Lowering his head, he kissed her. *"Later,"* he murmured against her lips.

"Promise?"

His answer was a wicked smile, and then suddenly he grabbed her and tossed her over his shoulder and went running. She shrieked as the water splashed off his shoes and hit her in the face.

Not stopping, he ran around the side of the house and to his truck, tossing her into the passenger seat, stopping to strap her in and kiss her again until she was quivering with much more than the chill now.

"You're kidnapping me?" she asked hopefully.

"Yes."

"A naughty sort of kidnapping, right? Where maybe you have to tie me up and everything?"

He flashed her a grin. "I won't need to tie you up."

A cocky statement, but the utter truth. She'd follow him anywhere and do anything he wanted, and he knew it.

The drive to his place took two minutes. He parked in the back. They got out of his truck, but before she could dash inside he pushed her up against the passenger door.

He was soaking wet, his eyelashes so long that drops clung to their tips and slid down his face, and when he smiled at her, she melted.

All hers . . .

Reaching out, he brushed the wet hair from her face. "Cold?"

"Not anymore." She fisted her hands in his shirt and rocked into him. The rain fell all around them, further drenching them, soaking the land, hitting the roof of the truck with a drumming sound that matched the beat of her heart. "Do you ever get enough?" she whispered.

"Of you? Never." He led her to his patio deck and to one of his huge lounge chairs.

"Is it later?" she asked with great anticipation.

"Yes," he said, and unzipped her while she did the same thing to his pants.

Her dress fell around her ankles and she kicked out of it. Her nipples contracted into two tight beads as his gaze skimmed her body, his eyes hot. He sat on the lounge and pulled her down to straddle him. She tilted her hips and rubbed herself against him, aided by his big hands at her hips.

His head fell back to the lounge pillow and Darcy bent over him, trailing kisses down his throat. Slipping a hand between her thighs, he scraped the material of her panties out of his way, tracing circles with the rough pad of his thumb until she was slick and ready for him.

"Now," she gasped.

He cupped her ass and squeezed. "Up on your knees."

She lifted up, shoved his pants to his thighs, fully freeing the beast, and then slowly lowered herself on him, taking him deep.

They moved together, the heat building to an unbearable ache inside Darcy that she knew he could assuage.

Only him . . .

Lowering her head, she sucked the raindrops off his bottom lip, letting her hands trace the lines of his chest and abs.

She was never going to be able to get enough of this, of him. Once upon a time that thought would've terrified her. Now it gave her comfort and security, and a sense of love such as she'd never known. "You're like my mac and cheese," she said against his mouth.

His chest shook with his laugh. "Something that's bad for you?"

"No, something that makes me happy."

He brushed the hair out of her eyes and held her face in his hands. His gaze was lit with passion and affection and so much love it stole her breath. "You're so beautiful, Darcy."

It was one thing to say it, another entirely to make her believe it. But looking into his eyes, Darcy absolutely believed herself beautiful.

He slid his hands out of her hair and back down to her hips, guiding her into the rhythm he wanted. She arched her back, her wet hair brushing the tops of his thighs as they rocked against each other, his hands stoking the heat from within while the rain cooled her off. "So good," she murmured, her eyes drifting shut.

"Stay with me, Darcy."

She slipped her arms around his neck and stared into his eyes, letting him see everything she felt as she started to pulse around him, pulling him into her vortex. When she came, she took him along with her. She fell forward onto his chest, feeling his heart racing with hers. Turning her head, she brushed her lips over his jaw. "I love you, AJ."

Holding her close to him, he laughed softly and kissed her.

"I know," she said. "Took me long enough to get comfy saying it without having a panic attack, right?"

He flashed a grin and softly kissed her mouth. "Some things are worth waiting for."

ABOUT THE AUTHOR

New York Times and *USA Today* bestselling author **Jill Shalvis** lives in a small town in the Sierras full of quirky characters. Any resemblance to the quirky characters in her books is, um, mostly coincidental. Look for Jill's sexy contemporary and award-winning books wherever romances are sold and visit jillshalvis.com for a complete book list and daily blog detailing her adventures.